Anthony Gilbert and The Murder Room

>>> This title is part of The Murder Room, our series dedicated to making available out-of-print or hard-to-find titles by classic crime writers.

Crime fiction has always held up a mirror to society. The Victorians were fascinated by sensational murder and the emerging science of detection; now we are obsessed with the forensic detail of violent death. And no other genre has so captivated and enthralled readers.

Vast troves of classic crime writing have for a long time been unavailable to all but the most dedicated frequenters of second-hand bookshops. The advent of digital publishing means that we are now able to bring you the backlists of a huge range of titles by classic and contemporary crime writers, some of which have been out of print for decades.

From the genteel amateur private eyes of the Golden Age and the femmes fatales of pulp fiction, to the morally ambiguous hard-boiled detectives of mid twentieth-century America and their descendants who walk our twenty-first century streets, The Murder Room has it all. >>>

The Murder Room
Where Criminal Minds Meet

themurderroom.com

Anthony Gilbert (1899–1973)

Anthony Gilbert was the pen name of Lucy Beatrice Malleson. Born in London, she spent all her life there, and her affection for the city is clear from the strong sense of character and place in evidence in her work. She published 69 crime novels, 51 of which featured her best known character, Arthur Crook, a vulgar London lawyer totally (and deliberately) unlike the aristocratic detectives, such as Lord Peter Wimsey, who dominated the mystery field at the time. She also wrote more than 25 radio plays, which were broadcast in Great Britain and overseas. Her thriller *The Woman in Red* (1941) was broadcast in the United States by CBS and made into a film in 1945 under the title *My Name is Julia Ross*. She was an early member of the British Detection Club, which, along with Dorothy L. Sayers, she prevented from disintegrating during World War II. Malleson published her autobiography, *Three-a-Penny*, in 1940, and wrote numerous short stories, which were published in several anthologies and in such periodicals as *Ellery Queen's Mystery Magazine* and *The Saint*. The short story 'You Can't Hang Twice' received a Queens award in 1946. She never married, and evidence of her feminism is elegantly expressed in much of her work.

By Anthony Gilbert

Don't Open the Door (1945)
  aka *Death Lifts the Latch*
Lift Up the Lid (1945)
  aka *The Innocent Bottle*
The Spinster's Secret (1946)
  aka *By Hook or by Crook*
Death in the Wrong Room
  (1947)
Die in the Dark (1947)
  aka *The Missing Widow*
Death Knocks Three Times
  (1949)
Murder Comes Home (1950)
A Nice Cup of Tea (1950)
  aka *The Wrong Body*
Lady-Killer (1951)
Miss Pinnegar Disappears
  (1952)
  aka *A Case for Mr Crook*
Footsteps Behind Me (1953)
  aka *Black Death*
Snake in the Grass (1954)
  aka *Death Won't Wait*
Is She Dead Too? (1955)
  aka *A Question of Murder*
And Death Came Too (1956)
Riddle of a Lady (1956)
Give Death a Name (1957)

Death Against the Clock
  (1958)
Death Takes a Wife (1959)
  aka *Death Casts a Long
  Shadow*
Third Crime Lucky (1959)
  aka *Prelude to Murder*
Out for the Kill (1960)
She Shall Die (1961)
  aka *After the Verdict*
Uncertain Death (1961)
No Dust in the Attic (1962)
Ring for a Noose (1963)
The Fingerprint (1964)
Knock, Knock! Who's
  There? (1964)
  aka *The Voice*
Passenger to Nowhere (1965)
The Looking Glass Murder
  (1966)
The Visitor (1967)
Night Encounter (1968)
  aka *Murder Anonymous*
Missing from Her Home
  (1969)
Death Wears a Mask (1970)
  aka *Mr Crook Lifts the
  Mask*

Death in the Blackout

Anthony Gilbert

An Orion book

Copyright © Lucy Beatrice Malleson 1942

The right of Lucy Beatrice Malleson to be identified as the author of this work has been asserted in accordance with the Copyright, Designs and Patents Act 1988.

This edition published by
The Orion Publishing Group Ltd
Orion House
5 Upper St Martin's Lane
London WC2H 9EA

An Hachette UK company
A CIP catalogue record for this book is available from the British Library

ISBN 978 1 4719 0974 0

www.orionbooks.co.uk

CHAPTER ONE

And many a burglar I've restored
To his friends and his relations.

—GILBERT.

I

IN THE LATE SUMMER of 1940, when Hitler's Blitzkrieg on London was staggering everyone except the English, one of his pilots, for reasons best known to the High Command, dropped a bomb uncomfortably near the roomy flat occupied by Mr. Arthur Crook at No. 1 Brandon Street, Earl's Court, S.W.5. The sight of so much debris, glass and rubble temporarily blocking the roadway and destroying telephonic communication, caused the tenant on the floor below to pack her traps and depart hastily for the country, thus leaving the house, consisting of a basement and four floors, virtually in Mr. Crook's possession. Since the outbreak of war the tenant of Flat 2 had remained out of London and, since she was responsible for the rent in any case, the agents had been at no great pains to secure a sub-let. In any case, at that time it seems doubtful whether they could have got one.

The ground floor and the basement comprised a maisonette let to a Miss Bertha Simmons Fitzpatrick, who "kept herself to herself," and for the good of the country joined Churchill's Silent Column and was very fierce at pinning down enemy spies, discovering them

1

in the most improbable disguises. She believed the Prime
Minister when he said they were all around her, and
would hardly have been surprised to see one climbing
up the bedroom wall. Her reaction to the bomb outrage
was characteristic. Collecting all the property she chiefly
valued, she migrated to the basement, where she lived
in the heart of her possessions, like some small underground creature, seldom coming up for air. Her presence
made itself felt to her neighbours by her constant prac-
tising on an antique harmonium, that she placed in the
window, so as to watch all the comings and goings of
the house, while simultaneously ensuring that Satan
should not find work for idle hands to do.

This harmonium was her especial consolation during
the raids themselves.

> "Nearer, my God, to Thee,
> Nearer to Thee,
> E'en though it be a bomb
> That raiseth me."

she would cry in her cracked, fervent voice, while the
bombs fell all round and great piles of masonry came
crashing to the ground, a new version of an old favourite
that scandalized the devout, and enchanted Mr. Crook.

"She'd be a daisy for crime," he would say respect-
fully, but unfortunately the attraction was not mutual.
He was aware that she regarded him with the deepest
suspicion, noting his comings and goings in a marble-
covered exercise-book in which she inscribed all the
movements of the house between daybreak and black-
out. When it was time to draw the curtains and switch
on the light, she ended her self-imposed vigil.

2

Crook had only spoken to her on one occasion, when she had appeared at the top of the basement-steps to inspect local damage that, on that particular day, was considerable. A bomb had fallen in the middle of the road not far off, and windows and their sashes were splintered in all directions. Crook tipped his common brown bowler and said cheerfully, "Nice work." But Miss Fitzpatrick would have none of him. Like a little shawled troglodyte she was, her sparse grey hair sticking out in all directions like a detachment of steel pins, casting suspicion on air-raid warden and A.F.S. man alike.

"It isn't the uniform that makes the man," she observed, darkly.

"Some of 'em 'ud look a lot less without it," suggested Crook.

Miss Fitzpatrick turned her spectacled, malevolent gaze upon him. Then, in a voice like a nutmeg-grater, she remarked, "It stands to reason someone told them whereabouts they were," and, turning, began to flap down the basement stairs to the back door, looking now like a very untidy penguin. Crook realized that he was suspected of flashing signals to the Junkers 88 as they flew overhead.

"Though why the old girl should imagine I want to hand in my checks is beyond me," he told himself.

Miss Fitzpatrick established herself at the back door, and watched him as he climbed the front steps.

"You stay at the top," she hissed unexpectedly, with all the suddenness of a concealed revolver going off in the dark.

"Right you are, lady," agreed Mr. Crook, in blithe

tones. "If we are all going to Kingdom Come, it's nice to know I'm nearest Heaven and will get there first."

Getting to any particular destination one field ahead of the hunt was one of Crook's peculiarities that hadn't endeared him to the police, who naturally don't like having their eye wiped by an amateur any more than anybody else.

Mr. Crook's relations with the basement remained on this footing until the curious affair of the Tea-Cosy's Aunt brought the tenants of the house into a closer relationship.

The Tea-Cosy, as Crook was to christen him, put in his appearance early in 1941. There was a rumour that he had been bombed out of his previous lodgings, which made Miss Fitzpatrick say indignantly, A Jehu, meaning by that cryptic comment a Jonah; but no one, not even Crook, who overheard it, had the courage to correct her. The newcomer was even more elusive than the tenant of the basement. During the early months of his tenancy Crook never spoke to him at all, and rarely saw him. In appearance he was something like a question mark with a halo atop—tall, lean and bowed, always wearing a large wideawake hat of black felt, and usually carrying a haphazard collection of papers under his arm and having an odd, slightly staggering walk that caused people to wonder if he could be just a little under the influence. To judge by the number of books that moved in with him, he was of a studious temperament. Crook saw him once or twice on the stairs on his way out in the morning, when the old pedant was en route for the British Museum, where he apparently spent his day, and usually realised that he was back when he (Mr.

Crook) returned at night, by the faint blue light shin-ing through the glass transom above the front door. Crook put him down as one of those amiable lunatics to whom the British Museum is the antechamber of Paradise, and concluded that he was hardly likely to be of use to an ambitious man.

In which, for once, the astute lawyer was at fault.

II

One evening in April it chanced that Crook returned earlier than usual, i.e., at about eight p.m. Mounting the stairs in his usual solid manner, he noticed the blue light over the door of Flat 3, and decided that his neighbour had, as usual, returned. As he came round the bend of the stairway to the floor above, however, he halted sud-denly. From the inky blackness beyond him (for a thoughtful landlord had painted the windows as being cheaper and safer than curtaining them) strange sounds proceeded. It became obvious to Crook that someone inexperienced was trying to break into his flat. The faint scratch of an instrument being unskilfully applied came to his keen ears. Frankly entertained, he leaned against the wall and awaited developments.

"I never was one for spoiling the fun," he told him-self, "and if things are going to happen I'm not one to hurry them."

He was further intrigued by the fact that either the amateur housebreaker had actually not heard his cheer-fully noisy ascent or else was waiting for the newcomer to reach his level.

"When in doubt suspect a trap," Crook reminded

himself. And waited a little longer. Job, he thought conceitedly, had nothing on him when it came to patience.

After two or three minutes the invisible cracksman stepped back with a sigh.

"It won't open," he announced to the unsympathetic night.

Like an actor entering on his cue, Crook stepped forward.

"Perhaps I can help," he offered briskly, "I have a key."

The ghost turned vaguely in the direction of the voice. Neither man flashed a torch, Crook because he was an old hand and could see in the dark anyway, and the house-breaker because he hadn't got one.

"How very kind," said a thin, old voice. "Mine, for some reason, seems quite useless."

"Jumping Moses!" thought Crook. "It's the old boy from downstairs."

Opening the door with a flourish, he ushered his visitor into the hall. From his gesture you might have thought it was Buckingham Palace, and from Crook's point of view it was better. The long corridor, with its shabby carpet and inevitable hatstand, was revealed in a faint blue glow. There was nothing startling, certainly nothing imposing, about the scene, but it seemed to fill the old man with a kind of awe, bordering on delight. He looked, thought Crook, like one of those noble but bewildered birds of prey a civilised society imprisons in cages and charges its enlightened members a shilling to view. His hair was grey and rather long, his bald forehead was magnificent, his nose like a beak economically covered with parchmenty skin, his mouth long, classical and severe. He still wore the wide, black hat and a very long, exceedingly shabby, black overcoat of old-fashioned cut, that came almost to his ankles. His voice was touchingly grateful, and though he seemed possessed by a surprised pleasure, he evinced no embarrassment at all.

"How exceedingly kind," he said. "I can't imagine why my key grated in the lock."

"I had a Parkinson put on," Crook told him cheerfully. "Any amateur could bust the kind the landlord provides. That's probably why you were in difficulties. I'm afraid you must have got cold hanging about on the stairs."

The old gentleman didn't appear to be listening. With every sign of confidence he had pattered after his host into what Crook called the sitting-room. This was a square, untidy, uncomfortable place, full of books, papers, hard chairs and dingy curtains.

"Make yourself at home," he invited.

If the hall and passage had appeared to astonish the old man, the sight of this room completed the miracle. He stood on the threshold goggling at the unappetising furniture. The two men formed as vivid a contrast as you could hope to find. Crook wore his business suit, a round coat and trousers of a brown shade he considered cheerful and the refined found vulgar. A brown billycock was tilted over his large aggressive nose, almost concealing his thick, red eyebrows. His brown shoes were pure gangster. Stamping across to a cupboard, he produced two bottles of beer; but when he turned to offer his guest the only thing he understood by hospitality, he was staggered by the expression on that gaunt, handsome face. It had passed through amazement to ecstasy; he was like a man who realises he is about to perceive the Beatific Vision and it was more than he could bear. He simply couldn't believe his luck.

"Wonderful," he whispered, just above his breath. "I could never have credited it. And yet—and yet the evidence seems invincible." Putting out a timid hand he touched a book-case. "Quite solid," he remarked. "I must certainly write to the *Review* about this. I believe there is only one similar record, and that not authenticated."

"Will you or won't you?" asked Crook, patiently, holding out the beer.

The old man stooped to read the titles of the books on the nearest shelf. Slyly his hand stole out and he abstracted one. There was nothing there that might be expected to interest a savant, but the old scholar seemed absorbed.

"*Blood at Wapping Stairs*," he read aloud, and turned to the title-page. "1938." He looked at Crook, questioningly.

Crook smiled in what he believed to be a reassuring manner. Bill Parsons said once that in a previous existence Crook had probably been an alligator.

"That's right," he said, kindly. "The year of the Crisis. That's why I bought it. For distraction."

"The year of the Crisis," his visitor repeated. "And—how long ago would that be?"

"Arithmetic not your strong point?" suggested Crook, in the same kind voice. "Say two and a half years."

The old man's face fell. In place of rapture dawned perplexity.

"So it is still the year 1941."

"Snap out of it," said Crook. "What did you think it was?"

He had not, by this time, the smallest doubt that his visitor was crazy, but he had no desire to be rid of him for that reason. Madmen, he knew, have a logic of their own, and madness, after all, is only comparative. Crook was determined to find out the meaning of the old man's presence here and what his speech was intended to convey. The visitor laid down the book and lifted his sensitive, troubled face.

"I simply do not understand," he confessed. "For an instant I believed—I hoped—that I might be a spectator, a privileged spectator—of some experiment in time. But you, sir, what is your view on the subject?"

Instantly Crook felt himself on familiar ground. "Actually, I've never done any, but I'm told by chaps who have that it's an education in itself. You may know nothing when you go in, but there's precious little you haven't picked up by the time you come out. Not that any of my clients do time," he added hastily. "I only defend the innocent. That's what they pay me for, see?"

His guest looked like a child who has suddenly been let loose in a toy bazaar. His attention was perpetually diverted from one prize to another. All the time Crook was speaking, his eyes were roaming round the room. Nevertheless he had heard what was being said, for as soon as Crook fell silent he inquired, "You mean—you claim to be infallible? Interesting, most interesting. That, naturally, raises the whole question of the power of thought. Which, in its turn, is inevitably linked up with my time theory." He paused for breath and Crook took advantage of this to say, "No need for anythin' like that. You've only got to be a bit less fallible—and gullible—than the old boy on the box."

His visitor gaped an instant before he realized that Mr. Crook referred to the judge in charge of the case.

"Any little thing I can do for you just now—as between friends?" inquired Mr. Crook, his eyes as bright as a canary's. "Hang it, man, you were damn-all keen to get into the place."

"Is that so strange at this hour?" the old man rejoined. "Naturally, I had not presupposed your presence here, and I hope you will not allow yourself to be inconvenienced by the fact that at this moment—my moment, that is, which may, perhaps, not coincide with yours—I am the tenant of these rooms."

Crook's elaborate expectations fell to the ground so abruptly he wouldn't have been surprised to hear them bounce.

"I get you," he said, in tones of extreme mortification. "You think this is your flat, don't you? Well, it ain't. It's mine—me, Arthur Crook, the Criminals' Hope and the Judges' Despair."

"Your flat?" The old man's face was ludicrous with dismay. "In that case, where is mine?"

"Where it was when I passed it five minutes ago. In fact, I thought you were in it. By gum, though, that's queer. When were you there last, Mr.—Mr. . . . ?"

"Kersey is my name. Theodore Kersey." He fumbled in his pocket and produced a battered visiting-card. "Mr. T. Kersey." Crook read aloud and grinned. "I bet they called you Tea-Cosy at school."

Mr. Kersey looked a little embarrassed. "As a matter of fact, they did. But I must confess I could never fathom the connection. Even as a boy no one could suggest any resemblance between myself and that very useful, but plump, article of furniture." He looked down at his spare form with a sigh.

"You win," said Crook. He was, as has been said, a patient man, but he claimed to know his limitations. "You didn't answer my question. When were you last in your own flat?"

"I left, as usual, about nine o'clock. My—er—female comes then and she doesn't care for me to be on the premises while she is at work. As a rule, I return about six, but to-day I attended a conference on the nature of time, which delayed me somewhat."

"Well, then, your skivvy must have left the light on in the hall," said Crook, sensibly. "It's quite usual."

"I thought," said the Tea-Cosy nervously, "I heard sounds in the flat."

"What sort of sounds?"

"It was like running water."

"She could have left the tap on," Crook reassured him. "That's another trick they're rather fond of. One of these days someone will invent the automatic tap, and then women like yours and mine will break their hearts looking for some fresh mischief. You shouldn't let a little thing like that keep you out of your own premises."

"You misunderstand me," said Mr. Kersey, with a very moving dignity—that is, it would have moved any man less hard-boiled than Crook—"I thought, in my absorption, I had paused a floor too soon, and I therefore climbed an additional flight of stairs, still under the impression that I was approaching my flat."

"You're not mistaking me for one by any chance?" suggested Crook, but the old gentleman only shook his head in fresh bewilderment. Crook saw that he was wasting his time. It hadn't occurred to the old bustard that his story mightn't be accepted.

"Actually," he was saying, "I anticipated an even later return, but eventually I decided not to remain for the dinner of the society. I had no inclination for that part of the programme."

He looked so like a big bird as he spoke that Crook almost expected him to add that what he really liked was a dish of caterpillars, with worms in dew for dessert. He nodded intelligently.

"So much to do, so little time," he agreed, under the impression that he was quoting some literary master. And indeed, even poets must have enunciated truisms on occasion.

"As to that," said Mr. Kersey, anxiously, "we are, as one may say, in the dark. You—er—misunderstood my question about time a little while ago. I am, as you are yourself, a spirit moving in the fields of eternity. Now, eternity of itself implies a condition of perpetual being." He rambled on very happily for a time, and Crook gave every appearance of absorption. In his heart he thought, Goofy old bird this, but you never can tell. And when he could get a word in edgewise he brought the conversation back to its starting-point by saying, "About that light. There shouldn't be any one on the first-floor either. So it looks as if someone's on your premises who didn't ought to be, or else, like I said, your Abigail is to blame."

"As a matter of fact," murmured the old man, "I remember now. There was a card in the hall from Mrs. Davis saying she was unavoidably prevented from coming this morning, but hoped to return to-morrow. It was sheer chance that I saw it—I have so few letters. A bad leg, I think she said."

"The number of bad legs these women develop you'd think they were centipedes," agreed Crook, genially. "Well, who else has a key? I take it you've one and she's another . . ."

Mr. Kersey wobbled on the brink of explanation. "It isn't so much that she has a key as that a key is available for her," he bumbled. "Actually, it is placed beneath the mat, and she replaces it when she leaves. That, in point of fact, is for my benefit. I am a little absent-minded" (Crook here reminded himself of the British genius for under-statement), "and I might well forget to take my key with me. In that case, I know that I shall find a duplicate beneath the mat."

"You find it works?" said Crook.

The Tea-Cosy beamed earnestly. "It has a double advantage. If I am detained—and I am expecting a visitor —he or she has simply to admit himself and wait."

"I suppose to a chap with his views on time, keeping a guest waiting an hour or so doesn't mean a thing," Crook reflected.

"That might be the explanation," he added aloud. "If you're expectin' someone."

But the Tea-Cosy shook his head. "I assure you that I am not. Indeed, I seldom expect any one."

"Have many unexpected visitors?" pursued Crook, but he knew what answer he'd get to that. The Tea-Cosy's wasn't the kind of establishment where people drop in without warning.

Mr. Kersey smiled vaguely. Crook kept a tight grip on his patience. "You don't think the charwoman recovered and decided to pop round after lunch?" was his next idea.

The Tea-Cosy's eyes nearly fell out of his head at this bizarre suggestion.

"I am the last man in the world to deny the possibility of miracles," he declared, "but even so . . ."

"I get you," said Crook. "A hundred to one, no takers. Well, then, it looks as though there's some villain rootling round your place."

But he didn't really believe it. He thought the Tea-Cosy had left the light burning himself.

The old man was looking at him imploringly. "If you could further extend your kindness to—er—aid me in my investigations," he suggested.

"Pleasure is mine," said Crook, who never refused a dare. He had been up since seven that morning, but was as fresh as a daisy and as curious as Peeping Tom.

"That would be most accommodating of you. It is very difficult for me to believe that any one would assume I have anything worth burgling in my possession. A few books, my notes for my monograph on time, but . . ."

"No one's goin' to move into Park Lane on their account," murmured Crook, rightly interpreting the old man's expression.

"Then, again, I find myself at a loss in dealing with

the Englishman's idea of American dialects. I was on the classical side myself, but . . ." his voice said that even classical scholars had to draw the line somewhere.

"You leave it to me," said Crook, reassuringly. "I know half a dozen languages even Oxford wouldn't recognise. But, first of all, how about a drop of Dutch courage," and once more he indicated the beer.

The Tea-Cosy looked doubtful. "Has it—er—recuperative qualities?" he inquired.

"Nothing like it at the price—or any price for that matter," Crook informed him enthusiastically. He found glasses and did the honours. "No, no," he exclaimed in horror an instant later. "You've got it wrong. This ain't port and it ain't sherry wine. You don't sip it or roll it round your palate. You just open your uvula and let the stuff roll around your Little Mary. That's where it does the most good."

Like a man dazed, Mr. Kersey did what was expected of him. Then, feeling considerably more dazed, he picked up his big black wideawake and followed his host.

Crook clattered cheerfully down the stairs. An amateur would have been disappointed in his technique. There was here no hint of the hooded figure, stealing on feet of velvet through the gloom, no sudden hiss of, "Got him, my dear Watson," no complacent recountal later over a pipe of opium and a violin. Crook pounded down those stairs like a sack of coals.

"Chaps are on the lookout for what they expect," he would explain. "If you're after a fellow he'll take it for granted you're coming like Old Man Possum, so, if he hears you tearing about, he won't take any notice, because detectives and policemen simply don't do things that way. *Crime Detection in Twelve Lessons* by Arthur Crook."

As he came round the corner of the stairs he saw that the blue light was still visible through the transom of Flat 3. Which might argue that the interloper, whoever he was, was still on the premises. Still, even Crook who, like his companion, cherished a belief in miracles, could hardly credit that the old man would have anything very valuable on the spot, nothing worth breaking in for, anyway.

When, slipping his hand under the mat, he found the front door key, he was convinced that the alleged mystery was all moonshine. Still, for form's sake, he examined the lock with his torch, and found, as he expected, that it hadn't been tampered with.

"Once more into the breach," said Crook gallantly, straightening himself from his croquet-hoop posture and wondering: Am I for it this time or am I? For he was sufficiently conceited to suppose that all this might be an elaborate plot against himself. He wasn't a psychologist, he couldn't tell you a man's secret history by looking at his handwriting; he knew that the poet was right (though he never read poetry) when he said that all things are not what they seem, and that though the Tea-Cosy looked like a goof of the most harmless variety he might conceivably be a murderer, a Fifth Columnist or the leader of a stick-em-up-shoot-em-in-the-guts gang. It didn't seem likely, but part of his success (and his annual takings would have made a prime minister sing small) lay in the fact that he didn't believe in the impossible. He said it didn't exist.

Fitting the key into the lock, he pushed the door open and waited politely for a man or a bullet to come through the aperture. It occurred to him a little late that he might have shoved the Tea-Cosy in front of him. All things come to him who waits, he knew, including a good wallop on the head, but it seemed that his hour was not yet.

"Got your blackout up?" he inquired of his invisible companion.

The old man poked his head over Crook's shoulder. "I—think not, but perhaps my visitor . . ."

"That's right," approved Crook. "Look on the bright side."

He stood very still for a moment. He said he had a sixth sense that warned him of danger. The fact that more than once murderous attempts had been made on his life, and twice at least had been almost successful, did not affect his belief in his instinct. He said that in his profession a man had to harden himself to take risks. That was what his clients paid him for, "and," he would add, "they pay damn well."

"Looks like the bird's flown," he observed cheerfully. "We'd better see what flew with him."

The flat was very quiet, except for the patient flow of running water. There was no sound of any breathing but their own, no betraying creak of boards or rustle of draperies. Crook, like a great dark cat, his torch shrouded, moved through the hall. Behind him the Tea-Cosy whinnied and whickered like a nervous horse.

All the doors of the flat were fitted with glass transoms, so that the merest flicker of a torch would be readily discernible. But if there was any one on the premises, he was playing remarkably canny.

"I've had enough of this," said Crook. "It reminds me of that silly game—Murder, they call it, don't they?"

The Tea-Cosy replied courteously that he didn't know—he'd never played it. Methodically Crook went round the flat, pulling curtains as he went, because at that time even a torch was enough to land you in court with a two-pound fine. Meanwhile the Tea-Cosy, anxious to be helpful, pattered into the kitchen and turned off the running tap. Crook arrived just too late to stop him. There was a notice on the wall about patriotism and waste of water, that seemed to stamp the interloper, whoever he might be, as a person of no good feeling whatsoever.

"One thing," said Crook patiently, "if there were any finger-prints on the tap you've blotted 'em out."

The Tea-Cosy looked startled. "I shouldn't have touched it?"

"It doesn't matter," said Crook, "now I'm on the fellow's trail, he can do with all the help he can get."

He turned back to the living-room that overlooked the street. Here the curtains were partly drawn.

"Is this the way you left it this morning?" inquired Crook.

Mr. Kersey said a little nervously that he was afraid he couldn't remember. Again Crook assured him it didn't matter. I daresay, to him, this morning's as far away as the Battle of Thermopylæ, he reminded himself generously, pressing the switch of the electric light.

Nothing happened.

"Bulb gone?" he wondered. But examination showed that the bulb had been removed.

It was a pitchy night; not a gleam came through the partly-drawn curtains and the pale beam in the hall was too faint to penetrate the blackness. Crook advanced with speed, but with some caution. But he need not have feared. There was no one in the room able to do him any harm.

"Well," he observed, switching the shaded beam from wall to wall, "it looks as though. . . . My gosh!" He stepped backwards on to the Tea-Cosy's feet. The Tea-Cosy instantly apologised.

"Don't mention it," said Crook. "You—er—you didn't tell me you had a lady on the premises. Or perhaps you forgot about her."

"I assure you," began Mr. Kersey in agitated tones, but Crook was well away.

"P'raps she turned on the light and—and washed her hands under the tap—come to think of it, I didn't see any kind of drying-up cloth in the kitchen—and then went to sleep and got tired of waiting for you. Anyway, there she is."

His torch showed an unforgettable hat resting on the top of an armchair turned backwards to the door. The hat was a staggering creation in black velvet, shaped like the Albert Hall and decorated with jet, marquisite, flowers, tulle and a number of small, black velvet bows, perched like careless butterflies over crown and brim.

"A woman?" repeated the Tea-Cosy. He might have been an evolutionist considering the possibility of yet another missing link.

"Well," said Crook in reasonable tones, "did you ever know a man who'd be found dead in such a decorated cartwheel?" and then wondered if perhaps his notorious tact had failed him for once.

The Tea-Cosy stared. "You don't mean that she—that she——"

"Did I say so?" demanded Crook, feeling he might quite well be saying so five seconds later.

He pounded between the piles of books, manuscripts and diagrams that scattered table, chairs and floor. And after him came the Tea-Cosy, falling over something at every step.

"You have to be up early in the morning to catch Crook," was one of Crook's mottoes. But it appeared that someone had been up early.

The two men came to a standstill beside the empty chair.

"My aunt!" Crook ejaculated, in a queer voice.

"No," said the Tea-Cosy, simply, "mine. I could never mistake that hat."

CHAPTER TWO

Get your facts first and then you can
distort 'em as much as you please.

—MARK TWAIN.

AFTER an instant Crook recovered his normal garrulity.

"You say you recognise this hat?" he demanded.

"Aunt Clara always said it was a model. I don't think there could be two."

"Only if you had D.T.s," acknowledged Crook, looking with fascinated eyes at the monstrosity. "Tell me more about her."

"She is a very independent person," said Mr. Kersey, hesitantly. "Actually, I don't see her very often, but she has been kind enough to be interested in my work. You will realise," he added more fluently, "that I am largely concerned with research along lines that do not appeal to the general public. I have, in fact, suggested to her that she should utilise part of her means to endow a scholarship for research in this particular field."

"Got a nice little bit, has she?" suggested Crook.

The Tea-Cosy looked slightly dazed. "I—really I hardly know. She has a house in the country, but, to tell you the truth, we have never discussed her affairs."

"Were you expecting her?" Crook wanted to know.

"I—as a matter of fact, I never expect her. She comes —and goes."

"And leaves her hat behind her, like the baa-lambs

21

with their tails. Or do you practise a code? Does that hat mean 'Ring me at eight o'clock to-morrow'?"

"I simply cannot understand how she came to over-look it," confessed the Tea-Cosy. "I can only imagine that she was waiting for me, and—and overlooked the fact that she had removed her hat."

"Are they all like that in your family?" inquired Crook, not rudely but from simple curiosity.

"I really scarcely know any other of my relations. I believe there is a cousin who lives with my aunt, but we have never met. My work keeps me in London, and I have neither the time nor the inclination for holidays."

"I get you," said Crook, "not only your bread and butter, but your meat and drink as well. Now get a load of this one. Had—your—aunt—written—to—say—she—was—coming—to—see—you?"

"Oh, I don't think so," said the Tea-Cosy, vaguely.

"Then you weren't expecting her?"

"No, no, certainly not."

"Would she know about the key under the mat?"

"Yes—oh yes, she would know about that. It is my invariable rule, and though she had never visited me here before, I have followed the same procedure at all my addresses."

"She sounds a methodical woman," remarked Crook. "She replaced the key all right."

"I understand she has considerable business acumen," said the Tea-Cosy in the same vague voice.

"And yet, though she didn't forget the key, she did forget the hat. Can you think of any answer to that one?"

The Tea-Cosy caressed his long, distinguished chin with his long, nervous hand.

"I really can't imagine." Suddenly he brightened a little. "All I can suggest is that we should ask her."

"You know where she's staying, perhaps?"

"She has a house at King's Widdows, called Swansdown."

Crook looked at him suspiciously. "You havin' me on?" he asked. "That's no name for a house."

"But it did," said the old man, earnestly. "The swan, I mean. In the garden. With a broken leg."

"I believe you," said Crook, with faint bitterness. "Now, when did you last see Miss Kersey? All right, have it another way. Is it a long time since you last met your aunt?"

The old man lifted his head. In the torchlight he now looked more like a tortoise than an eagle.

"It is a little difficult for me to answer," he returned, in troubled tones. "The division of time into periods is a mere arbitrary convenience to satisfy man's mathematical sense. And, of course, to simplify his experience. No such division can affect the true nature of time. You, of course, can appreciate as well as myself that these periods have little actual meaning. They are entirely dependent on circumstances. A year may pass like a flash, a day seem as long as eternity."

"How right you are!" his companion agreed, obligingly. He felt as though he had been closeted with Mr. Kersey for a couple of days at least, whereas actually he hadn't met him—not really met him—an hour ago. "Well, then, do you know any reason why any one should want her out of the way?"

"I am sure she had no enemies," murmured the Tea-Cosy in his apologetic voice.

"Don't kid yourself," Crook advised him. "Everybody has enemies—you, me, the whole world. Didn't you say she was a rich woman?"

"I believe she owned jewellery of considerable value," offered the old man.

"Ever set eyes on it?"

"She never offered to display it to me, and I was never sufficiently curious to ask for details. It has always seemed to me incomprehensible that what are, after all, merely coloured pieces of stone should arouse the most persuasive passions in the human heart. Even assuming that beauty is the great educator. . . ."

"If any one ever bangs you on the head I'll act for him free," promised Crook, bitterly. "Look here, can you get it into your head that there's probably been some hanky-panky here? Hats don't walk through doors by themselves, and elderly ladies don't go out without them—unless, of course, she bought a Paris model en route."

The Tea-Cosy looked quite horrified at the suggestion. "My Aunt Clara would never do that," he said.

"Bit near, eh?" Crook grinned. "All right then, what do you propose to do next? Because, if you don't do something p.d.q. someone else will."

The old man looked horribly startled. "You don't mean the police?"

"Be your age," said Crook, wearily. "I've got a reputation to keep up, even if you ain't particular. Do you believe the police aren't simply prayin' for a chance like this to have the laugh of me? Ever heard a professional actress talkin' about amateurs? Well, take my word, they're doves, just doves, compared with the police givin' you their opinion on a layman." As he spoke, it occurred to him it was just as well his clients couldn't see him standing beside that unbelievable hat, haranguing an elderly zany in a theatrically dark room. "No, we won't trouble them at this stage, but—don't the blood-tie mean anything to you? Don't you feel inclined to look up your lady aunt and make sure all's well?"

The Tea-Cosy now looked completely out of his depths.

"You really consider that necessary?"

"It was your own suggestion not so long ago," Crook pointed out, feeling more sympathy with murderers than he had ever done in his life.

"But—to-night?"

"What's the time? All right, I can see you don't run to clocks, but I ain't so faddy." He hauled a great turnip of a watch out of his waistcoat pocket. "Going on nine. Well, maybe that is a bit late, what with a war on and all." He considered. "How about the telephone?"

"In the hall," offered the Tea-Cosy, eagerly.

"I don't mean yours. I mean hers."

"I don't think Aunt Clara has a telephone. She says its inconvenience outweighs its value."

"Easy to see she don't have to earn her bread-and-jam. Well, it looks as though we'd have to wait till the morning." He flashed his torch upwards. "That bulb, by the way? You removed it?"

The Tea-Cosy looked very puzzled. "I distinctly remember reading in this room last night," he said. "And certainly I did not remove the bulb. This is very strange."

"Don't put it back now. There may be finger-prints."
He flashed his torch round the rest of the room.
"Hallo!" he continued, "don't you ever look at your
correspondence?" He nodded towards a letter that was
lying on top of a pile of papers on a side-table.

The Tea-Cosy ambled across. "How very remarkable!" He took up an envelope that lay on a newspaper.
It seemed pretty obvious that the old man's lack of
interest in his correspondence extended to current world
affairs also, since, although the paper was twelve hours
old it obviously hadn't even been unfolded.

"This," he announced in a surprised tone, "looks exceedingly like my Aunt Clara's writing."

"So perhaps she was expectin' to see you." He
watched the old man's fingers fumble with the flap of
the envelope. "When was that written?"

"The 3rd," said the Tea-Cosy, glancing at the single
sheet.

"And when did it arrive?"

"When I was out," returned the Tea-Cosy, simply.

"To-day? Here, let's see the postmark."

The postmark was rather thick and blurry, as though
the stamp had slipped, but Crook, who had experience
of these, made out 3 Ap. and a sufficient number of letters of the name King's Widows to establish the postal
town. The time of posting was indecipherable.

"Well," said Crook, "what does that tell us, beyond
the fact that it must have arrived a couple of days ago
and got overlooked?"

The Tea-Cosy nodded affably. "I daresay. As a rule,
Mrs. Davis props any letters that may come against the

clock the last tenant left on the premises, but on this occasion she must have forgotten and left it on the table instead. Had she put it in its usual place," he added earnestly, "I should, of course, have noticed it. As it is, but for your fortunate intervention, it might have remained untouched for many days more." He rubbed his hands together and beamed sweetly. "Everything is now quite simply explained," he announced.

Crook felt a little weak. "You tell me," he suggested.

"Aunt Clara wrote to warn me of her visit. Here is her letter. By a mischance this was not opened, and so I remained unaware of her intention. She arrived during my absence, presumably waited for a while, and then departed, leaving her hat as a token of her visit."

"Does she often do that sort of thing?" inquired Crook, really interested. "Wouldn't a note be simpler?"

"But not so much in character," the Tea-Cosy assured him.

"She must have a great number of hats."

"Oh, no." The Tea-Cosy seemed quite happy again. "It must be unheard-of for any one to fail to keep an appointment with Aunt Clara. She will probably mention it in the autobiography she frequently speaks of writing."

"What," asked Crook patiently, "does your Aunt Clara say in that letter?"

The Tea-Cosy referred to the sheet in his hand. "That she would be visiting me at three o'clock on the 7th April."

"That all?"

"She says it is a matter of considerable importance."

"Does she tell you where she's staying?"

"Dear me!" said the old man. "How very thoughtful —it never occurred . . ." He looked at the paper upside down. "The Warburg Court Hotel," he announced, reversing it. "She expected to arrive this morning."

"Does she give the telephone number?"

"Telephone number? I hardly think . . ."

Crook, sympathising with those progressives who advocate the painless extermination of the insane, took the sheet from him.

"Paddington 00991. How about ringing up?"

"At this hour?"

"I know it seems like to-morrow morning," agreed Crook, with elaborate courtesy, "but it's still only about nine o'clock. Anyway, you might apologise for not bein' in."

"If you consider that necessary . . ."

"I don't know about necessary, but I'm simply burstin' with curiosity to know what she meant by leavin' her hat here."

The Tea-Cosy offered him an amiable smile. Crook, repressing his obvious reaction, bustled into the hall and unshipped the telephone receiver.

"Warburg Court Hotel," said a mincing voice.

"Put me through to Miss Kersey," snapped Crook.

There was a pause, and he heard a protracted buzz that showed the room extension was being rung. After a while this noise stopped and the same voice informed him, "No reply from Miss Kersey's room."

"Have her paged," demanded Crook. "It's urgent. I'm a lawyer."

But, as he had anticipated, at the end of a long wait

he got the information that Miss Kersey was apparently not in the hotel.

"She might be takin' a bath," suggested Crook, resourcefully.

"The telephone is not connected with the bathroom," replied the clerk, icily.

"Find her chambermaid and ask if she's been seen since tea. Get hold of her waiter and ask him if she had dinner in the hotel. No, don't tell me he's gone off duty. If he's gone to Halifax get hold of him." He put the receiver down without listening to the clerk's refined clamour.

"Don't look too good," he observed to the Tea-Cosy, who had come to the doorway and was watching him with indulgent interest, like a zoologist observing reactions.

"Perhaps she went to the theatre," suggested the Tea-Cosy.

"Then wouldn't she have told the hotel to reserve tickets? Besides—how old's this aunt of yours?"

"Actually, she is only a few years my senior. I am sixty-eight and she is, I should say, a decade older. Measured, you will understand . . ."

"Yes, yes, yes," said Crook quickly, perceiving the rapt expression returning to the ancient face. Wonder if he understands anything about time, he reflected, waiting for his reply. If he'd told me he was eighty I'd have believed him.

"She is in possession of all her faculties," said the old man helpfully, and before Crook could retort that that seemed to be more than her nephew was, the clerk spoke at the other end of the wire and said that Miss Kersey had not dined in the hotel.

"Did she leave any message in case of calls?"

"There doesn't seem to be one," said the clerk.

Crook slammed the receiver back on its rest. "They appear to have got the original Aged Man at that desk," he announced. "Haddock's eyes and all. Well, we'll try a bit later."

He surveyed his companion speculatively. He didn't seem at all perturbed, but then he lived so utterly in a world of his own that normal considerations didn't occur to him. When, however, a later call elicited the information that Miss Kersey was still absent, Crook decided to call it a day. After all, old ladies have very odd views on humour, and it might be entertaining Miss Kersey enormously to think of a frantic nephew trying to get into touch with her. Perhaps all this time she was comfortably chuckling to herself at the Warburg Court.

"Or perhaps she's the leader of a gang. P'raps she's an agent of the Black Market. You never know."

His experience had proved that, no matter how wise you were, you could seldom be wise enough to allow for every eventuality.

He made a pact with the Tea-Cosy to visit the hotel first thing in the morning. True, the old lady was no affair of his, but there was still an element of doubt as to her fate, and, left to himself, the old gentleman would probably moon himself into another century and forget that Miss Kersey existed.

"I'll pick you up at nine-thirty," he said, firmly. "Don't touch a thing—not the bulb, not anything. By the way, where were you proposin' to sleep to-night?"

"I don't think there's any one in my room," offered the Tea-Cosy.

"You don't mind chancin' ghosts? Oh, but I forgot. You probably don't believe in them, or, if you do, you'd jump at the chance of meetin' one and havin' a nice chat on philosophy and the time theory." He walked towards the door. "I wonder," he went on, struck by a new thought, "if Bertha Simmons Fitzpatrick could help us. If anythin' was goin' on, you can count on her bein' around. The nosey kind—and quite right too. Gentlemen may have a fine time in Kingdom Come, but they miss a lot of fun on the road."

A kind of excitement was boiling up in him. The case was peculiar, it was crazy, it might be a fool's errand, or it might turn out a death-trap. Given such alternatives, it was bound to prove interesting.

"Remember," were his last words, spoken on the threshold in that unearthly blue glimmer, "don't touch anything and be ready at nine-thirty on the dot."

He thrust out his great ham of a hand. The Tea-Cosy put a long, dry hand into it. It felt so fragile you expected to feel the bones crack at a touch.

"Don't think yourself into the middle of next week before I get back," Crook advised, and with a chuckle for his own wit he clattered up the shabby stairs.

As he turned the bend he heard bolts being uncertainly shot into place in the flat below, and an instant later a clock chimed the half-hour.

All Crook's imperturbability fell from him as he slammed the front door.

"I don't like this," he told himself, candidly. "If it is a practical joke, it's being played by a fellow with a

31

very queer mind. Of course, if it does turn out to be a police case, there's going to be trouble. They'll want to know why the something something they weren't informed at the start. Yet, if I were to go to them and say I've got the wind up because a lady's hat was found in a bachelor's flat, minus the lady, they'd laugh their silly fat heads off."

There was an element of the unusual about this affair that nagged at his attention. He had other work on hand, yet, again and again, he would find his mind wandering back to that ghostly unlighted room and that incredible hat perched on the back of the chair. Was that deliberate? he asked himself. Was it put there to mislead a third party? And, if so, what the devil's behind it all? Is the Tea-Cosy just what he seems, an amiable lunatic, or am I the sucker? He couldn't make up his mind.

It was after midnight when he put his papers aside and went to stand by the window of the small room the landlord called the spare bedroom and that could, at a pinch, have housed a Pekinese dog, and that he never bothered to black-out. It was a night without a gleam in any direction. From here not even a street lamp was visible. No star, not a rim of moon showed in the impenetrable sky. Hitler was giving London a rest for once—or else the outer barrage had been too much for his planes. The air was very cold and appeared to have a density of its own.

"Lovely night for a smash-and-grab," reflected Crook. "Or a murder, come to that."

His imagination, stolid but persevering, conjured up a vision of black river banks, empty houses where no cry would be heard, black mews and alleys, where a body might lie for twenty-four hours before it was discovered. He found himself thinking of old Miss Kersey. She might be huddled somewhere under this sinister blanket of the dark. He recalled the panic and fury that had filled him the previous year when he had been hunting for Laura Verity, his fear that he might be too late. The same sense of urgency claimed him now.

"I'm getting the horrors," Crook told himself contemptuously, and went forthwith to bed.

He slept at once, as was his custom, but he woke in the night with that sense of urgency more powerful than ever. He knew how the night-hours make a fool of a man, the absurd fears and phantoms that are spawned by the darkness. Nevertheless, he was convinced that he had been awakened by some sound he could not identify. He lay very still, trying to let memory have its way, but no amount of thought or relaxation was of any avail. It might have been a step outside, a hand on the door, some sound from the street. He glanced at the watch under his pillow. It said four o'clock. Had he awakened five minutes earlier the whole history of the case might have been changed.

But, as it was, he only murmured, "Three hours to go!" and went to sleep again.

The woman who "did" for him came at seven-thirty and the post arrived at eight. By eight-thirty Crook had finished his breakfast and by eight-forty-five was on the line to Bill Parsons. At twenty-five minutes past nine he tilted his bowler hat from the back of his head to the front, refilled his cigar-case and went down to the next floor. He heard the electric bell shrill through the flat and grinned at the prospect of the day before him. He had forgotten the sense of unease that had irked him in the night.

He appreciated the thought of the Tea-Cosy's aunt. She would, he was convinced, repay a visit to King's Widdows, and if she should not be there then he was on the threshold of a new original crime.

He rang twice before he got any reply. Then the door flashed violently open, and he found himself face to face with an aggressive-looking female; she wore a makeshift coloured apron and downcast black plimsolls; in the corner of her mouth drooped a cigarette stub.

Crook stared at the apparition.

"Want something?" demanded the female, without removing the cigarette.

"Mr. Kersey?" hazarded Crook.

"Gone out," said the female.

"Already?" exclaimed Crook.

"That's what I said," snapped the female.

"That's the worst of these fellows with time obsessions," observed Crook, chattily. "No sense of keeping a date. Did he, by any chance, mention where he was going?"

"Gone before I come," said the female, beginning to close the door.

"Now, now, Boadicea," remonstrated Crook, placing a large, well-polished brown shoe across the threshold. "Don't be hasty."

" 'Oo are you calling names?" demanded the female.

"She was a British Queen," said Crook.

"First I've 'eard of 'er," sniffed the female, beginning

to close the door against that intrusive foot, thus disposing of Boadicea.

"I had an appointment with Mr. Kersey for nine-thirty," Crook explained.

"You've an 'ope," said the female.

Crook was frowning. "Look here," he said. "Have you done the living-room yet?"

"What do you think I am?" demanded the female. "One of 'Itler's tanks?"

Crook didn't waste any more time. Suddenly he pushed his compact, sturdy body into the flat.

"You come out o' that or I'll scream," said the female.

Crook grinned. "No one 'ud believe you, lady," he assured her, opening the door on the right. The blackout curtains had been roughly drawn back, and when he put his hand to the switch a light sprang up at once.

"Who put that bulb back?" Crook demanded.

"I did, o' course. Expect me to see in the dark, p'raps."

The lawyer looked round him. The chair on which the hat had rested the previous night had been pushed back into its place beside the hearth. A sort of makeshift dusting and tidying had taken place. There was no sign of the hat anywhere.

"Where did you put it?" he demanded, over his shoulder.

"Put what?"

"The hat."

"If you're asking me," said the female coldly, "he most likely went out in it. 'E 'asn't but the one."

"I mean the lady's hat," Crook corrected her.

He could feel her stiffen. "Come to the wrong place, ain't you? This is a respectable 'ouse."

"A big black hat covered with flim-flams," elaborated Crook. "And if ever I saw a hat that spelt respectability that was it."

"Y'orter be ashamed of yourself," said the female virtuously. "If I couldn't see nothing better than that of a night I'd take the pledge." She regarded him with scorn. "Well, can I get the police now?"

"I'd wait a bit if I were you," said Crook, thoughtfully. "You'd look no end silly if it should turn out to be a practical joke. Though nothing," he added candidly, "to the fool I'd look."

He walked slowly across the room. Suddenly he stooped and picked up something the slapdash sweeper had missed.

It was a small, black velvet bow.

"Well, that shows I'm not crackers," Crook told himself with a spasm of relief. "I was beginnin' to wonder." He came back to the door. "I'll be seein' you," he said, and went out.

The voice of the Tea-Cosy's charwoman followed him as he ran hotfoot for the basement.

"The last time I saw Paris," she shrilled.

Crook, who could enjoy anything except cocoa, grinned afresh. To reach the basement he had to descend the front steps leading to the street, and then go down a further short flight to the house's back door. All the basement windows were heavily shrouded by thick lace curtains, and defended by wicked-looking spikes. In the central pane a canary swung in a gilt cage. In the little patch of earth in front of the windows Miss Fitzpatrick had sowed runner beans, leggy growths that now sagged in every direction.

"She can't have much light in her room," Crook reflected, but when he got inside he realised that the vegetable thicket couldn't make much difference. There was so much furniture, so many pictures, such fantastic draperies in every corner, that light retired defeated. When he halted at the door he listened a moment, and heard the harmonium being played full blast.

The tune was "Abide with me."

Crook hammered on the back door, and when his summons met with no response, not even a diminution of the volume of sound from within, he hammered on the window instead. This time he was more successful. The playing stopped abruptly, and Miss Fitzpatrick crawled off her stool and peered through her Swiss lace barricades at this intruder on her peace. When she saw Crook her mouth drew down and she violently shook her head. Crook nodded his. Miss Fitzpatrick shook both hands at him; Crook waved amiably back. Two errand-boys and an A.R.P. worker stopped to see the fun. Crook paid not the slightest attention. The canary, apparently disconcerted by the cessation of the music, broke into a song of his own in B flat. A voice from the street opined loudly that that bloody canary was really a bloody sparrow.

As though this were her cue, Miss Fitzpatrick left the room and opened the back door.

"What do you want?" she demanded.

"A little help," responded Crook.

"You should be ashamed," said Miss Fitzpatrick in

wrathful tones. "Begging at your age. What's the relief for?"

"Interested in murder?" asked Mr. Crook.

"Yours?" inquired Miss Fitzpatrick.

"It could be," acknowledged Mr. Crook.

"You'd better come in," said Miss Fitzpatrick, unexpectedly.

"I can see we're going to understand each other," said Mr. Crook, and followed her down a dark passage.

The room into which she led him was so cluttered with furniture that it was at first difficult to find a chair on which to sit. Leaning against one wall was an enormous and eerie oil-painting of Big Ben, with a real clock where the clock should be. This stood permanently at ten minutes to twelve. There were four other clocks in the room, only one of which was going, and this was wrong.

Crook nodded appreciatively.

"You ought to meet the Tea-Cosy," he said. "You'd get on like a house afire. You have the same time theories."

"If it's collecting for anything," said Miss Fitzpatrick, forbiddingly, "I don't give at the door, and if more people were to follow my example there wouldn't be so many murders."

"You're about on his level for logic, too," approved Mr. Crook.

He slammed his brown bowler on to the table, between the heel of a loaf and a packet of birdseed.

"Hullo," he commented, affably, "that's a nice thing you've got."

He indicated an enormous framed text done in needle-work that hung on the opposite wall.

"Knock and it shall be opened unto you," he read. "You ought to hang that outside by rights."

Miss Fitzpatrick looked affronted. "This neighbour-hood's gone down enough as it is," she said, severely, "without anything of that kind. Sometimes I find myself wondering what sort of a house this really is."

"Shake," said Crook exuberantly, putting out his tre-mendous fist. "I'm wondering, too. Still, there's some-thing you can tell me. What time did the old lady come yesterday?"

Miss Fitzpatrick stared. "There wasn't any old lady."

"Caught you napping, did she? I thought you were never off duty."

"No more I am, not so long as it's light. If your friend came, it was after the black-out."

"I don't think so," said Crook.

"Well, no stranger came to this house yesterday after-noon, bar the girl about the first-floor flat."

"Which girl is this?"

"I'm telling you. She came to look at the first-floor flat. Bombed out, she was, just like Old Wideawake from the second floor. Works for the Ministry of Secret Supply, she told me, and sleeps, when she does sleep, at that rest-shelter place in Pieman's Row. Nice little thing she seemed, though you can't go by appearances. Said it was all right but something shocking."

Crook felt his own level head begin to swim.

"She doesn't seem difficult to please," he suggested. He felt he could have made the world in the time it took him to get stories out of people like the Tea-Cosy and Troglodyte.

"I mean she liked the place, but the last owner left it in a dreadful mess, all bits of old furniture and pictures and whatnot. She came to ask if I knew who the lady was, but I don't, of course. Not that she's what I'd have called a lady, anyhow. A slummocky piece, and so I always said. Well, would a lady have let That Man drive her out of her own house?"

"She hadn't got your spirit," suggested Crook.

"What I say," continued Miss Fitzpatrick belligerently, "is—Hitler can pour all over Europe, but he won't get me out of my place, I can promise you that."

"What made the girl come down here?"

"I happened to be standing in my doorway as she came down the steps and she called down to ask if I knew, like I said. Taking little thing, blue eyes, fair hair, little short blue coat, and her head tied up in a scarf. I told her to tell the agents. Mind you, I wouldn't sleep in a flat that wasn't even self-contained, if it is a low rent."

Crook thought of the house's three occupants. You couldn't imagine either the Tea-Cosy or Miss Fitzpatrick doing a little burgling as a side-line.

The old lady suddenly chuckled.

"One thing did make me laugh. I'd asked the girl to have a cup of tea with me—well, it was about three o'clock—and she was talking about the flats she'd seen. She said the minute she got inside this one she got the creeps. Funny whispering noises all round her, sort of shivering noises, she said. She couldn't make it out. It seemed to come from the big room in the front, but when she opened the door it was all black—and then, of a sudden, the noise stopped. And do you know what it was?"

"I'll buy it," offered Crook, obligingly.

"Someone had left a roll of paper on the window-sill and the wind caught it. Ever so creepy it was. Chatter, chatter, chatter—like mice or worse. Oh, and there's a painting of a heathen Chinese worse than life, she said. That made her jump, too."

"How long did she stay?" asked Crook.

"Say half an hour. I showed her my photographs after tea."

"Your photographs?" Crook glanced round interrogatively.

"Oh, none of these. The pictures of me as a professional, I mean. They're on the staircase. With the Burlington Rep. I was for years. Could have come to London if I'd had a mind, but I always did like a change, and if you come to London what happens? You're playing the same part for a year or more."

"It doesn't always follow," murmured Crook. "Well, then, while you were having your nice cosy chats and lookin' at photographs and whatnot, any number of old ladies could have pattered up the front steps."

"Not without me hearing them," said the Troglodyte firmly. "I was on the stairs, remember."

Crook was quite unaffected by this logic. He had learnt what he came to find out—that Miss Fitzpatrick couldn't help him at the moment.

The old creature fixed him with a buttony eye. "What's that you were saying about murder when you came in?" she demanded.

"Sister," said Mr. Crook earnestly, "there are strange things goin' on."

She nodded. "All the same," she continued obstinately, "it 'ud be a funny thing if a strange party was to come *and go* without me seeing her. Why, I see every one. There was the undertaker on Saturday afternoon."

"Undertaker?" exclaimed Crook. "A bit previous, wasn't he?"

"It was a mistake, of course. He thought someone had died on the second floor."

"He must be a relation of the Tea-Cosy. Got his times mixed and come a bit early."

"He seemed most surprised when he got no reply."

"Did he expect the corpse to open the door?"

"He said he had been knocking and ringing for some time, and asked me if I knew when the tenant would be home. I told him he was always out in the afternoon and lived alone, so I didn't think there could be a funeral there. A wrong address, of course."

"Odd," commented Crook.

"A very gentlemanly fellow," said Miss Fitzpatrick. "Speaking as one with a wide experience of undertakers —for I was a clergyman's daughter—very gentlemanly indeed."

"Always happy to learn," said Crook, referring to her confidence about her parentage. "Did he find his corpse, do you know?"

"How could he? It wasn't in this house. But we had a very pleasant conversation on funeral hymns and the new method of embalming. Quite a charming interlude."

"Of course," Crook reminded himself earnestly, "be-cause you find yourself living in a bat-house, it doesn't make you a bat. You're just an investigator and the rest is pure coincidence." After his encounters with his brother-tenants he felt a little less happy about this conclusion than he would have liked.

"Look here," he said, leaning forward, "you lend me a hand now. Goodness only knows where all this is going to end, but you watch out to-day and keep a note of who comes and goes, and if you see an old lady, you pop up and offer her a cup of tea, and one of these days you may see your picture in the papers."

The old creature reared her head haughtily. "That wouldn't be any treat to me," she said. "You seem to forget . . ."

Crook soothed her.

"By the way, I suppose you didn't see our friend from the second floor going out this morning?"

"Which I did not," replied Miss Fitzpatrick. She pursed up her little puckered mouth. "All things that are done in the dark shall be revealed in the light," she added in oracular tones.

"Have it your own way," said Crook, who considered this undue optimism. "Question is, will they be revealed in time?"

"Why not?" demanded Miss Fitzpatrick, small bright eyes twinkling behind her steel-rimmed glasses.

"Of course"—Crook cheered at the thought—"I'm on the case now. Like to make a bet on it?"

But Miss Fitzpatrick assured him that she didn't bet, and it was time for her thinking anyway. Pressed for an explanation by a fascinated Mr. Crook, she said she devoted a proportion of each day to thinking right thoughts for those that needed them. To-day, for instance, she had a well-known statesman in mind.

"Don't let me discourage you," said Mr. Crook, "but you'll have to think a hole into that chap's head before you can think any sense into it."

"More things are wrought by thought than this world dreams of," the old woman misquoted, to which Crook replied that thought might be very well, but a blunderbuss was generally a lot quicker.

"I'll be seeing you again," he promised her, as a sort of *bonne bouche* as he rose to leave.

"You come before black-out," she warned him, darkly. "I wouldn't let the Prime Minister himself in once my curtains are drawn."

CHAPTER THREE

A Woman doth the mischief brew,
In nineteen cases out of twenty.
—GILBERT.

THE FACT that his would-be companion had given him
the slip seemed to Crook no reason for abandoning his
plan of visiting the Warburg Court Hotel. On the contrary, it seemed to him more important than ever.

Although he had no reason to suppose that his expenses would be reimbursed to him—since you could
scarcely expect the Tea-Cosy to recognise financial lia-
bility—Crook thought the situation sufficiently important to warrant a taxi. He was anxious to learn whether
the old gentleman, perhaps forgetting their original
arrangement (if the old cock ever took it in, that is,
he told himself) had preceded him. Or perhaps there
really had been an accident and he had had a telephone
call. Perhaps that had been the noise that roused him
in the night. Or perhaps his sub-conscious had heard a
slamming door. (The trouble with the sub-conscious is,
that—like a successful criminal—it never comes openly
into the field.)

The Warburg Court was a large, prosperous, second-
class hotel catering mainly for commercials and passers-
through London. Since the war it had abandoned its pre-
tensions to being residential, and indeed, the raids in its
neighbourhood would deter the least superstitious from
seeking permanent accommodation there. This was a

disadvantage from an inquirer's point of view, since it was unlikely a casual traveller would notice one old lady in particular, even in so monstrous a hat, whereas residents are always quick to spot the unusual and the unfamiliar.

Crook went through the lobby, in which a number of people were sitting writing letters or waiting for telephone calls while their accounts were being made out, and asked the clerk at the desk if Miss Kersey were in.

The man looked at him in some surprise. "I'm afraid," he said rather uncomfortably, "Miss Kersey is no longer with us."

"She was with you last night," said Crook, in sharp tones.

"Are you a relation, sir?" the clerk wanted to know.

Crook produced a card. "Lawyer acting for the family," he said briefly. "I was expecting to see her this morning," which wasn't, perhaps, quite accurate, but Crook agreed with the man who declared that truth is too valuable and too rare to be wasted on those who won't appreciate it.

"Perhaps," suggested the clerk, "you would like to see the manager." He dispatched a pimply little boy to find him.

Crook wondered if for once he had missed the bus, and the police were already on the trail.

The manager, a plump, brownish, rather shiny man, adroitly buttoned into a morning coat, came out, rubbing his hands in an uncertain way, as though against his better judgment.

"Good morning, Mr.–ah–Crook," he said. "You've

come about Miss Kersey. I'm afraid I—er—have bad news for you. I had—er—hoped you might hear it from the family."

"Don't tell me she's dropped down dead," said Crook.

"Well—er——" the manager contrived a smooth, brownish-shiny smile. "I'm happy to say it's not so bad as that. The fact is," he paused. "I must admit I am surprised Mr. Kersey has not communicated with you."

"It surprises me too," Crook agreed. "But perhaps the shock's been too much for him."

"The fact is that Miss Kersey, in spite of her age, most courageously insisted on remaining out in the black-out, with the consequence—the not unnatural consequence—that she was knocked down by a motor-bus."

"I shouldn't have thought any bus would take the liberty," said Crook, simply. "What happened after that?"

"We—er—didn't get news of the accident till after ten o'clock, when her nephew telephoned to say that she had been taken to a nursing home. . . ."

"Nursing home," said Crook, sharply. "Why not a hospital?"

"I really couldn't say," said the manager, looking rather surprised. "I can only suppose the nursing home was nearest."

"And, of course, you can't have inquiries made so easily at a nursing home."

Mr. Prince looked as though he thought his visitor had gone mad.

"He said he would be coming along to collect her luggage and settle her account," he added.

"What—this morning?"

47

"No, no. He came last night. Miss Kersey required her luggage—naturally."

"Naturally," agreed Crook. "Would you know him again?"

"Mr. Kersey?" The manager looked shocked. "I do hope, Mr. Crook, you are not insinuating there is anything wrong."

"If there is, you'll know soon enough. The police don't let the grass grow under their feet. They have to be on the stretch all the time, if they're going to stay one jump ahead of the amateur."

"Naturally it never occurred to me that there was anything—unusual—about the affair. The quota of accidents in the black-out is lamentable, and we were only sorry that the poor lady had been so rash."

"Did you get the address of the nursing home?"

"He gave us the telephone number, as a kind of guarantee, I understand. He said he realised we didn't know him, and we might want to check-up on his story and the home would verify it."

"Ever noticed how much more honest rogues are than really honest men?" inquired Crook. "An honest man wouldn't have thought of that. Honest men have the kind of conceit that goes with virtue—they expect you to take their word for things. Very simple of 'em, but there it is."

"But really, Mr. Crook," protested Mr. Prince in horror, "I assure you, you are quite mistaken." He drew out a silk handkerchief and rubbed his hands. "There is no deception here. I myself telephoned immediately, just as a precaution, you understand, and I was informed that the old lady had been brought in suffering from a broken thigh. Her nephew was on the premises if I wished to speak to him, though on the point of leaving."

"All very pat," said Crook. "Tried the number again this morning?"

"Naturally, I intended to telephone," said Mr. Prince, who probably hadn't thought of doing anything of the kind. And indeed why should he? Clara Kersey was not an individual to him, but No. 48. She always had 48 if it was available. "We know Miss Kersey quite well. She always stays with us when she comes to town."

"That sort of evidence ain't worth the breath it takes to give it," returned Crook, a shade irritably. "How can you possibly know that? No, don't tell me. Because she says to you, Mr. Prince, I wouldn't dream of going to any other hotel when I come to London. I'm always so comfortable here. But she may be sayin' that to half a dozen other hotel managers on her other visits, the ones you don't know about. Well, did you try the home this morning, and did you press Button A?"

The manager said coldly that they had their own lines, twelve of them.

"I mean, was it Bob's your uncle?"

The manager, abandoning any hope of understanding this extraordinary visitor, said more coldly that he had not yet rung up. Nursing Homes were notoriously busy at this hour of the morning, doctors' visits and so forth, but the matter had not slipped his memory.

Crook grinned at him. "Be a good chap and risk hurting the porter's feeling," he suggested. "I'd like to hear the latest bulletin. Besides, I want to know if I can see her."

"Have you got the number there, Miller?" asked Mr. Prince. "Tell them to put the call through to my private room. If you'll come this way, Mr. Crook . . ."

Crook followed him into his office, a big, square room furnished in tasteless luxury, designed to impress the sort of people who patronised the Warburg Court. After a minute a message came through that the number was engaged.

"So, y'see, chaps do phone a nursing home at this hour," was Crook's unkind comment. "Wait a minute and we'll try again."

Later they made a second, and then a third attempt, but always with the same result.

"Never mind," said Mr. Crook, heaving himself out of his chair that was too deep in the seat and too short in the back for real comfort, "give me the number and I'll have a shot myself later on."

The manager accompanied him through the hall. "I do most sincerely trust you will find everything is all right," he said. "In fact, I am convinced you will. The gentleman telephoned to Miss Kersey's home address to warn them of the accident."

"Why didn't you say that before?" demanded Crook. "Got the number?"

"It was a long-distance call. The operator . . ." He sent a page scurrying.

"This would be about ten o'clock, you said?"

"Say ten-fifteen. He had already paid the bill and was collecting the luggage."

"Did she have much?"

"Just a zipper bag and her umbrella that she took with her when she left the hotel. She never travelled anywhere without the umbrella. I never saw her put it up, but she liked it to lean on. She was like that," he continued, proud of his perspicacity, "quite an old lady but she didn't like you to think it. That's why it was an umbrella, not a stick." He smiled fatuously. "Quite a little joke between us, it was. One of the Chamberlain tradition, I'd say. . . ."

You would, thought Crook. "And what," he inquired, "was her snappy come-back to that?"

"That she was carrying umbrellas before Mr. Chamberlain knew what they were meant for. But it was as a stick that she really used it. Never went anywhere without it. Her little joke, you see," he added, explanatorily.

"You must have had a roaring time," acknowledged Crook. And then the page came back and said the telephone number was Minbury 7612.

"Damned odd," said Crook, thoughtfully.

"I'm afraid I don't understand you, Mr. Crook."

"I didn't expect you would. But I don't mind letting you into the secret. You see, the fact is—Miss Kersey didn't have a telephone at her house."

He made one or two more inquiries before he left the hotel. He asked for the chambermaid and asked about the hat, and the girl said at once that she certainly remembered it. She had passed the remark to a friend that when Miss Kersey came to stay she felt as if Queen Victoria had come up out of her grave.

"She was old-fashioned," said the manager, with a generous air of one passing half a crown to a porter. "But then, so was the nephew."

"Oh? So you knew him too?"

"Not till that night. But he had a sort of old-world air and wore a big, black hat—quite a distinguished-looking personage really. But then Miss Kersey was distinguished. I mean, you couldn't overlook her."

But Crook mystified him by saying that he feared that was just what someone had done, and asked if Mr. Kersey had said anything about calling for letters? Mr. Prince said he'd spoken of looking in, but he didn't suppose there'd be any.

"And are there?"

"Not yet," said Mr. Prince.

"Okay," said Crook. "Well, I dare say you'll be hearing from me." And off he marched.

The telephone number of the nursing home suggested the district of King's Cross, and he wondered what an old lady like Miss Kersey was doing in that part of the world at nine o'clock at night. But already he had his own ideas.

Crossing the street to Paddington Station, he waited in a line for an empty telephone booth.

"Always like this at a central station during daytime," he reminded himself philosophically. But presently his turn came, and he shut himself into the little box and put two pennies in the slot. Again he got the engaged signal and pressed Button "B." Regardless of those waiting outside he had another shot a couple of minutes later, this time with more success. The bell had scarcely begun to ring when the receiver was lifted.

"Who are you?" demanded a voice, both startled and annoyed.

"Is that Euston 00182?" inquired Crook.

"Half a minute," said the voice irritably. "Yes, it is. Who are you?"

"Put me through to Miss Kersey, will you?" said Crook.

"Look here, you've got the wrong number," shouted the voice, now yielding to complete exasperation.

"Who are you?" demanded Crook, in his turn.

"This is a call-office in Euston Station," yelled the unknown.

"Thanks a million," said Crook, and hung up. "Simple enough," he acknowledged, stepping out of the box, that was instantly occupied by someone else. "X gave the number of the phone he was using, hung up, and waited for Prince to come through. He knew the fellow would ring at once if he rang at all, and he stayed in the box to keep other people out. There wouldn't be much of a jam at ten o'clock at night."

It next occurred to him that it might be possible to trace the taxi in which Miss Kersey's luggage had been removed, and he tackled a driver on the rank nearest the hotel. The driver was an elderly man with the look of one who knows that he is himself Hitler's especial target.

"Cab, sir?" said the elderly driver, but without enthusiasm.

"I'm trying to track down a cab that went to the Warburg Hotel last night to pick up an elderly gentleman and a small case. It probably came off this rank."

"It wasn't me," said the driver, briefly.

Crook jingled some money in a suggestive fashion. "It might be important."

"Well, I'll ask," the driver promised, unbending a little. "Of course, some of the cabs are out."

Two returned to the rank as he spoke, but their drivers knew nothing of any call at the Warburg Court. Crook handed the first driver a ten-shilling note.

"When you see the others you might ask them. By the way, this isn't a night-rank?"

"There isn't, as you might say, any night-ranks now," the man informed him. "What with blitzes and so on. Not but what things haven't bin a bit more quiet these last few nights," he added in the voice of one who knows that fate has a yet worse blow in store.

"Well, if you pick up any information you might pass it on. Here's my number, day and night." He scribbled some figures on a bit of paper and went away, saying, "You might ring this evening in any case."

"You want 'im bad, don't you?" called the driver. "Oh, 'ere's Lefty."

Crook halted his departure as Lefty drove in.

"Lefty, did you go to the Warburg about ten o'clock last night? Though, as a matter of fact," he added to Crook, "it's not likely there'd be any cabs on the rank that late. If you wanted a taxi you'd be more likely to pick one up."

Lefty said with vigour that he'd been driving a lady round the houses and eventually she gave him five shillings for a four-and-ninepenny fare and had threatened to report him to the police when he remonstrated. She had also observed that it was terrible and un-English to complain of raid dangers when you remembered what our wonderful men went through at Dunkirk.

"It's not the murders that are committed but the ones

that ain't that surprise me," agreed Crook, pleasantly, and this time really did go away. He thought most likely the driver was right and X had collected a crawling cab, just to make things a bit more difficult. Still, it seemed obvious that that taxi would have to be identified if the luggage were to be retrieved.

He rang Bill Parsons to give him an outline of the latest developments and went to the booking-office to take a ticket for King's Widdows. A little to his surprise, the clerk did not throw back his head and roar with laughter or call a policeman, but clipped a ticket and said the fare was ten-and-tenpence, please, and there was a train at 11.6.

"Just time for a quick one," said Crook, philosophically, gathering up his change.

The journey was long, slow and picturesque, with changes at little stations with names like Tempest Green and Barnham Thicket. Not many people seemed interested in this part of the world and Crook, who could hustle all right when he liked, enjoyed himself as the train ran through little villages and green fields that might have belonged to a world at peace, but for the persistent roar of planes overhead and the prevalence of khaki and air-force blue among his few fellow-travellers.

Just before one o'clock the last of the three trains decanted him at a little station that looked as though it came out of an Ivor Novello musical comedy. But it was a bustling little place for all that. From every wall posters exhorted you to buy National Savings Certificates, hit back with three per cent War bonds, join a Savings Group. It had been having a war-weapons week between 30th March and 5th April, and Crook could just imagine that intrepid old lady, Clara Kersey, pouncing like a cat on all the local mice and squeezing their last farthings out of them. It wasn't nice, really, to think that now, perhaps, someone had pounced on her.

A very brief search discovered for Crook the nearest public-house, called the Three Kings and Bowling Green, and with a sigh of satisfaction he swung open the door of the public bar. An elderly man, looking so like a well-known comedian that the theatrical impression produced by the station was greatly enhanced, brought him some really excellent beer and agreed to supply some sandwiches of potted ham. Over this cheerful meal Crook inquired for the whereabouts of Swansdown. Once he had set eyes on the village he had no doubt whatsoever of the existence of such a house. He wouldn't, indeed, be surprised to find that its neighbour was christened, "Where The Bee Sucks." The barman told him to walk three hundred yards, turn right by the post-office, go through the common and Swansdown was the first house at the farther end.

"Wonderful old lady, Miss Kersey," offered Crook, returning his tankard to be refilled.

The man agreed that she was wonderful and added, after a moment's consideration, that if the gentleman had come to see her he would be unlucky because she had gone to town the previous day.

Crook's thick, red brows lifted. "That's bad luck," he said. "When is she due back?"

The barman said he didn't know.

"I suppose they'll know at Swansdown."

The barman said he doubted it. Miss Kersey was a

very independent old lady, and really she seemed the best of the three.

Crook said *which* three? and the barman said her niece, the other Miss Kersey, and the maid that liked to be called a companion, though how one old lady could want two companions like them two you could search him. After which he departed to the farther end of the bar. As Crook was finishing his third pint, the man returned to add, as though the conversation has been consecutive, that no doubt the gentleman did brighten things up a bit, and he wouldn't be surprised if the old lady was his favourite, and no particular compliment to her at that.

Crook adjusted his bowler and said perhaps they'd meet again sometime and walked out on to the ridiculously picturesque village green. Following the barman's instructions, he soon found Swansdown, a pleasant, modern house on two floors, standing in its own garden. Crook wondered if they'd erected a memorial on the spot where the swan alighted, and thought it probable, and while he was still surveying the landscape, a man came round the corner of the house, whistling gaily.

He looked about thirty-five years old, and wore nothing more military than a pair of slacks and a pullover.

"Hallo!" he exclaimed, sighting Crook. "Didn't you come down on my train? I'd have showed you the short cut if I'd known you were coming my way."

"I stopped for a breather at the Three Kings," said Crook, smiling happily at the recollection.

"Wish I'd thought of it," said his companion. "This place is like that poem you learn in the Lower Fourth—'Water, water, everywhere, and not a drop to drink.'

Still, I'm afraid it's N.B.G. if you're selling anything—even tracts go into the salvage bin."

"Hell!" said Crook, looking hurt. "What do you think I am? A strolling preacher?"

"Never can tell," said his companion. "Speaking as an ex-diplomatist . . ."

"So that's who you are," said Crook. "I thought maybe the gardener."

"Strictly amateur," returned the other. "Well—I mean to say I'm not actively lengthening the war by pruning cabbages, whereas in my professional capacity . . ." he broke off with a grin.

"Medicine man?" hazarded Crook.

"Liaison officer to the Ministry of Suppression," corrected the young man.

"It does run in the family," decided Crook. "By the way, my name's Crook. I'm a lawyer."

"And an honest one," said the young man, taking the card. "Y'know, I'd never have guessed. Does Miss Flora expect you?"

"That's the other Miss Kersey?"

"I dare say."

"And the Tea-Cosy's cousin?"

"D'you mind being a bit more explicit?" his companion suggested. "We whacked it up pretty late last night and—well, humiliating as it is for a diplomatist to admit it, I don't get there."

"Mr. Theodore Kersey. You've heard of him?"

"So he really does exist? I've often wondered."

"Doesn't he ever come down here?"

"I always understood from Auntie that he was more or less in a bat-house in London."

"Thanks a million," said Crook. "He lives in the same house as I do."

"Look here," urged the young man, whose name was Hilary Grant, "you did say you were a lawyer, not a doctor, didn't you?"

"It's evident," said Crook, in pitying tones, "you don't know much about the law."

"The law sees to that," returned Grant, and then stopped. "Good Lord, you're not the Mr. Crook, are you?"

"I never heard of another, and I wonder if you really ever heard of one."

"I told you I'd been in the Diplomatic, and the idea of the Diplomatic is to teach you how not to do it—put your foot in it, I mean—and if you have got it in, how to get it out, without smashing the other fellow's face."

"What made you give it up?" asked Crook.

"I never learned how to put my foot in it—and so, of course, I was on the list of the permanently unemployed."

"And after that?" said Crook.

"Stage," said Hilary Grant apologetically. "Well, there's one thing, the Diplomatic was a good grounding for that. Then I wrote a few little numbers of my own. 'The Not So Young Young Man,' and 'So We Hid the Ukulele Under Auntie's Bed,' but the Ministry of Suppression soon stopped that one. Thought we might be giving information to the enemy. And they offered me a job instead where I couldn't do any harm, because they saw to it I should never do anything at all. It's a very sore point with Miss Flora. Every time I wake up I expect to find all the feathers in my pillow on the out-side of the case."

"Then you're billeted here, are you?"

"That's it. But, I say, who was it you really wanted to see? Auntie? Because, if so, you're unlucky."

"So they told me at the pub."

"But Miss Flora's here. She'd be fascinated to hear more about—what did you call him?—the Tea-Cosy. Come to that," he added, "so should I. What's he like? I always thought of him as a clock-shaped little chap, round and beaming, to match his theories."

"He may match his theories, which are certainly tall," Crook agreed, "but he's not clock-shaped, unless you're thinkin' of one of these elongated atrocities women seem to fancy. He's one of the long, bony kind, all beak and brain."

At this instant a voice as cold as the northern snows inquired, "Is this a friend of yours, Mr. Grant, or has he come to see one of the household?"

"Miss Flora Kersey?" suggested Crook, stepping for-ward with his best bow. "I was wondering if I should find your cousin, Theodore, here."

"No," said Miss Flora, with exquisite simplicity, as though that finally disposed of Mr. Crook.

"Is Miss Kersey here?" Crook persisted.

"I'm afraid it's quite impossible for you to see her."

"I was afraid so," said Crook. "Well, if Theodore isn't here, where is he?"

Miss Flora's mouth tightened. It was a difficult mouth at the best of times, the mouth of a woman who has known stress and danger and suspense, and has become embittered in the educational process.

"Since you appear to be a friend of his," said she, with a biting emphasis on the word friend, "you can tell him that his presence is not appreciated here."

"Not even by his aunt?"

"The man is a mountebank," exclaimed Miss Flora, clasping her hands, passionately. Crook's interest was rising with every second. When the woman first made her appearance he had thought, "Here's a nice bit of ice," but already he realised his mistake. She wasn't ice, she was fire, smouldering, dangerous, suppressed fire. When she burst into flame she would burn up everything in sight, ruthless, fearless. He wondered what her history was.

"A mountebank?" he repeated. "Well, I don't say his theories are the same as mine, but . . ."

"I don't wish to hear any more about him," Miss Flora interjected.

"It might be better to talk to me than the police," suggested Crook, mildly.

"The police!" She wheeled sharply. "You mean, he has got himself involved in some disgraceful scandal? I always warned my aunt—but if it is money he wants, as I suppose it is . . ."

"Look here," said Crook, "I didn't say he wanted money or even that the police wanted him. They don't —yet—but they will if he don't turn up soon. And the same, of course, goes for your auntie."

Miss Flora's dark, uncompromising brows drew together. They were too heavy for a woman and they added a sort of ferocity to her rigid expression.

"Now I am completely at sea," she acknowledged. "What have the police to do with my aunt?"

"Nothing—if you know where she is."

"She is staying in London."

"Know the address?"

"Certainly."

"Well, well," said Crook, "I must say I'm surprised. I thought you'd have gone dashing up to sit by the sick bed . . ."

"Sick bed?"

"Yes. Nursing home. You know. After the accident she had last night."

Crook saw that he now had the complete attention of both members of his audience.

"I think," said Miss Flora, "there has been some mistake."

"I think so, too," said Crook.

"I have heard nothing of an accident."

"That's queer. Because at the hotel they said the gentleman rang up Miss Kersey's home. I thought it a bit queer, as I understood from your cousin that Miss Kersey isn't on the phone."

"She wasn't," said Miss Flora emphatically, "but she had an instrument put in after Mr. Grant came to stay here. He represented it as a necessity . . ."

"Well, I ask you," said Hilary Grant, in a deprecating voice, "how are the ministry going to stop me going in to do some work if they haven't got a phone to stop me with?"

"Please, Mr. Grant." Miss Flora's voice was as definite as a slamming door. "Will you explain?" She turned back to Crook.

"She was out in the black-out and was knocked out by a bus and taken to a nursing home," returned Crook in a rapid sing-song voice. "At least, that's what the gentleman said."

"The gentleman?"

"The chap who telephoned the news to the hotel and afterwards called for her luggage and said he rang you up."

Miss Kersey lifted a face from which every atom of colour had drained.

"Mr. Crook," she said, "you must forgive me if I didn't take you seriously at first. I realise now that something terribly grave has happened. Perhaps you would come in."

Crook followed with alacrity, and behind him with equal eagerness, trod Hilary Grant. But on the step Miss Flora turned. "We mustn't keep you from your work, Mr. Grant," she said.

Crook shot a malicious glance over his shoulder. "You didn't stay in the Diplomatic long enough," he said.

"She don't like me, do she?" murmured Grant. "I say, about Auntie. Are you pulling our legs or . . . ?"

"My dear chap!" Crook looked honestly shocked. "Do I look as though I'd get any kick out of pulling that sort of leg?"

He hurried into the house after Miss Flora, barked his shin on a large suitcase deposited by the casual Mr. Grant in the hall and made a more or less decorous entrance into the morning-room. Here Miss Flora indicated a chair, small and stiff, with straight wooden arms, but Crook, saying he'd be stuck like jam in the pot in that one, moved to a position that enabled him to see her clearly while she talked.

"Mr. Crook—you spoke just now of a telephone call

63

received here last night. You were right—there was one. But not from a man or so I supposed. Someone rang up purporting to be Aunt Clara, saying she had finished her business more quickly than she had anticipated and would be down to-night. She even said we were to get a chicken for dinner."

"And you did?"

"Yes. I've told Watson to cook it. But now, if what you say is true, I mean, if there has been an accident—or worse—I don't know what my aunt would wish. She certainly wouldn't expect us to have the chicken in her absence. On the other hand, if it is you who have been misled and she does arrive for dinner, she will be furious if the chicken isn't waiting for her."

"The problems women have to face!" said Crook. "I don't think you need bother about her coming down to-night, though."

Miss Flora wrung her hands. Crook, who had never seen this done before, watched her, fascinated.

"I should have suspected a trap," she cried. "It is the first time I have ever known my aunt put through a long-distance call. Oh, but where do you suppose she is now?"

"That's what a lot of people will want to know."

"And you," continued Miss Flora, "how exactly do you come into this?"

Crook explained. Miss Flora's brow grew dark.

"That man again!" she cried. "It's been the same for years—sponge, sponge, sponge—he's absolutely shameless."

Crook recalled the stooping, remote figure. Shameless seemed a queer word to use.

"Why can't he earn his living like other men?" Miss Flora demanded.

"He'd say he does."

"Not a paid living," she contradicted.

"I thought Miss Kersey was paying him."

"Why should she?"

"Only because it's her money and that seems to be the way she likes spending it. After all, it's the privilege of the rich to foster the arts." He grinned as the smooth words rolled off his tongue.

"You talk about my aunt being rich. Do you know that all her life until these last few years she's had to work from morning till night to keep her head above water? I know. For years I worked with her. She was left with nothing—nothing—and she had to go out as a companion and put up with everything that that involves. People think if they pay you a few pounds a year they own you—your time and your spirit and everything you have. Now perhaps you understand why I grudge this mountebank practically blackmailing her."

Crook pricked up his ears. "Blackmail?"

"Oh, I don't mean he's done anything the law could touch him for—not so far as I know, that is—but he must know she wouldn't let her own flesh and blood starve. And I dare say he's like Mr. Grant—has a certain sort of charm and exploits it."

"I'm glad you allow him charm—Mr. Grant, I mean."

"Who was it who said that charm is the least deserving of all human qualities? People do nothing to get it— it's like the shape of your face or the colour of your eyes—and then they proceed to—to——" Indignation choked her.

"Cash in on it," said Crook, watching her with a wary gaze. Poor woman, to fling her cards so passionately on the table! Of course, she hadn't a ha'porth of charm, and like most unattractive women, resented it desperately in others in consequence. "But that's common sense. If they didn't they'd be like the chap who hid his talent in a napkin. It may be the only one they've got."

"At least they could do honest work," cried Miss Flora, bitterly.

"Don't Mr. Grant work?"

"I don't trust him, Mr. Crook. Well, consider his own version of his life. He's been in the Diplomatic Service, on the stage, in the army during the early part of the war, and now he's in a Government Department. And he's—what? Thirty-five. No honest man has time to do all that in thirty-five years."

"And he's crept up your aunt's sleeve?"

"Of course he has. Do you think I don't see his little game? He's trying to come between her and me."

"For the sake of what she's got?"

She turned to him in desperation. "I believe he'd be capable of proposing to her for her money."

"And from all accounts she'd be capable of acceptin' him."

"Look at the way he fussed over her yesterday. I don't believe he had to go up to town on the Ministry's business. He just wanted to ingratiate himself. As a rule, she won't let any one travel with her, but she made an exception in his case. Of course, she's getting old. She was a very good business woman once, but now she's more easily taken in."

"If she was a companion for so many years how **did**

she become a landowner?" Crook wanted to know.

"She got a little legacy from one of the ladies she nursed. She was a Mrs. Phillips, a doctor's wife in Hampstead. She'd been an invalid for a long time—though, actually, Watson could tell you more about that than I can. Watson was employed by Mrs. Phillips as housekeeper, and that's where she met my aunt. After about two years Mrs. Phillips died and left Aunt Clara enough money to start a business of her own."

"What sort of business?"

"She had an employment agency. She said she had so much experience of households it was a pity to waste it. She went in for companions and upper servants and occasional governesses, mostly the uncertificated kind. She was very successful for several years—I met her that way quite by chance, going in to see if she had anything on her books that would suit me. I hardly even knew I had an aunt until then."

"And you've been with her ever since?"

"She wanted an accountant and general clerk, and in an emergency I could go out and fill a temporary job. But most of the time I was in the office. But about five years ago the doctor told her she'd have to give up . . ."

"So she sold the agency?"

"She gave it up. I don't know if it exists now. I don't think it does. It was her personality that made it such a striking success. And she came down here and bought this house and asked me and Watson to come with her. Watson had been with her ever since Mrs. Phillips died." She moved restlessly.

Crook looked thoughtful. "Any reason you can think of why any one should harbour a grudge against her?"

"Why do you say a grudge?"

"Well, don't it look like that to you?" demanded Crook, genuinely surprised. "Here she is, disappeared, leavin' her hat behind her. . . ."

"You've only got my cousin's word that it was her hat. It might have belonged to someone else."

Crook shook his head. "Don't you believe it. There couldn't be two. Look at this." From his pocket he took an envelope, from which he shook something into the palm of his capacious hand. It was a little black bow.

"Recognise that?"

"It does look as though it came off my aunt's hat," Miss Flora conceded. "Mr. Crook, what do you really think has happened?"

"That's where I'm lookin' to you to help me. Now, did your auntie say anything about goin' to see her nevvy while she was in town?"

"I—don't—know," said Miss Flora slowly. "But I can tell you this. She wrote to him one day last week—Thursday, that was—I remember, because it was market day, and I was going in to Minbury. She had just finished the letter and was sealing it up, and she shouted to me to take it in so that it could catch the mid-day post. We only have one from here at ten-thirty in the morning. She didn't tell me what was in it, but I suppose she was making an appointment to meet him."

"If it's the one he showed me that's what she was doing," Crook agreed. "But he forgot to open it and she came and found him out and went away, leaving her hat as a sort of message."

Flora frowned. "Mr. Crook, this is no joke. My aunt would never dream of doing such a thing."

"That's what he seemed to think. In fact, he was coming down with me this morning."

"Why didn't he come?"

"Because, by morning, he'd disappeared, too. Now, now don't get anxious. You know my motto. Crook always gets his man—living or dead."

"Why do you say that? As if you expected someone to be dead."

"Doesn't it seem that way to you?"

She looked at him in amazement. "But—why?"

"Well, where do you think your aunt is? Or is this the kind of practical joke she's accustomed to play? Her luggage is called for by an unknown man, we're given the number of a nursing home that turns out to be a telephone booth in Euston Station, you get a fake telephone call—if that doesn't seem a bit irregular to you, I don't know what is."

"I always felt that one day Aunt Clara would tackle something beyond even her astounding strength. She was so reckless, and lately she seemed even more so. In a way, I suppose, she missed her work. A little establishment like this didn't give her nearly enough scope. She was like a theatrical producer who suddenly has to retire and spends his time coaching amateurs."

"You mean, she got a bit restive?"

"I mean, she was ready to take any risk that offered. She kept up with a good many of her London correspondents, and every now and again she went up there. But—she had something on her mind. I don't know what it was, but I'd lived with her too long not to know."

"She didn't say anything, give you a pointer?"

"No. Perhaps six months ago she would have done,

but—well, she liked new interests as I told you, and . . ."

"And Bonnie Prince Charlie's stepped on the grass?"

"I may be doing him an injustice," admitted Flora coldly. "But . . ."

"But you don't think so."

"No."

"Now, comin' down to brass tacks," said Crook, "this voice that spoke to you on the phone last night—did it sound like your aunt's?"

"It's never very easy to be sure of voices on a long-distance, and then Aunt Clara has a very deep rather masculine voice at all times. Perhaps, if anything had happened to arouse my suspicions, I might have doubted, but nothing had."

"But you don't feel you could go into court and swear it wasn't her?"

"Surely the facts you've given me prove it couldn't have been. Mr. Crook, who do you suppose this man was? Do you think he might be . . . ?"

"Now, now," Crook admonished her, "no ridin' in front of the hounds. Next, I'd like to have a word with Watson."

Like an actor arriving on her cue the door burst open to reveal a little, skinny woman with gold rings in her ears, dressed in black.

"Miss Flora," she cried, apparently oblivious of Crook's existence, "just look at this. Madam's pearls. They're gone."

"Gone!" Flora turned sharply, but her voice was vague, as if she scarcely realised what the woman had said.

"Yes. I was surprised to see the case not locked-up,

knowing how careful Madam is about her jewels, and then I saw why—because it was empty."

For the first time she seemed to see Crook, and she flashed him a suspicious glance.

"Don't mind me," said Crook, "what pearls are these?"

"A string Madam particularly valued," said Watson in an aloof voice. "I'm sorry, Miss Flora, I didn't know you had any one with you."

"This is Mr. Crook, Watson. He was asking for you anyway."

"For me?"

"Yes. The fact is, we're afraid something may have happened to my aunt."

It was a queer household. When she heard that, Watson clasped her hands tightly over the jewel-case and exclaimed, "I always knew it, travelling alone at her age. Let me come with you, Madam, I used to beg, but she'd say, 'When I'm a dodderer, Watson, I'll let you know.' What is it, Miss Flora?"

"According to her hotel, it was an accident in the black-out," said Crook.

"And—how bad is it? You don't mean Madam's dead? Oh no, Miss Flora, you couldn't mean that."

"We don't know," said Flora, slowly. "We only know she's disappeared. Though as to the pearls," she went on, "you needn't worry about those not being in the case. My aunt took them to London with her."

"Took her pearls?" Watson looked incredulous.

"Yes. She didn't say anything to you—she knew you'd worry . . ."

"And not without cause, as it's turned out," retorted Watson grimly. "Why didn't she take them in the case?"

"Because she thought it would be safer to wear them."

"Wear them? Wear pearls worth five thousand pounds?"

"She argued that no one would believe they were real."

"She knows better now," said Watson, fiercely.

"We don't know that the pearls have anything to do with her—disappearance," Flora pointed out.

"I was taught arithmetic when I was a girl," said Watson grimly, "and they taught me that two and two make four. Why, any one might be murdered for pearls like those."

"We don't know she has been murdered," Flora exclaimed.

"On the other hand," pointed out Crook, "we don't know she hasn't."

"Have you called the police?" Watson demanded.

"Give Miss Kersey a chance," Crook suggested. "She's only just heard there's any mystery about her aunt. All the same, if nothing turns up by to-night I'd be inclined to get in touch."

"What can have turned up?" Watson demanded.

"There's the bare chance that in his anxiety X gave the hotel the wrong number. My partner, Bill Parsons, is combing that part of London for news of nursing homes. When I get back to-night he'll tell me what luck, if any, he's had. Besides, there's the Tea-Cosy. We shall have to find out something about him."

Miss Flora offered them both her tight-lipped smile. "It's possible the two mysteries are linked."

"I'd say it was a lot more than possible. I'd say you could put your shirt on it."

"I still don't know why Madam took the pearls to London," continued Watson.

"She said she wanted them restrung."

"Restrung? But there was nothing wrong with the string."

"I only tell you what she told me. Perhaps Mr. Grant could tell you more. She showed them to him quite recently. That I do know, because he said to me how beautiful they were, and what a pity it was she didn't wear them sometimes."

"Didn't she ever?" asked Crook.

It was Watson who replied. "I think she liked to feel she had them. She said that what had cost so much should be carefully looked after. Besides, down here, what chance had Madam to wear any of her nice things?"

"Quiet place?" murmured Crook. "Well, I daresay we shall wake it up before we're through."

Watson turned to him with an air of passionate intensity. "I don't know where you come in," she said, "but I tell you this. I'd give my life for Madam."

Crook thought it not entirely impossible that she might be called upon to do so.

CHAPTER FOUR

Something will come of this.
I hope it mayn't be human gore.
—SIMON TAPPERTIT.

I

IT WAS from Watson that he presently extracted the information that was to form the foundation of his premises in this extraordinary affair. When Miss Flora left them together the housekeeper made exactly the opening he had anticipated.

"That Miss Flora," she said, "she takes too much on herself. You'd think she was the only one to take any interest in Madam, just because she happens to be her niece, and grudging any one else so much as saying good-morning."

"Very devoted to Miss Kersey, isn't she?" suggested Crook in his most guileless voice.

"And well she may be," returned Watson, darkly. "It's not many as 'ud have done as much for her as Madam did. And no obligations, neither. It's a pity really she sort of hides her feelings to Madam's face."

"Perhaps she's afraid of being accused of trying to—er—make up to her aunt."

"Madam's no fool. She knows what people are after. Mind you, I'm not saying anything against Miss Flora, but all said and done I knew her aunt before she did.

We were together when life was more difficult than it was afterwards, in Dr. Phillips' household."

"Oh yes. She was companion there, I understand."

"Companion to Mrs. Phillips, yes."

"A tough assignment?" murmured Crook.

"I always say we've no right to judge the sick. Suppose they are a bit difficult, well, so might we be if we had to lie down all the time and just be waited on."

"That's plenty of people's idea of Heaven."

"It wouldn't be mine. I was always one for wanting to do a job myself. Miss Kersey was the same—but there's no getting away from it things weren't always easy."

"Was Mrs. Phillips an old lady?"

"A lot younger than I am now, though a bit older than her husband. No, she wasn't above five or six and forty, but she'd been out of sorts for a long time."

"What was wrong with her exactly?"

"No one seems quite to know. Dr. Forster was always in and out, and he gave her tonics and sleeping-draughts and things, but she used to say he didn't really understand. The least little thing upset her—if a tradesman made a mistake of a shilling on the wrong side of the addition, even if it was quite late at night, she'd be all of a fret until she had got it put right."

"Bit careful with her money, eh?"

"She said she knew she was an expense to her husband, even though, being a doctor himself he didn't have to pay the big fees, you or me would have to. You know," continued Watson thoughtfully, "she was a bit queer in a way. Always day-dreaming, saying how wonderful it would be if she suddenly heard of an uncle dying in Australia and leaving her a fortune. She said she had to be careful about the household books, because it was the only way she could help her husband."

"Very fond of her husband?"

"Well—in a way. Of course, she did feel it that he went about without her sometimes. Well, it was natural. It wasn't much of a life for him just going round sick beds all day and coming back to a sick room at night. But she felt she was a burden to him. It would be better for every one if I were dead, she'd say to me and Miss Kersey."

"And you, naturally, couldn't agree with her. What did she die of in the end?"

"It was about two years after Miss Kersey came. She'd had influenza and you know how it is, how low it makes you; and she didn't seem able to pull up. Still, she did get a bit better and it was arranged she and Miss Kersey should go away a bit to convalesce, but I suppose she lost heart suddenly or something, because one night she just died in her sleep."

"Heart failure?" suggested Crook, his small eyes as bright as those of the Troglodyte's canary.

"I think that's what the death certificate said. But, of course, things were pretty bad just then. It was the big epidemic after the Armistice, and no one had any time to spare, doctors least of all. I dare say it was hard on Mrs. Phillips, her husband being out day and night, but he said people were dying like flies, and they couldn't get enough doctors out of the army right away."

"And after she died?" suggested Crook.

"The doctor shut up the house. He had the 'flu himself when every one else was getting better, and he never came back to Hampstead. Later on he married again, and went to Kensington, I think it was. Madam used to hear from him every now and again."

"And you?"

"It was after that Madam opened her agency. She told me Mrs. Phillips had left her two thousand pounds."

"And you didn't think that queer?"

"Well, in a way I did, seeing Mrs. Phillips had always said she hadn't got any money. You see, it meant either she had had some, or else that it was the doctor giving it to Miss Kersey in his wife's name."

"Any reason for him to do that?"

"She was ever so good to Mrs. Phillips, nursed her when they couldn't get a proper nurse. I'm sure no one could grudge her the money."

"And—did you get a legacy, too? After all, you'd been there a lot longer than Miss Kersey."

Watson looked offended. "I never thought of such a thing," she said, and it was obvious that she was speaking the truth.

"Very nice feeling on your part," approved Crook. "All the same, if the doctor was going to be so generous to Miss Kersey, he might have remembered you too."

"I had my wages," said Watson, with dignity. "Besides, there's no two ways about it, Mrs. Phillips did put on Miss Kersey. Making her darn old towels that in any other house where I've worked would have been used for polishing rags; and sending her down to fight with the grocer over odd pence and ha'pence. Oh, she earned her money all right."

"And after Mrs. Phillips, you joined up with her?"

"She told me she was starting this agency and asked me if I'd like to be housekeeper to her. Well, Dr. Phillips didn't want me any more. He sold the practice, like I told you, and set up somewhere else. And then I'd taken a fancy to Miss Kersey, and being together so much during Mrs. Phillips' lifetime—well, I thought it would suit me nicely, and so it has."

"And where exactly does Miss Flora come in?"

Watson folded her lips tightly. "She came into Madam's agency one morning—just by chance, as you might say."

"Attracted by the similarity of the name?"

"Madam called it the Kay Agency. I don't see how she was to know. Anyhow, she was in a pretty bad way —and it's not every auntie that would be as good to her as what Miss Kersey was."

"When you say a bad way . . ." insinuated Crook, delicately.

"She was out of a job," said Watson, "and she was finding it hard to get one."

"What was her line?"

"I think she'd had charge of some accounts, and—well, it's not the way she put it, of course, but there was some dissatisfaction. I heard Madam say once she was lucky not to get six months. Well, naturally, on references like that you're not likely to go far, but Madam said blood was thicker than water . . ."

"She realised she was a relation?"

"Oh, she's a niece all right, but Madam said you couldn't blame Miss Flora for her father's bad blood. He's been dead a long while now, and a good thing for every one. Well, Madam talked to Miss Flora, and then she gave her a post on her own staff for a time, and now and again she'd send her out, but Miss Flora always knew she was safe. Oh, Madam treated her well. It's a shame really that Miss Flora gets so short with her sometimes. And with me, too, come to that."

"She doesn't seem to have much affection for Mr. Grant either," Crook suggested.

"She's soured in a kind of a way," acknowledged Watson. "Mind you, she's the greedy kind. I don't say she minded about Madam's money or her jewels, but she doesn't like Madam to confide in any one else."

"Little green-eyed monster," said Crook, cheerfully.

"There's times I've seen her watching me as if she'd like me to have a stroke. And it was the same at the Agency. Madam wasn't the kind to have favourites. She was good to all her girls, and that's a fact. Well, the proof of the pudding—you know what they say—and the girls 'ud come back again and again whenever they wanted jobs—and the number of jobs some of those girls could get through in a couple of years would surprise you—and when they were away they'd write and Madam 'ud write to them, and if they were in a tight corner she'd tide them over. Wonderful she was."

"Quite the philanthropist," agreed Crook.

"When I'd say to her, 'Really, Madam, you shouldn't let yourself be so put upon,' she'd say, 'It pays to be kind, Watson, really it does. If I help these people over bad times, then when staffs are wanted they'll come back to me.' And they did. She had a very distinguished clientele. The Kay Agency was known everywhere. All the big houses came to her."

"What made her give it up, if it was doin' so well?"

"She had a kind of heart attack, and the doctor told her it 'ud be death to carry on. And seein' what she was, she knew she'd never stay in London and do nothing, so she packed up and came down here."

"Who's carrying on the agency now?"

"There isn't an agency any more. Well, it was Miss Kersey's special organisation. It would never have been the same with any one else."

"Still, she might have got something for the good-will."

"She wouldn't have liked to think of it being run on different lines and p'raps not so well. No, she'd rather let it go."

"It was pretty successful, eh?"

"It was the best-known agency in town."

"It must have done pretty well for Miss Kersey to be able to invest in jewellery. Nice stones cost money."

Watson was becoming momentarily more confidential. "I've often thought it takes them like that, when they've not had much in youth, I mean. There was Miss Kersey, always worked hard, never had any fun, not much money, and suddenly she was in a way to become quite rich. And she fancied the things she'd never had."

"Fur coats and all that?"

"No. It's funny but she didn't care much about clothes. Didn't care what she wore. And in a way it suited her, if you know what I mean. Some people are all clothes and so they have to dress to the nines, but some people, and Miss Kersey was one, only need clothes for a covering."

"I get you," said Crook, soberly. "Did she flash her jewels much?"

Watson looked puzzled. "You mean, wear them? No, she never wore them. That's why I was so took aback to hear she'd worn those pearls to go up to London. There's no sense in being reckless, after all."

"What was the sense in having the stuff if she never wore it?" inquired Crook reasonably. "Or did she keep it as an insurance against old age?"

"It takes them like that sometimes," said Watson, seriously. "When they've had to work hard, I mean, and not had much for themselves. I was with an old gentleman once, who came into money when he was nearly seventy. Regular miser he was. Never spent a shilling but he'd say good-bye to it as if it was an old friend he'd never see again. Hours he'd sit playing with his money. And Miss Kersey was a bit the same. Sometimes of an afternoon she'd lock herself in her room and go right through everything she had."

"All on her lonesome?"

"Once or twice she asked me up."

"Not Miss Flora?"

Watson shook her head. "Miss Flora always said she couldn't see any sense in hoarding a lot of coloured stones. Oh, but they were beautiful, some of them. There was a green cross she was specially fond of. Emeralds that was. She'd turn it about in the light and it was like green fire, really it was. And then she'd laugh."

"What at?" asked Crook, prosaically.

" 'Think of the people who've worn that,' she'd say. 'Think of the parties it's been to. The Ronald Cross they call that, Watson, and it's famous. I don't suppose any one ever thought it 'ud come to me in the end.' "

81

"You're right, lady," Crook agreed in sincere tones. "Life is queer. I don't suppose any one ever did."

"There were others, too. She looked at them like she loved them. It gave me a creepy feeling, because after all Miss Flora was right, they were only stones."

"You never knew her give any away, I suppose?"

Watson looked astounded. "I don't think she would, and anyway who would she give them to? You can't see Miss Flora wearing gems."

"She didn't send any to the old gentleman?"

"From all accounts, he wouldn't know what to do with them either. It's not as if he was married. Or if he was, he didn't seem to know it. No, she'd have parted with her life as soon as those stones. 'I've worked hard for those,' she'd say. 'No one knows how hard. . . . They represent more than you guess. Power, Watson.' And she'd gloat. I must say that cross did nearly take your breath away."

"When do you say you last saw it?"

"It 'ud be about three months ago. As a matter of fact, it was my birthday, though, naturally, Miss Kersey didn't know that. It was a real treat. Of course, I know things like that were never meant for such as me, but I must say I liked to see them. I used to be sorry Madam didn't keep more state so she'd have a chance of wearing them now and then. But perhaps she got as much pleasure out of just looking at them."

"Very interestin'," said Crook, thoughtfully. "Very interestin' indeed. Specially as I happen to know where the Ronald Cross has been for the past six months and that isn't at King's Widdows."

Disregarding Watson's start of indignant disbelief he went on, "By the way, you didn't tell me where the Phillips lived in Hampstead."

The change of subject seemed to bewilder his companion. She said in a rather flat voice, "It was Paulton Terrace, No. 19. The house on the curve. There was a lovely view from the dining-room window."

"I must remember to take a look," said Crook warmly. "One more thing. I suppose you haven't got a picture of the old lady?"

Watson said decorously that she would see, and after a moment or two rejoined him carrying two silver photograph frames that she had looted from the drawing-room. One was of a short determined woman with dark hair, untidily looped up from her ears.

"Miss Kersey," said Watson, triumphantly. "Well, of course, that was taken some time ago . . ."

"I'll say it was," agreed Crook, heartily. "All of twenty years."

The other he recognised as the Tea-Cosy, also taken a score of years earlier.

"It's a very good likeness," said Watson approvingly of the first picture. "And really she hasn't changed much. Of course, her hair's turned colour, and perhaps she's got a few more lines, but you'd recognise her as easy as easy from that picture."

"It all depends," said Crook, meaning Depends on the state she's in now, but this last bit he kept to himself.

As Crook came into the hall Hilary Grant appeared from a room on the other side of the passage. He had an open telegram in his hand.

"Kismet," he observed, cheerfully, passing it to Miss Flora. "Summons to the W.O. Now I can start looking for Auntie at the Government's expense."

"You are pleased to make a joke of this, Mr. Grant," snapped Flora. "Mr. Crook thinks it may be less of a joke to my aunt's own family. As for this . . ."

She handed back the telegram.

"It's quite genuine," protested Grant, looking a little hurt. "I believe you think it's code and really means, 'Put a bomb under Churchill's chair three p.m. to-morrow.' "

Miss Flora disregarded him entirely. Quite unper-turbed, Mr. Grant stooped and picked up the suitcase on which Crook had already stubbed his toes and went towards the stairs remarking, "Shan't want anything so voluminous as this for one night."

Flora turned back to Crook. "Will you give me your telephone number? Can I get in touch with you to-night?"

"Hitler permitting," agreed Crook with his usual ready wit.

"Then, if my aunt does not arrive for dinner, I will let you know."

"Let the police know," Crook advised her. "And p'raps you'd like me to broadcast it at my end, too. That is, if Cousin Theodore hasn't shown up by the time I get back."

"I am not interested in Cousin Theodore," said Miss Flora, icily.

"Then you're goin' to be Britain's exceptional woman, because the rest of the world's goin' to be on its toes about Cousin Theodore before the curtain drops."

He tore himself away and accompanied Hilary Grant down the diminutive drive.

"That household would be an absolute gift to Professor Freud," he observed.

Grant surprised him by saying, "You know, I'm sorry for Miss Flora. Oh, I daresay she's soured now, but no one would get a chance next to a woman like her aunt. She'd take the shine out of a tin of Nugget Boot Polish."

"How does she hit it off with the old lady?" inquired Crook.

"Oh, all right. She's inclined to fuss about her a bit. Of course, she and Watson are at daggers drawn. Trust one another about as much as a couple of cat burglars."

"It doesn't seem a very lively existence for a woman of her age," said Crook. "She can't be much above forty."

"Ah, but if she cleared out, that would leave the field to Watson. Whenever Miss Flora becomes restive Miss Kersey says, 'Pity to spoil the ship for a ha'porth of tar. You'll find it was worth while being patient after I've gone.'"

"Meaning she's left everything to the niece?"

"Mind you," said Hilary Grant, thoughtfully, "I don't know how much there is to leave, any more than I know if all the old lady's talk is so much blarney and she's really going to donate it all to a home for tom-cats. But it wouldn't surprise me to hear that the will is in Miss Flora's favour. It's the sort of thing I'd expect her to do. And why not? She'll have had her fun during her lifetime. She enjoys teasing, you know, and, of course, her niece plays up the whole time."

"Cat and mouse," said Crook, intelligently. "Is she a millionaire in disguise, do you suppose?"

"She's got some damned fine pearls," the young man assured him. "And she told me that one day, if I was interested, she'd show me something else that was even better. Well, paupers don't generally have jewels like that, and Miss Flora hasn't a thing and doesn't care who knows it—which means that Miss Kersey carries all the expenses of the house—and a pauper couldn't do that."

"She might have put her money into an annuity," reflected Crook. "You never can tell."

"I hadn't thought of that," Hilary Grant admitted. "And I don't think Miss Flora had, either."

"Miss Flora open up much about the future?" inquired Crook.

"Only to say that the money won't be much good to her when she's too old to enjoy it. And yet I somehow don't believe the money motive is the determining factor in the case where she's concerned. I don't mean she couldn't use the cash, but even more, she wants to stand first with her aunt. I suppose she feels she's never been of paramount importance to any one. I don't know if you get me . . ."

He looked at Crook a little helplessly, asking to be met half-way.

"Sure you haven't been in Harley Street just as a make-weight?" suggested Crook, and grinned. "All that psychological flapdoodle and laws of compensation make me thirsty. Plain fact is she and Watson are as jealous as hell of each other. Hallo! Is that the post office? I want to ring up Bill Parsons in case any bodies have come to light. Thought I wouldn't actually do it from the house."

"You won't get in there till half-past two," Grant warned him. "It shuts from one to two-thirty. No business done, not even if peace were signed in the lunch interval."

"And it's now two-twenty. They do look after themselves in the country, don't they? Ah well, it's an ill wind that blows no one any good. I said I was thirsty."

And, his cheerfulness unimpaired, he crossed the street to The Three Kings.

At two-forty he was speaking to Bill. "I suppose," he suggested, "you didn't find that nursing home."

"Quite right," said Bill. "I didn't."

"Nor any bodies?" pursued Crook.

"I haven't," Bill agreed, "but the police have been a bit more enterprising."

"You mean, they've got a body?"

"Asking for you to go down and identify it."

"Where did they find it?"

"Flat below," said Bill, laconically.

"Golly!" said Crook. "Poor old Tea-Cosy, after all."

But as it happened what the police had really found was the body of the Tea-Cosy's aunt.

II

While Crook was being leisurely conveyed to King's Widdows, the pretty girl, Sigrid Petersen, was paying her second visit to the flat in Brandon Street. As she had told Miss Fitzpatrick, she was bombed-out of a neighbouring road in March, since when she had been living very uncomfortably between her office and a shelter, where she did canteen work. Three weeks after the

bombing some of her furniture was rescued, and she de
cided to rent another flat. There were a good many ii
the district, but the one she preferred both for conven
ience and for the size of the rooms was the flat on the
first floor in Mr. Crook's house. She hurried round
therefore, at noon on the day of the Tea-Cosy's mys
terious disappearance, to take measurement for curtains
etc., having obtained the specious promises of the house
agents to get into touch with the original tenant and
have her belongings shifted without delay. Although thi
time she was prepared for the sight of that grim Chinese
face lurking just inside the door, and had herself taken
steps to suppress the mysterious heart-shaking rustle tha
had alarmed her the previous afternoon, she knew a sud
den and quite unaccountable dread, as she thrust her key
into the lock. It was so definite it was like a voice crying
to her from the other side of the door: "Don't come in
Don't come in."

Shaking off this ridiculous fear, she turned the key
and stepped into the dark passage. She was prepared for
the ramshackle sitting-room, with its flotsam and jetsam
of an incurable hoarder providing stumbling-blocks fo
the unwary.

"This flat must have looked very odd when it was fur
nished," she told herself. "Everything looks as though i
came out of the Ark and got thoroughly well soaked.'

The room looked eerie and dim in the faint light com
ing through a crack in the shutters. Only the outlines o
the furniture were visible, the broken-springed sofa
piled with cushions and old, coloured counterpanes, and
covered with a moth-eaten rug, the overmantel leaning
against the wall, the chipped standing lamp with its bat

tered shade askew. She moved cautiously amid the ruins.

She felt something crack under her careful tread and supposed that she had stepped on some unnoticed ornament. Hurriedly stepping off it again, she reached the window and folded back the shutters. Then she turned to see what damage she had done. The object, she found with some surprise, was a flat gold watch attached to a scrap of chain that must have fallen out of some bundle of rubbish and been overlooked.

"At least they might have got something for the case," reflected Sigrid, stooping to pick it up. The glass had been cracked across by her foot, but the face of the watch was unharmed. By an odd coincidence, it stood at 12.10.

"Even an old watch must tell the right time twice in twenty-four hours," she reminded herself, laying the watch on one side and looking for some perch on which to stand while she measured the curtains. Long net for the windows, she decided, and then her cream chintz with little blue flowers scattered on it, the whole lined with black to shut out the light.

"Any one dishonest might take the watch," she was thinking. "It's worth two or three pounds for the gold alone."

There was a pelmet here, and she had to measure that too. It took her about five minutes to work out the necessary calculations, a slender pretty girl, rather below average height, smiling with pleasure at the thought of once again having a home of her own, and with no notion of who shared the room with her. As she stepped down from the rickety cupboard on which she had been standing her eye again fell on the watch. The hands now said 12.15. Sigrid's brows, like little gold feathers above those eyes of brilliant blue, drew together in astonishment. She glanced at the diminutive watch on her own wrist.

That also said 12.15.

"I must have made a mistake," she told herself, picking up the gold watch and automatically putting it to her ear.

The next moment she had an appalling shock.

The watch was still ticking.

She could scarcely be blamed if for the first instant she failed to grasp the implications of that. A watch ticking in a room that had been shut for months and months!

The agents had warned her everything would be in a very dirty and dishevelled state, because no one had looked over the flat for a year. The facts began to hammer themselves more insistently into her intelligence.

A WATCH WAS TICKING IN A FLAT NO ONE BUT HERSELF HAD ENTERED FOR TWELVE MONTHS!

And—wasn't it strange that she shouldn't have seen the watch yesterday? It had been lying in the middle of the floor where, you would say, it simply couldn't be overlooked.

Then—had someone else come on a tour of inspection since yesterday? But the agent had handed her the key again, saying, "You might as well keep it really. No one else seems to want it." So that wasn't the explanation.

"But watches, telling the right time, don't fall from Heaven," she told herself. "Someone brought it here."

She looked round vaguely, as if expecting the person concerned to materialise from the wall. Her glance fell

on the sofa. It was odd she hadn't noticed that the cushions, flung carefully—carelessly?—you couldn't tell—
upon it, looked remarkably like a body under the rug.

"It's a good thing I wasn't so imaginative yesterday,"
she told herself. "I should probably have had hysterics
before I realised they were only cushions."

Nevertheless, her fascinated gaze strayed back to the
sofa. In spite of its suitability, she had a sudden feeling
that it would be wiser not to take the flat after all.
Rooms retain influences and atmospheres, and she knew
she would never find herself alone here without a sense
of being haunted.

She looked from the watch in her hand to the laden
sofa.

"Oh, pull yourself together," she adjured herself in
disgust. "You know they're only cushions."

Putting out her hand, she tweaked the moth-eaten rug
aside.

A terrible shriek rang through the house. It seemed
to splinter against the ceiling, crash into fragments and
come echoing back again. For an instant Sigrid had no
notion whence the sound came. She thought perhaps the
Thing on the sofa—the Thing on the sofa. . . .

She put her hands over her eyes. There was a foot in
a black patent shoe that had been caught in the fringe
of the rug, and that still waggled a little. . . . In the
silence that followed the scream she could hear the
watch ticking quite clearly.

Tick-tock, tick-tock—quite dead, quite dead.

"I'm going mad," she thought, and the watch echoed
Tick-tock, tick-tock, quite mad, quite mad.

And still she couldn't move.

Slowly her hand fell away from her eyes and she stared and stared at the Thing that seemed to stare back, but couldn't, of course, whatever a disordered imagination might suppose, because the dead can't see, the dead can't see.

And, beyond all question, the Thing on the sofa, choked and gagged by a common or garden dishcloth, was absolutely dead.

When the scream first resounded through the house Mrs. Davis, from Flat 3, put down her cup and came on to the landing. Simultaneously, Mrs. Tate from Flat 4, laid aside her glass and leaned over the banisters. The two ladies knew one another by sight, though they were careful to obey the dictates of their class, which precluded intimacy.

"Did you think you 'eard something?" inquired Mrs. Davis, after an instant.

"As a matter of fact, I did," agreed Mrs. Tate. "Gave me quite a turn. Lucky I was sitting down at the time."

"Me, too," said Mrs. Davis. For both ladies had taken to heart the Government's appeal to use household goods, such as brooms and dusters, with economy and care, since they would soon be irreplaceable. "Wonder what it could 'ave been."

"Not the kind of sound you'd expect to 'ear in a respectable 'ouse this time of day," observed Mrs. Tate, as though frenzied shrieks after nightfall were quite normal occurrences.

"Don't know 'oo it could 'a' bin neither," contributed Mrs. Davis. "That lower flat's empty."

"By rights," added Mrs. Tate, darkly.

Then another sound began. It wasn't a scream now, but something more terrible still, something to freeze the blood and chill the flesh of the least imaginative. A kind of sobbing gasp reached their ears.

Oh-h-h! Oh-h-h!

It was like a beast in pain, thought Mrs. Tate uncomfortably.

"Sounds like a murder to me," remarked Mrs. Davis.

A voice called from the floor below. "Is there any one there?"

Neither lady answered at once. It wasn't compatible with dignity to admit to listening on staircases.

"Please!" The anguished voice swept up to them again. "Is there any one there?"

Mrs. Davis, as being the nearer of the two, inquired in refined tones, "Did someone call?"

"Oh please come down, come down. Something—something's happened. It's terrible."

The conventions having been satisfied, the ladies descended the stairs like a tidal wave. They flowed all over the slender shaking figure in blue.

"There, there, dear," said Mrs. Tate, authoritatively. "What's happened? Had a nasty fright?"

Frantically Sigrid gesticulated at the door behind her.

Mrs. Davis drew herself up stiffly. "She's seen a black beedle," she said. "It takes some gels that way. When I was a gel . . ."

"When I was a gel," said Mrs. Tate, tartly, "my mother 'ud 'ave took a stick to me if I'd roused the 'ouse for a black beedle. But I don't believe it was a beedle, was it now, dear?"

Sigrid turned her head so that they saw her face for the first time. Both ladies looked rather startled.

"She's 'ad a shock," said Mrs. Tate. "I told you it wasn't no beedle. Now then, dear, you tell Mrs. Davis and me . . ."

"In there," whispered Sigrid, pointing with a shaking hand.

"But the flat's empty," remonstrated Mrs. Davis.

Sigrid shook her head. "Not now. It was empty yesterday afternoon, but it isn't empty any more."

"We better see what the girl's talking about," said Mrs. Davis.

Sigrid put out a hand to detain her.

"No, don't," she whispered. "You don't know. We must get the police."

"I'm sure I've never been mixed-up with the police," said Mrs. Davis. "I'm going to take a look."

Together they pushed their way through the door and stood blinking in the dark passage. Mrs. Tate turned her head over her shoulder.

"Where, dear?" she asked.

"In there. On the left. But don't go in, don't go in."

A wild bull wouldn't have prevented her two companions from breaking-down the door, if necessary, after these passionate adjurations. And, after all, they had been hardened by attendances at child-births, fatal illnesses and death-beds. All the same, Mrs. Tate hurriedly replaced the rug, saying something about respect for the dead, to which Mrs. Davis replied that whoever was responsible for that bit of work hadn't had much respect for the poor soul. Then they rejoined Sigrid, who had turned green, and told her she'd have to go to the police, and though they had neither of them had any truck with such folk in their lives before, seeing as she was a girl alone, they'd come with her.

"Thank you," whispered Sigrid, faintly.

"Foreign, aren't you, dear?" asked Mrs. Tate.

"Norwegian," whispered Sigrid.

"It do seem hard," said Mrs. Tate. "First 'Itler in 'er country, then a bomb in 'er belongings, and now a body in 'er flat, or as good as 'er flat."

On the way downstairs they tried to coax further information out of her, but she weakly shook her head.

From her place at the basement window, Miss Fitzpatrick saw the three of them emerge into the street. When she had noted the fact in her exercise book, she took a little refreshment. Seated at the harmonium she played, with vocal accompaniment:

All things bright and beautiful.

She was still playing when the police arrived; she saw them from her place in the window. Some time afterwards—quite a long time afterwards—there was a heavy tread on the basement steps and "they" knocked on the door. ("They" in Miss Fitzpatrick's mind were always the police, just as "they" to Mr. Crook were always houses of refreshment.) They told her that the body of a woman had been found on the first floor and asked a number of questions.

"Ha!" said Miss Fitzpatrick, profoundly. "I expect that's Mr. Crook's old lady."

Detective-Sergeant Benham looked to her for further explanation. He wasn't sure if she referred to a Mrs.

Crook, of whose existence he had never guessed—or some other person.

"He came down to see me this morning to say he'd lost an old lady," Miss Fitzpatrick supplemented. "Wanted to know if I'd seen her, but, of course, I hadn't. Well, he said, keep your eyes open in case she turns up to-day, though I don't suppose he expected her to turn up where you found her."

"Mr. Crook's not in," said Benham, unnecessarily.

"He's coming in to-night," Miss Fitzpatrick assured him. "Said he was coming to have a word with me. You come before black-out, I told him, or you won't get in, not if you're Mr. Churchill himself."

The police remained to ask further questions, none of which, so far as she could see, threw any light on the affair. She wouldn't come and look at the body because, she said, she'd seen plenty of bodies since raiding began, and where was the sense in upsetting yourself? Whoever the dead woman was, it wouldn't be a friend of hers, because she hadn't any. After the sergeant had reluctantly left the imprint of his large boots on her polished linoleum, Miss Fitzpatrick sat down and played, "My God, I love Thee . . ."

CHAPTER FIVE

This is the place. Stand still my steed,
Let me review the scene,
And summon from the shadowy Past
The forms that once have been.
                                    —LONGFELLOW.

I

CROOK and his companion had a very comfortable journey to town.

"Pity one ever has to travel down," said Hilary Grant,
thoughtfully. "Think of this morning's jam and compare
it with this. We can have a carriage apiece if you're feeling fussy."

Crook, however, was in a convivial mood and they
didn't separate until they reached Paddington. As they
passed through the barrier, Grant said, "If you should
want me for anything, I'm staying at the Sporting and
Dramatic. Can't say for how long, because I'm not in
charge of the war, but I'll be there to-night anyway."

"You'll be God's gift to the police force," Crook assured him. "They'll want someone to identify the body
—or not, as the case may be. I'm no good to them. What
the soldier said ain't evidence, and after all, I never saw
the old lady in life."

"I didn't want to scare Miss Flora," said Hilary Grant,
soberly, "but I don't mind admitting to you I don't like
it. After all, her hat was as famous in its own locality as

Beachy Head, and it don't seem likely she left it in your friend's flat for fun."

"That," agreed Crook, "is the way I see it, too, but then you and me, Grant, we ain't the police. There's no knowing what they'll see—the Loch Ness monster, I shouldn't wonder."

He saw Hilary shout at a taxi-cab, leap into it and give an address in Whitehall, whereafter he himself travelled less expensively, if less expeditiously, to Earl's Court. As he set his foot on the lowest step, he heard a sound at once furtive and imperious and, lowering his eyes, perceived the Troglodyte at her basement window. When she saw that she had caught his attention, she beckoned mysteriously, and Crook, never in a hurry to establish communications with the police, went cheerfully down to the back door.

"Come in quietly," she warned him. "You'll wake Garry." Garry was the canary. "They're still up there," she went on. "Been there on and off all the afternoon. Waiting for you and that man—what did you call him? —to come back, I suppose."

"Why should they expect me to know anything?" Crook demanded.

"Well, I told them it might be your old lady."

Crook grinned. "And what did they say to that?"

"Just asked when you'd be in. They've been taking fingerprints I shouldn't wonder."

"From the old lady?"

"Anyway, they've been going up and down and that woman who works for you, if you can call it work, she said they were taking photographs and she didn't know what else."

"There can't be much else worth taking in that flat," Crook consoled her. "What about the body?"

"They've taken her away—after I told them she was most likely yours." Her voice sank to a thrilling whisper.

"I suppose in a minute you'll tell me they really found her under my bed," said Crook in a resigned voice.

"Oh no. And she was on it—the sofa, I mean—not under it."

"Who did the finding?"

"That girl who came yesterday. She wanted another look round."

"Must have been a nasty shock for her."

"She screamed."

"I don't blame her. What about the second floor? Seen anything of him?"

The Troglodyte shook her fierce little head. "If you ask me, they'll find him in another flat."

"Uncommonly likely, I should think," Crook agreed.

"From the way the policeman talked, you'd have thought I had him hidden inside the clock." She brooded. "It's no thanks to him"—she meant Detective-Sergeant Benham—"that there wasn't another body on the premises."

"I must tell him that," said Crook approvingly. He gave a noisy fillip of his big fingers in the direction of the bird-cage. The canary instantly woke up and sang. Crook came out of the flat and climbed the stairs.

On the first floor a door moved and a voice said, "Mr. Crook?"

"Sorry you have been troubled," said Crook, backing noiselessly, because you can't be too careful, and after all, if one body why not two?

Benham introduced himself. Crook invited him up for beer, but it transpired that even when off duty the sergeant didn't drink beer. He played hockey for the police at week-ends, and he was afraid beer might spoil his style.

Crook was speechless, which gave Benham his advantage. "There's a body been found on the first floor, that we want you to see," he remarked. He was a big tower of a man, with so long a chin his mouth seemed to come in the middle of his face.

"Any hat?" murmured Crook.

Benham looked startled. "Hat?"

"Belonging to the lady, I mean."

"We didn't find one. But then ladies don't always wear them these days."

"She wore one all right when she left King's Widdows—that is, if she is my old lady. I wouldn't know."

"Your old lady?"

"Name of Kersey."

Benham stiffened. "Same as the party on the second floor."

"It could be his aunt," said Crook, dreamily. "He was wondering about her. And so were some other people."

"Mr. Kersey hasn't been in all day," said Benham.

Crook looked at his watch. "Bit early perhaps. I wouldn't know. Never back at this hour myself as a rule."

"He seems to have gone out very early."

"I always say you have to be up early to catch me," Crook told him, "but he was up earlier still this morning. Y'know, this house'll get a bad name. Gent spirited away overnight from one flat, body found next morning in another. Hope it's not an omen. As a matter of fact," he went on, "if it should be Miss Kersey, the man you want is a fellow called Hilary Grant. He's been living at Miss Kersey's house for some weeks and knows her well. I never set eyes on her in my natural. He's at the Sporting and Dramatic—Grant, I mean, that is, if the War Office has done with him, *pro tem.*"

Benham borrowed Crook's telephone and had the good fortune to find Grant at his club.

"It was all a mistake," he told Crook resignedly, when he appeared at Brandon Street. "They seem to think I'm too valuable to risk in Egypt after all. They're keeping me for a really big affair." His levity dropped from him. "I say, is there any news?"

"The police are hoping you can tell them," said Crook, and the three of them went round to the mortuary together.

The body proved to be that of a short, elderly lady, looking, as dead people usually do, one size smaller than life. She had, it appeared, been wearing a black dress much trimmed with jet, dangling jet ear-rings, old-fashioned black shoes, with straps and a lot of black beading, and a variety of chains and bracelets. No hand-bag had been found in the flat, and there was no way, short of identification by a relative or close friend, of discovering who she was. Of the pearls there was no trace.

"That's Miss Kersey all right," said Grant in sober tones. "I say, she's not a very pleasant sight, is she?" He turned away abruptly. "What in Heaven's name did they do to her?"

"She was struck on the head and stunned," returned Benham, unemotionally, "and then choked."

"Found a weapon?" asked Crook.

"There were a number of articles in the flat that might have been used, but most of them were so thick with dust and grease they'd have yielded finger-prints, and we couldn't find any. But, of course, we had nothing to tell us where the murder took place. Now, from your story, Mr. Crook, we'd be justified in searching Mr. Kersey's flat, supposing he doesn't return."

"Good Lord!" exclaimed Grant. "You don't think something's happened to him too?"

"You can't tell with a fellow like that," Crook assured them. "He might suddenly find himself back at the Court of King Arthur. That's his particular bee."

Benham said morosely, Ho, that might be very convenient, but the law was the law. He questioned Hilary Grant about Miss Kersey's journey to town and said they'd have to get into touch with the niece. It would be necessary for her to attend the inquest. Then they returned to Brandon Street and Benham went inch by inch over the events of the previous night.

"You didn't think anything queer about this man trying to get into your flat?" he demanded suspiciously. "It's not what you'd normally expect."

"You can't use a word like that about the Tea-Cosy," expostulated Crook. "What's normal to us would be haywire to him and vice versa."

He didn't take the police into his confidence about the suspicions rampant as lions on an heraldic shield in his own breast. If the police have a patron saint it must be St. Thomas Gradgrind with his insistence on facts, nothing but facts, whereas what Crook cherished in his brain was an enthralling and far-fetched fantasy.

When they reached Brandon Street there was still no sign of the Tea-Cosy. A paper bundle of laundry lay on the step outside his flat.

"He generally comes back when the British Museum closes," murmured Crook. "I don't know what time that 'ud be."

"He should be here before this," returned Benham firmly.

"And actually he had an engagement with me at nine-thirty a.m.," Crook added. That seemed to decide the police.

"We're going into this flat," the sergeant said.

"You'll probably find the key in its usual place." Crook hurriedly anticipated an assault on the door with a truncheon.

Mrs. Davis had presumably done as much in the way of clearing up as usual. That is to say, she had smudged and rendered valueless any finger-prints a possible assassin had left on the premises, had redistributed the dust and left a grimy cloth in one corner of the room, like an ill-scrawled signature. On the table was a note in an illiterate hand saying, "Regret shall not be coming to-morrow." The letter from Miss Kersey still stood on the mantelpiece and Benham took the sheet out of its envelope and glanced at it.

"He opened that in my presence," said Crook helpfully.

The policeman lifted his big unfriendly face.

"For the second time," he said.

Crook's red brows squirmed. It wasn't often the police scored off him.

"This envelope," Benham amplified, "has been opened and carefully stuck down again, and then reopened in not quite the same place. Now, you didn't see Mr. Kersey reseal this yesterday evening?"

"Not while I was here he didn't."

"And it wasn't sealed when we came in. That means, it had been opened before your arrival. There's another thing," he added, making his survey of the room, "there don't seem to be any other unopened letters lying about. Where do you say this one was?"

"On top of those newspapers."

"And he recognised the handwriting at once? And she sends him money from time to time? And yet he didn't bother to open it. H'm."

He went out of the living-room into the bedroom, but this told him nothing. The bed was made after a slummocky fashion, and without Mrs. Davis to question it was impossible to tell if it had been slept in the previous night. Benham asked for the woman's address, but no one knew it. Crook said you could ask Mrs. Tate, but most likely she wouldn't be able to help.

"Most likely not," assented Benham in forbidding tones. "I'm going to leave a man outside and if he sees any one coming in he'll stop him. If you hear anything of this Mr. Kersey, Mr. Crook, we should like to know."

Crook was recalling the events of the previous night. At the time he had told himself he might be putting his head into a trap, and yet—and yet—why drag him into it, a man called Crook who both looked and behaved like a bulldog, and could be trusted, if once he got hold, never to let go?

After the police had taken themselves off, he turned to Hilary Grant.

"Beer?" he suggested. "Right. I could do with it myself."

"This is pretty damned awful," said Grant. "What sense is there in any one knocking the poor old lady on the head? I can see the police are putting two and two together all right."

"Twice one is two," quoted Crook, "and twice two is four, but twice four is ninety-six if you know the way to score. That is, if you're in the Force," he wound up.

Crook was never fair to the police. He said it wasn't his job to work miracles.

They talked for a little of this and that, and then Grant said, "I've been thinking about Miss Flora. I suppose the police will ring her up or something?"

"They'll get in touch with the local police," said Crook, "and they'll tell Miss Flora what's happened."

Hilary sighed. "I wish she weren't always so antagonistic. For her own sake, I mean. I say, will she have to see—what we saw?"

Crook nodded. "I'm afraid so."

"She's pretty devoted to her aunt. As far as I can see, she's more or less built her life round her. I don't know what she'll do now."

"There's a war on," said Crook, unemotionally. "Any one can get a job. Besides, if the old lady was eighty she must have known she couldn't go on for ever."

"All the same, her death—like this—will be a bad shock to her."

"I'm beginning to wonder if perhaps her life—like that —may not turn out a bit of a shock, too," said Crook oracularly and opened another bottle of beer.

II

Since, slightly transposing the psalmist, Crook could say, "Darkness and light to me are both alike," it was natural to him, although it was long past black-out, to return to his office in Bloomsbury Street, and natural, too, to find Bill Parsons waiting for him. Bill was a tall man with a face that had once been handsome, and a slight limp when he walked. This limp was a reminder of his unregenerate days, when he played against the forces of law and order, and generally won hands down. Years ago Bill had been one of the country's most notable jewel thieves, but an unsporting policeman having lodged a bullet in his heel during a particularly warm chase, he had abandoned his career at a comparatively early age, and had, as Crook said, appeared on the side of the angels. That is, he was Crook's aide-de-camp at a salary that would have made a good many business men open their eyes. But Crook said he was invaluable because he knew both sides of the medal. He had stipulated that he should never be involved in the prosecution of a man with whom he had once worked, but as a large part of Crook's flourishing practice lived in the underworld, this contingency seldom arose.

The virtuous have the whole of the police force on their side, Crook used to say. You must allow vice one special pleader. Besides, whatever vice may be, it's not ungenerous. It expects to pay handsomely for proof that it hasn't done something which it knows it has; a virtuous man expects you to take his word for his innocence, and resents having to put his hand in his pocket to prove it. And so, most of the time, it doesn't get very far in.

"Anything new?" asked Bill, as Crook entered.

"Well, as you and me know, it don't always pay to tell the police everything," replied Crook. "They ain't grateful, and they always know they'd have found it out for themselves, at compound interest, if they'd had half your chances. But this is goin' to be damned interesting, Bill. F'r instance, what do you know about the Ronald Cross?"

"I know it's not in this country and hasn't been for the past twelve months," returned Bill, promptly.

"Know who smuggled it out?"

"Andersen handled it, but where he got it from—no, I can't tell you that."

"I can," said Crook, simply. "From Miss Clara Kersey. And I'd give a lot, my boy, to see the rest of her collection."

"The devil!" said Bill, equally simply. "How did she get hold of it?"

"There are only two ways of getting hold of stuff like that," Crook reminded him. "One's paying for it, and somehow I don't think she did that, the other involves pressure. . . ."

"Blackmail?" Bill's brows rose to his dark, silvered hair. "So that's her game?"

"I think so, Bill, I think so. But, bein' a careful man and havin' a reputation to keep up, I'm goin' to put it to the touch. Now, accordin' to Miss Flora and to the housekeeper, Mrs. Phillips, wife of a doctor, dyin' of

'flu in 1918, left her companion two thousand pounds.
But, also accordin' to the housekeeper, Mrs. Phillips
hadn't got a penny, and the doctor was a bit old-fashioned about paying a companion's wages. Moreover,
though she's said to have left the companion two thousand for less than two years' devotion, she didn't reward
the housekeeper's fidelity with as much as half-a-crown,
which seems fishy to me."

"A whole whale, in short," said Bill, drily.

"Well, how does it strike you? Of course, I know
getting something out of nothing is a sure recipe for a
millionaire, but if she was goin' to provide for our Miss
Kersey, why didn't she at least pay her wages in her
lifetime? Answer: Because she hadn't the necessary . . ."

"And the doctor had? And Miss Kersey knew it?"

"And knew somethin' else and cashed in on it." He
stroked his pugnacious jaw with his big mottled hand.
"Wonder if there was any funny business about the late
Mrs. Phillips' decease," he observed. "Watson said the
doctor had married again."

"1918's a long time ago," Bill suggested.

"Might check-up on that," said Crook, paying no attention. "Hang it, even a philanthropist don't shell out
two thousand for nothing. Besides, he left the place after
his wife died, set up somewhere else."

"Meanin' Hampstead was a bit too chatty for him?"

"You've said it, Bill."

"Were you thinkin' of lookin' him up?" Bill wondered.

"To ask if he murdered his wife twenty years ago?
Likely. No. Forster's our man. Forster's the chap who

was attending Mrs. Phillips at the time of her death. Well, if there was any monkey business, he won't have forgotten."

"He will, if he's got any sense," said Bill.

"I might be able to stimulate his memory," proposed Crook.

"Proof . . ." began Bill, but the Criminals' Hope interrupted without ceremony.

"You don't want proof. A doctor's reputation's a damned sight more delicate than a debutante's. Just a whisper would do him harm, irreparable harm. I don't often see eye to eye with the Tea-Cosy, but on this issue I do agree that twenty years are the same as yesterday. Besides, Bill, what the hell does a woman like Clara Kersey know about the Ronald Cross, so long as she's on the straight and narrow? Oh, she had a secret life all right, you can bet your last pint on that."

"Didn't get any hints about the other pieces, I suppose?" murmured Bill, thoughtfully.

"I gather it was kept under lock and key—all but this mysterious string of pearls, valued at five thousand pounds. Don't ask me who by," he added quickly, "because I don't know, but according to Miss Kersey's niece the old lady was wearing them to come to London, and according to the housekeeper she wouldn't be such a fool."

"And according to the police?" prompted Bill.

"The police don't seem to have heard of the pearls," replied Crook in his most guileless tone. "Funny, when you come to think of it, Bill, ain't it?"

"She'd spread her net a bit, hadn't she?" Bill observed,

not without admiration. "A couple of thousand from the doctor is one thing, but things like the Ronald Cross would be right out of his line of country."

"Know what she did with her two thousand?" inquired Crook. "I'll tell you. Opened an employment agency. Companions, private secretaries and upper servants."

"I suppose she knew the ropes, seeing the houses she'd been in."

"You bet she knew the ropes. Knew 'em well enough to keep in touch with her employees. They kept on coming back to her for the next job. She wrote to 'em, asked 'em to tea. And during the years she ran the Kay Agency she also amassed a few trifles like the Ronald Cross and the missing pearls, and I daresay a number of other museum pieces."

"And since she abandoned the Kay Agency—as I take it she has—she's parted with the Ronald Cross and perhaps the missing pearls as well?"

"And the rest, Bill, and the rest. You might put a man on to the Kay Agency. Watson who, I should say, is perfectly safe because she knows nothing and wouldn't believe it if she were told, says Madam gave up the agency on account of her health about five years ago. I asked about good-will; it ought to have been worth something, but she didn't think there was anything like that. Of course, the town may have got too hot to hold the old dame. Perhaps she'd been putting on the screw too tight. A woman in her position is a hell of a game to the rest."

"Big fleas have little fleas," suggested Bill, and became thoughtful. "How are you going to find out about this?"

"There's only one line left open," said Crook, sensibly.

"Not the Cross?"

"Not likely. Is Andersen goin' to come forward and say he dealt with it? Or any other middleman? You bet they're not. Too many questions might be asked. The Cross is as well-known in certain circles as a greyhound in others. And those pearls—suppose they do exist, and the odds are they do. Who did Miss Kersey take them along to? Andersen again? Or Purdy Martin? Or Freddie? We don't know, and what's more, we shan't. I don't mind telling you, Bill, I wouldn't be Benham in this side-show. Half his witnesses have their own reasons for keepin' out of the limelight. Look here, I'm goin' to look up the deceased's record where Dr. Phillips is concerned. That's our one chance up to date."

"Think Forster will open up after twenty years?" Bill sounded sceptical.

"Doctors aren't the only chaps who know how to operate," Crook retorted, dryly. "Of course, I'm allowin' he's still alive. I'll pop along and see him in the morning. Meanwhile, you follow up the Tea-Cosy and the Kay Agency—not that there's any reason to suppose they're linked, except by the corpse. I don't have much use for the poets, as you know, Bill, but now and again they say a bit of sense. Something about things not being what they seem, though, come to that, it was probably some other fellow who really said it, and this poet chap pinched it for his piece."

With which pleasant and characteristic observation, Crook clapped his hat on his head and returned to Earl's Court.

III

The following morning, from sheer force of habit, he pressed the bell of Flat 3, but, getting no reply, he clattered down the rest of the stairs and went by tube to Hampstead West. A combination of the medical and telephone directories had discovered for him a Dr. Erskine Forster, who might, he decided, be the man he wanted. To make things doubly sure, he went to the registrar's office, and explained that he was a lawyer who required to establish, on a client's behalf, the death of one, Mrs. Phillips, wife of Dr. Charles Phillips, who was alleged to have died in the influenza epidemic of 1918. The registrar was what was called in 1915 a dug-out. With care and the expenditure of much time he succeeded in turning up in his records an entry regarding a Mrs. Muriel Phillips, who had died of influenza on December 3rd, 1918; the death certificate had been signed by C. Erskine Forster.

"He's still in these parts?" inquired Crook, without apparent enthusiasm, and the registrar agreed that he was. Crook, therefore, proceeded to Bryning Street, where he was shown almost at once into the presence of a red-faced little man in the sixties, at sight of whom Crook instantly diagnosed high-blood pressure.

As soon as Crook came in, Forster said waspishly, "Well, what's the matter with you? Not that you need ask me for a certificate. You're as right as rain. I'm sick of all this shamming."

"Well, that's a relief," returned Crook, heartily, dashing his bowler hat on to the table, "gloves off and all the cards where we can both see 'em—that suits me."

The little doctor glared. "What the devil d'you want?"

"No certificate, no tonic, no 'Say 99.' My name's Crook, and I'm a lawyer, and I want a bit of information from you—about a murder."

"What the devil!" said the doctor again, but this time he looked at his visitor more carefully. "I don't know anything about a murder."

"Oh come," remonstrated Crook, "I never met a doctor yet who hadn't at least suspected murder among his patients on at least one occasion. All the hearties who write detective stories insist on that."

"Perhaps, sir," glowered the doctor, "you don't realise I'm a busy man."

"I'll lay you are. And so am I. So that makes two of us. Now then, I'll come down to bedrock. I'm investigatin' the case of a lady who died in the influenza scourge of 1918. You signed her certificate. You might remember . . ."

Dr. Forster looked like a barrage balloon in process of expansion.

"Have you any notion, sir, of the number of people in Hampstead alone who died of influenza during that epidemic?" he thundered.

"You tell me," said Crook, engagingly.

"And then you expect me to remember one isolated case." He now looked like a barrage balloon about to explode.

"She was rather special," said Crook. "For one thing, she was a chronic invalid, and for another she was the wife of a brother practitioner, a man called Phillips. Does that rouse anything?"

It was perfectly obvious that it had.

"I do remember her," Forster was compelled to admit. "But not because she died of influenza. There was nothing unusual about the case. Heart failure—it was happening all the time."

"That's what you say? But can you remember if you actually saw the body? It's important," he added, as Forster began to rise from his chair with the clear intention of throwing him out.

"I don't know who the devil you may be, sir," he began, but Crook stopped that by saying, "Well, I suppose you'd rather have me than the police?"

"The police?" Forster stared.

"I'd better explain. If you remember the case, you may remember that Mrs. Phillips had a companion called Kersey."

The doctor made grampus-like noises. "I don't remember the woman's name."

"Still, you remember there was one."

"I do remember that. Phillips was against it from the beginning. He believed—and he was right—that these women encouraged his wife to be more hysterical than she'd otherwise have been."

"Dear me!" sighed Crook. "Not a very sympathetic husband, I'm afraid."

"Damned sight more sympathetic than most men would have been in his shoes. Mrs. Phillips was one of these women with nothing to do and no friends to speak of, so she organised a state of invalidism. Lots of women do. It's their substitute for a career. No children, nothing. Nowadays, I suppose she'd have gone to Harley Street and for a fee of twenty-five guineas some jumped-up Johnny would have diagnosed repressions and God knows what."

"It could be," suggested Crook, soothingly, "that the jumped-up Johnny was right."

"Meaning?" snapped Forster.

Crook took out his cigar-case. "Some talk of suicide, wasn't there?" he offered.

"Don't know where you got that idea from," exclaimed Forster. "There's not a word of truth in it."

"No? Funny how ideas go round."

"Who put that one into your head?"

Crook leaned forward. His bearing was now that of the simple honest soul who wouldn't know deception if he met it served up on toast.

"There was some funny business, wasn't there? Well, look here, Mrs. Phillips was a lady with independent means."

"I don't know where you get your facts, sir," snapped the doctor, "but I happen to know she hadn't a penny. Any one who had attended her professionally—or privately for that matter—must have known that."

"Queer," mused Crook. "Did you know she left her companion a couple of thousand pounds?"

"Someone's been pulling your leg," said the doctor contemptuously.

"Fact," said Crook, quite unmoved. "She opened an agency on the money."

"It's out of the question," said Forster, flatly.

"Have it your own way," said Crook, "but—the fact remains that when she went to Mrs. Phillips she hadn't a penny but her pay, and when she left less than two years later she had two thousand pounds. If that didn't come out of Mrs. Phillips' pocket—why, the doctor must have given it to her. There wasn't any one else in the household who owned as much."

"And why do you suggest he should want to set her up? My God!" he added, a new consideration occurring to him, "you don't imagine it was anything like that, do you? That woman was fifty if she was a day."

"Well, there must have been something," argued Crook. "If he hadn't been holdin' her hand it was something else."

"If you take my advice," said Forster, ferociously, "you'll let sleeping dogs lie. Mrs. Phillips is dead and her husband's been married to his present wife for twenty years. Besides, who cares?"

"I told you—the police."

"The police can't start making inquiries now about a thing that may have happened twenty-two years ago."

"Then you think it may be true, that she did commit suicide?"

"I've no reason whatsoever to suppose she did. In fact, from what I remember of her, she's the last person living to throw in her hand."

"And leave her husband free? H'm. You may have got something there."

"Look here," said Forster impatiently, "what is all this about?"

"Did you know she kept up with him?" said Crook. "Miss Kersey, I mean?"

"Kersey? Oh, the companion. Well, I shouldn't be likely to remember her name. I wouldn't even know her if I met her."

"I'll lay you wouldn't," said Crook, softly. "Not in the state she's in now?"

"You mean, she . . . ?"

Crook nodded.

"That's why they're turning up all the back history. And it's some history, believe me. And the interestin' part seems to start with Mrs. Phillips' death."

"Now," said Forster, very firmly. "Get this into your head, if you can. I know nothing about Mrs. Phillips' death, nothing out of the ordinary, I mean. I'd been attending her for influenza, and I got a message that she'd died of heart failure—not at all an unusual occurrence in the circumstances—and I sent up a certificate. That's all there is to it."

"You sent it up? You didn't go and see her?"

"If you'd been a doctor at that time you'd have known you hadn't much leisure for standing by death-beds," was Forster's grim retort. "I'd been attending the woman . . ."

"Had you expected her to die?"

Forster became evasive.

"You have to be prepared for any emergency in influenza. Anyway, I'm convinced she didn't commit suicide. She wasn't the type."

Crook spoke softly.

"But she was the type that sometimes gets itself murdered."

"Murdered?"

"Well, have it your own way," said Crook patiently. "Somebody gave Miss Kersey two thousand pounds, and it wasn't pure charity. You can't tell me. I've been a lawyer too long."

Forster digested that for a minute or two. Then he said, "What the hell's the sense of dragging up the affair now, anyway. Is this Miss Kersey making trouble?"

"Someone's been makin' trouble for her."

Forster looked unsympathetic. "I've no doubt she deserved it."

"Murderees generally do," agreed Crook in his unscrupulous way.

The doctor stared. "What's that you said?"

"Want me to say it again?" inquired Crook. "I thought not. Well, now d'you see why we're diggin' up the past?"

"You mean, someone's murdered Miss Kersey?"

"At all events, the police think so."

"But—why drag Phillips into this?"

"My dear chap, he is in. He's been in for twenty years. She came to town to see someone. So far we can't say who."

"But you think it may have been Phillips?"

"It could be," murmured Crook. "Oh yes, it could be. Well, thanks very much."

Forster started up from his chair. "Where the devil's this going to end?"

"No one's going to blame you," Crook soothed him. "And if Phillips can supply an adequate reason for settin' up Miss Kersey in business, no one'll bother him. Question is, if he can."

After his visitor had departed, Dr. Forster sat immobile for some minutes. Crook's questions, the suspicions he hadn't thought it worth while to conceal, were stirring the doctor's recollection. No, he was convinced he hadn't seen Mrs. Phillips. Well, why should he? Phillips was the last man who'd be up to any monkey business. He mightn't have cared for his wife, and there Forster was the last man to blame him; but he cared all right about his profession. Forster remembered he'd had an uneasy qualm when he heard that his recent colleague had married the daughter of a patient within two years of his wife's death, but after all, he'd told himself, you couldn't expect the fellow to stay a widower for the rest of his days, and a doctor has to meet his bride somewhere. Life being the way it is, what more likely place than a patient's house? All the same, he didn't feel happy about it. That fellow with the curiously apposite name, if appearances were to be trusted, was about as shy as a ferret. You could trust him to dig out anything hidden, and Forster himself had been a bit surprised at Phillips' abrupt departure from Hampstead. There'd been a few tongues wagging, too. It wasn't as if it had been such an ideal marriage that he wouldn't be able to stand the neighborhood without her, and all the alternative explanations were a bit less convenient. The story about the two thousand pounds had jolted him considerably. It was one thing to put on a contemptuous expression and express disbelief, but it didn't seem very probable that Crook had made the journey to Hampstead to start a crippled hare.

He was so much engrossed in his reflections that his receptionist actually had to touch him on the arm to recall him to the present and the next case.

CHAPTER SIX

I only ask for information.
—DAVID COPPERFIELD.

I

CROOK, armed with the knowledge of Phillips' whereabouts, had little difficulty in tracking him down. He
was less fortunate here than at his first essay, and had to
cool his heels for some time while the doctor kept ap-
pointments. But he wasn't a man to waste even half an
hour. There was a receptionist here, too, and a couple of
patients in the waiting-room, and he egged them on to
talk. It sounded as though Phillips was both popular and
likeable, and when at length Crook was ushered into the
doctor's presence this impression was confirmed. Phillips
was a tall, rather thin fellow with a distinguished sort of
face and a slight limp, his legacy from the first world
war. He had, Crook had learned from his inquiries,
served at the front during 1914 and 1915, returning at
the end of the latter year "unfit for further service."

"You look a pretty healthy specimen," was his greeting of his visitor. Crook, who never consulted doctors
professionally, presumed that this discouraging greeting
was automatic. "Hope you're not going to tell me there's
anything wrong with you."

"I've not come on my own account," Crook admitted.
"I'm here in connection with a Miss Kersey, one-time
companion to your first wife."

The man in front of him seemed to grow rigid. He nodded towards a chair and Crook sat down. Then the doctor said, "What exactly is the relationship between you and Miss Kersey?"

"I'm a lawyer—ask any one east of Charing Cross. Or you might try Scotland Yard. I'm not altogether unknown there. Miss Kersey's nephew is a client of mine."

"I'm afraid I can't help you," said Phillips, looking perplexed.

"Miss Kersey came to town a couple of days ago, with the intention of payin' a number of visits."

"She wasn't expecting to see me," said Phillips, sharply.

"Well, that's one of the things I wanted to know. You see, we're trying to get in touch with any one who can help us."

"Do you mean, she's—disappeared?"

"Well, she did for a short time, but have to hand it to the police, they do know their onions. They soon unearthed her—but naturally they're a bit curious."

"Do you mean that she's dead?"

"Very dead," said Crook, grimly. "I believe you've kept up with her since she left your employ at the end of 1918?

Phillips looked as if he'd deny it if he could, but gave up that idea when he caught another glimpse of Crook's face.

"As a matter of fact, she asked for assistance now and again. She must be quite an old woman now, and I've never cared to refuse . . ."

"She wasn't an old woman when you made her a present of two thousand pounds," Crook pointed out, bluntly.

"I . . ." But the doctor seemed to think better of his

instinctive denial. "She seems to have confided in you," he said.

"Now, I don't imagine you gave it to her for any sentimental reason," continued Crook, galloping ahead like a steeple-chaser. "She'd been with your wife less than two years, so she'd no kind of claim on you, but naturally, if that fact comes out, as it easily may, a lot of awkward questions are pretty certain to be asked."

"Why should you suppose anything should come out, as you call it?"

"Well," said Crook, adopting his most reasonable air, "what do you think yourself? Remember the facts. This woman has been found dead in damned suspicious circumstances. In short, by violence."

"That's no concern of mine," protested Phillips. "She was a very difficult woman. I don't doubt she had a good many enemies. . . ."

"Don't say that kind of thing to the police," Crook warned him, dryly. "Oh yes, you'll very likely be seeing quite a lot of them. She appears to have been a woman of mystery, and naturally they want to find out as much about her as they can. Sooner or later they'll trace her back to your household. . . ."

"I don't know why you should be so sure of that," muttered Phillips.

"Well, for one thing, she's still got your ex-house-keeper, Watson, with her."

Phillips smiled wryly. "She's covered herself at every point, hasn't she? Of course, Watson believes whatever Kersey may have chosen to tell her."

"All the same," said Crook slowly, "not being quite a fool, Watson has drawn her own conclusions."

"Meaning?" The doctor's voice was sharp.

"Well," Crook sounded slightly apologetic, "she does realise your first wife didn't leave her companion two thousand pounds, for the simple reason that she hadn't two thousand pounds to leave."

Phillips drew a long breath. Crook watched him intently.

"See where that gets you?" he suggested.

"All right," said Phillips, suddenly throwing up the sponge, "you can have the truth. I gave Kersey the money to save my wife's good name, and, incidentally, my own. It doesn't do a doctor any good if it gets about that his wife committed suicide."

"So that's the way of it. The death certificate said heart failure, following influenza."

"That's not Forster's fault. The man was run off his feet. I phoned him to that effect and he sent the certificate round. All quite in order. We were all doing that all the time. They couldn't get the doctors out of the Army fast enough to cope with civilian casualties. It was an unprecedented opportunity for unscrupulous men." His mouth twisted as he spoke.

"And women," Crook agreed. "But, seein' that influenza's known to be a most depressin' disease and your wife was in bad health at the time, at any time, come to that, plus the fact that just after the Armistice people were mostly off their dot, would it have been so damagin' to admit that she'd taken an over-dose or whatever it was?"

"You've missed the point," said Phillips, patiently. "In the circumstances, there could have been no proof that she did take her own life. Indeed, to have urged that solution would have involved saddling her with a degree of malice that no man, even a brute, could face with equanimity."

Crook looked at him slyly. "Are you tellin' me you don't really know how your wife died?"

"Not beyond doubt," said Phillips, slowly. "Though, if you were the police, I should say suicide while of unsound mind."

"But you couldn't prove it wasn't—the other thing?"

"No," agreed Phillips, very quietly. "I couldn't prove it."

"You don't feel inclined to open up? Remember, I'm a lawyer, not the police."

"But—you're on their side?"

Crook grinned. "Crook on the side of the angels? You tell them that and see what happens."

"I suppose I may as well give you the facts, since it looks as though they're likely to come out in any case. Actually, Kersey didn't play any trumps till after the funeral."

"Begin at the beginning," Crook urged. "Where did she find her trumps anyhow?"

"The circumstances themselves were enough for that. Any hint of—foul play—especially in a doctor's household—spells ruin for the man concerned. Even a whisper of murder in his practice does him no good, Heaven knows why."

"Guilty conscience," said Crook, briskly. "The average man can never be sure when he won't have a brainstorm himself, and a doctor who's already nosed out one murder isn't the man for him."

"You may be right. Anyhow, here are the facts. My

wife had had influenza, like several thousand other people. Both Forster and I considered the crisis past, and that she was definitely gaining ground. She'd talked a lot, of course, about being a burden and being ready to go; doctors hear a good deal of that sort of thing, so I didn't pay too much attention. But that last night she said it all over again, with variations, when I went up to see her after dinner. I had an urgent call, and even during epidemics misguided people go on breaking their legs and having babies and getting measles. Muriel asked for her sleeping-draught, saying that Kersey was often so immersed in her own affairs she forgot about it and had to be asked. I reminded her that we were employing Kersey for just that kind of thing, but she said, 'I know, but I hate feeling a perpetual nuisance.' I got the bottle and glass and put them by the bed, and then she asked me to pour the stuff out. It was rather a strong mixture that Forster had given her, and I told her to be careful how she took it. She said she only had it when she felt particularly exhausted, but she was sure she'd need it that night. I mixed the draught and put the bottle back in the medicine-chest. It was about a third full. I met Kersey as I came down to the hall, and she said my wife seemed better. I said, 'Yes, but I wanted her kept very quiet, she seemed to me a bit hysterical.' I added that I'd mixed her sleeping-draught, and I thought it would be a good thing if she settled down early. Then I went out.

"I didn't get back till nearly six o'clock—a.m., I mean. The baby I had to bring into the world took an unconscionable time putting in an appearance and I had a call from Shaw House, where Lady Shaw was dying, asking me to go along if I could. I went along there about four o'clock, just in time, as it happened, and as I say, came back to my own house at six. I met Kersey in the hall. She said at once, 'Oh Doctor, I'm worried about Mrs. Phillips. I think—I'm afraid—something's happened.' I suppose," added Phillips, but not as though he really believed it, "you legal fellows feel all in sometimes. That night I felt I could sleep on my feet. I hadn't had a break for almost twenty-four hours. Kersey couldn't have chosen a worse moment from my point of view or a more advantageous one from hers, to explode her bombshell."

Crook nodded. He knew what was coming and he sympathised with the doctor, without at this juncture making up his mind if the fellow were a murderer or no.

"Naturally," the other continued, "I asked her what she meant, and she said, 'I can't wake her. She feels very heavy.' I asked if she'd sent for Forster, and she replied in an odd way that at that stage I didn't understand, 'I thought perhaps it would be better to wait till you came in. I've been trying to get you but I didn't know where you were.' Actually, I'd said I might go on to Shaw House, but when I reminded Kersey of this she said, 'I know, but I thought you'd rather I didn't ring you there.' I didn't argue the point, but went up to my wife's room. These wasn't the smallest doubt, of course."

He stopped, looking at Crook, who said, "Well, these things will happen," in an unhelpful sort of way, and Phillips, after waiting for a more sympathetic comment which didn't come, continued his recital.

"I asked Kersey when she had last seen my wife, and she said, 'About ten o'clock, when she took her sleeping-draught and said she wouldn't be wanting me till she rang.'"

"And did she ring?"

"Apparently not, but Kersey went into her room about five o'clock. As a rule, she liked a cup of tea at five. And as soon as she came in she realised something had happened. Well, I was surprised, but not unduly so. These excitable people are like a game of snakes and ladders. Up one minute and down the next and, though I hadn't expected this development, I'd been a doctor too long not to realise that you can never be absolutely sure. I told Kersey she'd better ring up Forster and tell him what had happened. She said: 'Do you mean you want him to come round?' and I said it would do if he sent a certificate, as he'd been attending the case."

Again the doctor paused. He was proceeding with his story very carefully now, as if he felt every word counted.

"She said, 'You mean, you'd prefer me to tell him not to come.' I didn't understand at first. I said, 'When he's rushed off his feet like the rest of us, there's no need to insist on his coming in person.' She nodded and murmured in a considering sort of way, 'No, I suppose not.' But she didn't make any move towards the telephone, and I said a bit sharply, 'You may as well get through at once.' She just looked at me. 'Well?' I said. 'What is it?' She said, 'You poured out Mrs. Phillips' sleeping-draught last night, doctor. Did you notice how much was left?' I said, 'About a third. I couldn't be more exact than that.' She nodded. 'That's what I thought. But—look at the bottle now.' She went to the cupboard and took it out. It was stone empty."

"Jam for Miss Kersey," said Crook in approving tones.

"She had me on toast and she knew it," Phillips agreed.

"I asked her where she'd found the bottle, and she said in the cupboard. I said, 'Who's tampered with that?' And she just looked at me. You see the position?"

"Juicy," Crook agreed. "Only three alternatives. Either you poured in an overdose, or your wife slipped out and took the extra herself in the hope it would ruin you, or Kersey was responsible."

"My wife wouldn't have allowed Kersey to tamper with the dose I'd poured out for her," said Phillips, sharply.

"Suppose Kersey saw her chance and managed to up-set the glass. Oh, I admit it was risky, but she's a lady who deals in risks. Or—suppose your wife hadn't died of an overdose at all, and Kersey had taken another chance and just poured the stuff away."

"An inquest could have settled that," said Phillips, slowly.

"Point is, could you afford the inquest? The fact that the bottle was empty was bound to come out, and tongues would have wagged. They're better at that game than a dog's tail. No, I think Kersey knew you wouldn't call her bluff—if she was bluffing. What happened next?"

"Nothing happened till three days later. When the funeral was over I began to lay plans. I didn't mean to stay in Hampstead. It had too many unfortunate mem-ories, and I had the chance of buying this practice, while there was no difficulty in disposing of mine. My partner wanted to bring in a son—it all hung together very well. I gave the servants notice, and if they looked a bit odd, that didn't seem important then. Kersey had played her cards well. All the servants liked her, Watson in particular. I'd always suspected that Kersey played up to my wife. Certainly my affairs became even more complicated after she joined us. Though even then I didn't realise what she had in mind."

"This is an innocent man," reflected Crook, hopelessly. "No criminal's such an ass."

"Naturally, I gave her notice with all the rest. That couldn't surprise her. She'd realise there was no place for her in my household now that I was a widower. I gave her a cheque for a month's pay and told her she could look to me for a reference. She didn't take the cheque—have you ever thought how silly a man looks holding out something to someone who isn't interested?—and then she said, 'I'm past fifty, Dr. Phillips. I'm getting old to work in other people's houses.' I didn't quite know what to say to that. She went on, 'If I'm ever going into business on my own this is my last opportunity. Five years hence will be too late.' I said in a civil sort of way, 'What kind of business did you fancy?' And she said at once, 'I thought we should understand one another, Dr. Phillips. I thought of running an employment agency, but, of course, you need capital.' I asked her if she thought she would really like that—it was a lot of responsibility—and she said, 'Oh, I'm used to responsibility, and in my kind of work you learnt to be discreet. I don't suppose you can understand what it's like, always to be at someone's beck and call,' she wound up."

"Hadn't you got a lawyer?" inquired Crook, pityingly. "It would have worked out cheaper in the end."

Phillips shook his head. "In the circumstances, it wasn't possible. Kersey went on, 'It would cost two thousand pounds, Dr. Phillips.' 'Well,' I said, 'do you know where to put your hand on so much?' 'I think I could raise it,' she said. 'How do you feel about it?' To say I was staggered is to put it mildly. Mind you, I'd never liked the woman, thought she was a bad influence for Muriel, but I'd never thought of her as downright—dangerous. I said, 'Can you tell me any reason why I should set you up in business?' Because it was obvious that was what she meant, and she said . . ." Phillips hesitated and Crook filled in the gap.

"Don't," he begged. "My mother sang me to sleep with that one. She had something you might like to buy. Isn't that about the size of it?"

Phillips nodded.

"The chap that taught people to write made more trouble than our Mr. Hitler," Crook murmured. "I suppose there were letters. . . ."

"How in Heaven's name she laid hands on them I'll never know. Still the fact remains, there they were, and she offered to sell them for two thousand pounds—to the first bidder."

"They weren't worth that to any one but you," Crook assured him.

"And to me they were worth about two millions."

Crook looked out of the window. "And the writer of the letters was—the present Mrs. Phillips?" he suggested.

Phillips nodded. "I suppose you chaps are up to everything. Well, you see the position?"

"Shootin' a sittin' bird ain't sportsmanlike, but it is a temptation, y'know," Crook told him gravely. "Well, you gave her the two thousand. Did that close it?"

"I didn't hear from her again till I married Miss Shaw.

Then she wrote that she was having a hard fight of it, perhaps, seeing she'd been a member of my household—you know the kind of thing."

"Didn't occur to you to refuse?"

"I wasn't in a position to refuse."

"I thought you said she'd handed over the letters."

"Ah, but not the negatives. She had them all photographed before she sent them to me, dates and all . . ."

"And now she's featherin' her nest sellin' the negatives?"

"Yes. She had one more."

"On offer?"

"Yes."

"When were you expectin' her?"

"She never made a definite appointment, just walked in when she felt like it. Never mind what patients were waiting, she just chose her own time. . . ."

"I expect she wanted something pretty healthy for the last of the collection, the flower of the flock?"

Phillips nodded.

"Were you goin' to pay her?"

"We'd have to have agreed on a price, but actually, she never turned up. Well, there's the story. You know," he added, coming to his feet, "I wouldn't be surprised if she made a regular profession of it, blackmailing, I mean."

Crook looked at him with some admiration.

"Pity you weren't as fly as that twenty years ago," he remarked. "Matter of fact—nor would I."

II

His receptionist announced Dr. Phillips' next patient, a gouty and restive gentleman, and Crook taking the hint returned to his office.

"I've got some stuff for you about your precious agency," Bill told him, in his disinterested voice. "Your Miss Kersey seems to have been fairly hot stuff. It's not surprising she closed down in a bit of a hurry. The really surprising thing is that she got away with it for so long."

"Cover, I suppose," said Crook a little obscurely, hanging his hat on a peg behind the door, a sure indication that he intended to settle down to business.

"She specialized in temporary servants—ladies'-maids and so forth. You could practically always get someone—at high wages, certainly, but if it was the Kay Agency you could count on getting an expert. What happened was that Marie or Alphonse or Miss Smith came to you with excellent references and stayed, say, six months; after he or she had departed to another job, unpleasant things started happening. The ex-employer would get letters reminding her—it was generally her—of indiscretions that might prove damned expensive if they were publicly aired. It was suggested it might be worth her while to keep the writer quiet. Occasionally photographs of letters were enclosed."

"Be sure to look for the trade-mark," murmured Crook. "I begin to see how our Miss Kersey amassed her nice little collection."

Bill nodded. "You know how it is with people. Not one in a hundred has the nerve to go to the police—afraid of publicity, family to be considered, all the rest of the flapdoodle. As a rule, the money came and the evidence would be returned. But sometimes, even without concrete evidence, you can pull down a very pretty plum, and Miss Kersey seems to have known all the answers. Of course, she chose her clients with a good deal of care. Now and then she landed a stumer, but she soon pushed them out. Quite often the employees had something against them, like that niece who had been sacked for embezzling petty cash. She hadn't much hope of getting another job, not at a living wage or with an honest firm. Miss Kersey sent her out to see what she could learn. If nothing was forthcoming in six months, the employee gave notice. Some houses, of course, you could tell would be no good straight away, and then the servant said it was too quiet or she had a sick mother, or just that she didn't feel at home in the place, but not often, because Miss Kersey didn't want to get the reputation of having capricious servants. She only supplied to big houses and large staffs, and she specially liked the sort of house that gives week-end parties. Week-end parties give a lot of scope for blackmailers and there's a lot of truth in the saying that every family has its skeleton. The difference between the skeletons is that some are worth money and some you could hang out on the top of St. Paul's Cathedral and no one would take any notice."

"I guessed it was something of that kind," said Crook. "Well, it must have been a paying racket while it lasted."

"Nothing's more expensive to both sides than black-mail, or so I'm told," agreed Bill, who had no first-hand information. He had been a jewel thief, but a jewel thief is a gentleman and does not walk in the same street as a blackmailer.

"I suppose she'd have to pay these people a hell of a lot," Crook ruminated. "Otherwise they might start out on their own."

But Bill demurred. "Takes some nerve even for blackmail, if you're on your own. If you are found out, you're for it. I wonder if we can get anything out of the niece."

"Not if she's got the brains of a louse, you won't," said Crook. "How did the agency fold up in the end?"

"One of those developments that was practically bound to occur sooner or later. Mind you, Miss Kersey must have been a clever woman. She had to be sure she wasn't sending her people to households constantly in touch with one another, who might compare notes and draw their own conclusions, but in this instance she slipped up. One of her employees, Miss A., went as companion-secretary to a Lady Z. After some time, she left—a sick mother or something—and soon after she had gone, the mysterious letters started coming. Lady Z. paid up—goodness knows how—and hoped the matter was closed. Some time later, visiting a friend in the country, she found Miss A. there, as secretary. She asked after the mother, all the rest of it, and later happened to mention that Miss A. had once been employed by her. None of that would have mattered if Miss Kersey had realised the two employers had met, but one imagines the girl didn't mention the fact. Well, things followed their usual course. Miss A. left because she had to go back to town, for family reasons. Soon afterwards—the usual procedure. But in this case the wretched woman couldn't stand on her own feet, she had to confide in someone, and she chose to tell her story to Lady Z. Lady Z., not being a fool all round the clock, began to put two and two together. When Mrs. X. said, 'I can't imagine how any one found out. I was most discreet,' Lady Z., who also thought she'd been discreet, looked for the common denominator and found—Miss A. They talked it over and it seemed to both of them damned fishy that history should repeat itself in every detail. Lady Z. then did what she should have done a year before, took her courage in both hands and went to see Miss Kersey. She asked if Miss K. had any references for Miss A. She said that, though she very much disliked drawing inferences of an unpleasant nature, some important papers had disappeared from her house at about the time Miss A. left it. She had made no accusation, since she had no proof, but precisely the same thing had happened in the case of a friend of hers, who had also employed Miss A.

"Miss Kersey, of course, had wonderful references for Miss A.," contributed Crook. "And, of course, there had never been any previous complaints."

"Never," Bill agreed. "All the same, once on the war-path, Lady Z. was about as easy to stop as a young tank. She remembered that when she applied to the agency for someone to replace Miss A. the agency hadn't been able to help, and the same thing had happened in Mrs. X.'s case. How far the conversation went one can't be certain, but Lady Z. seems to have made it pretty clear that she meant to turn up all the stones and release all the things hidden under them. At all events, Miss Kersey seems to have realised she'd shot her bolt."

"If she'd called Lady Z.'s bluff, the odds are she'd have got by," said Crook, unsympathetically. "She's got a rich husband and two sons. She can't afford to come into that kind of limelight."

"Perhaps the affair got about a bit. Anyway, it was given out that Miss Kersey wasn't well. She left some-one in charge—presumably this niece you saw down at King's Widdows who must have been in her aunt's confidence all along, and a printed circular informed clients that, owing to a serious heart attack, the agency's proprietor had had to give up the concern and retire to the country. A chap in the same building was glad enough to take over the premises, and the Kay Agency just died out."

"And the men and women who'd gone there for their jobs?"

"I bet you Clara Kersey was much too fly to give 'em anything they could pin on to her in court. Besides, they were in it up to the neck themselves. The odds are most of her victims don't know to this day how it was done or who did 'em."

"It's an ill-wind that blows no one any good," said Crook, philosophically, "think of all the people who'll be able to lie quietly in their beds now the news has gone round."

"If they don't know they can lie quietly in their beds, it won't help them," objected Bill.

But Crook was following his own particular hare.

"It's too bad about the police," he said. "They ought to show more enterprise. Now, a murder like this does more social good than harm. They ought to take that into consideration when they hand their Johnny over to the court. But they won't, Bill. You take my word for it, they won't."

And he sighed for the blots on the fair shield of Justice.

CHAPTER SEVEN

Every why hath a wherefore.
—PROVERB.

I

THE INQUEST was held twenty-four hours later. Flora
Kersey had arrived in London, obstinately accompanied
by Watson, who said she had known Miss Kersey longer
than any of them, and what would the poor lady think
of her stopping down at King's Widdows at such a time?
She didn't ask to travel with Miss Flora and she would
pay her own fare, but come to the inquest she would—
and did. Hilary Grant was there, too; when he saw Flora
he went over to speak to her, but she must have sent him
away with a flea in his ear, because, after a minute, he
left her side and crossed the room.

There wasn't much to be done at this stage. Flora gave
evidence of identity, and the girl, Sigrid Petersen, looking pale and smaller than ever, repeated her story of the
finding of the body, after which the coroner announced
that the inquest would be deferred pending further
police inquiries.

Flora saw Crook and asked for news of Cousin Theodore.

"He's vanished as clean as a whistle," said Crook. "You
can draw your own conclusions."

"I always knew he'd ruin her in one way or another,"
said Flora, in a fierce, subdued voice. "When I heard the

rumour that he'd been killed in an air-raid last autumn I was glad. I thought there'd be one person less to prey on her. But, of course, he had to be the one member of his household to be out of the house that night, and turn up again like a bad penny at a new address a few weeks later."

Crook nodded sympathetically. "Hitler made a bloomer there," he agreed in serious tones.

"In any case, what are the police doing that they haven't found him?" Miss Flora continued, in the same voice.

"They do their best," said Crook, tolerantly. "But he may be somewhere where it won't be too easy to find him."

"That," agreed Miss Flora, viciously, "is quite probable. That was my aunt's weak point. She had been successful and taken risks for so many years she had come to regard herself as invulnerable. She couldn't believe, not only that any one could be as shrewd or far-seeing as herself, but that any one would dare to set him or herself up against her. I warned her. . . ."

"What against?" inquired Crook, intrigued.

"Taking people at their face value. But she wouldn't listen to advice. 'Don't teach your grandmother,' she'd say. 'How do you suppose I got where I am now, except by believing in myself and taking chances?' And now she's taken one chance too many."

"She had a good run for her money," Crook pointed out in what he intended to be a soothing voice.

"She'd had five years to enjoy what she'd spent a lifetime accumulating," flashed his companion. "Why, she was good for years yet. And she enjoyed life so. She liked its irony, the way things change. It's like a raft, she used to say. You never know when it's going to capsize and throw all the people who feel they're so safe into the water. And then she'd laugh in that subtle way of hers, and add, 'Ah, but it gives those who're already in the water their chance. When the raft rights itself, some of the others will have vanished, and if you're quick you can climb on. Always remember that, Flora,' she'd tell me. 'If the water's cold and you feel you must go under, remember that at any moment the raft will turn over and give you your chance.' She was a sportsman," Flora added simply. "She took risks and she knew she took them, but she wouldn't have lived any other way."

"She certainly doesn't give the impression of a lady who would be content to die quietly in her bed," Crook agreed.

He didn't want to continue the conversation. He didn't think there was anything else Miss Flora could tell him, at present anyhow. Of course, there was a number of questions on the tip of his tongue, the correct answers to which would, he felt, go a long way towards elucidating the mystery, but he sensibly assured himself that he wouldn't be likely to get the correct answers, so he left Miss Flora to make arrangements about the funeral.

But he was not yet finished with the household. After Flora had been shaken off, Watson approached him rather timidly.

"Excuse me, sir," she said, "but I don't quite know what to do next, and I thought, you being a legal gentleman, you might be able to help me."

"You wait till you hear the contents of the will,"

Crook advised her. "There may be something for you there; and even if there isn't, I suppose Miss Flora . . . ?"

But Watson shook her head.

"I wouldn't wish to stay with her now Madam's gone," she said. "Madam made it sort of home for me, but Miss Flora—she's different."

"I get you," said Crook, in his shrewd vulgar way. As indeed he did.

Watson had her pride like any one else, and she didn't propose to take money or orders from one who had, to all intents and purposes, despite the tie of blood, been a servant herself, and a dishonest servant at that. No, Watson wouldn't take service under Miss Flora. But she was by no means a young woman. Crook put her down at sixty-seven or eight, and hoped Miss Kersey had had the decency to make provision for her.

"Who was Miss Kersey's lawyer?" Crook went on.

"I think he's that gentleman there, that little gentleman. He telephoned to Miss Flora to ask about the inquest."

"Is this his first appearance?"

"Yes. Miss Flora told him they could discuss things when that was over. Oh, she's careful, Miss Flora is."

But Crook made no comment on that. He didn't imagine Miss Flora would save much on her lawyer's bill by cutting down the number of his visits.

"Well," he now told Watson, "he's the chap to tell you where you stand. In the meantime, you take my tip and stay at King's Widdows. There'll be plenty to do."

"Miss Flora spoke of closing the house," hesitated Watson. "But I tell her, the Government will take it over and she won't do so well over that."

"In any case," Crook observed dryly, "it might be as well to wait and make sure it's hers to close."

"Oh, I hadn't thought of that. Do you think—oh, but Miss Flora took it for granted it would come to her."

"Well, when Miss Flora's my age she'll learn not to take anything for granted," Crook told the woman, genially. "I suppose it was Miss Kersey's property?"

"Oh yes. Madam bought it. She never could see the sense of spending hard-earned money keeping up some-one else's house, and after the war she'd always be able to sell at a profit, she thought."

"If the place hasn't fallen down from old age by that time," Crook agreed. "And then, well, naturally, I don't know anything about her relations with her niece. . . ."

"Madam didn't altogether trust her," Watson announced in her flat, deliberate way. "That I do know. I don't mean about money or anything of that sort, but—well, I overheard a word or two she said to Mr. Grant once. Flora's longing to step into my shoes, she said. It doesn't seem to occur to her that our feet may not be the same size."

"You must have had a grand time," approved Crook. "What were you thinking of doing yourself?"

"I've got a sister at Basingstoke," said Watson. "I thought of going there. But, of course, I'd like to know just how things stand." She sighed. "Mr. Grant's moving out. Would you believe it, she told him to his face last night, with me there, that he'd been making up to her aunt ever since he arrived, and she knew it. It was awkward, it was, really."

"Awkward's hardly the word," murmured Crook,

appreciatively. "All right I'll have a word with the lawyer. What's his name?"

"Mr. Maxwell."

Crook went across. "I'd like a word with you on behalf of my client," he said. "My name's Crook, and I'm representing Mr. Theodore Kersey, who's unfortunately prevented from being present to-day. I don't want to keep you, but I'd be glad to know if he benefits in any way under the will."

Before Maxwell could answer, Miss Flora swept up. Paying no attention to Crook, she said, "I shall see you then at half-past two, Mr. Maxwell. I have to arrange about the funeral first," and strode off again.

"I'm afraid," began Mr. Maxwell nervously, looking after her retreating figure.

"I don't blame you," said Crook, warmly. "I'd as soon act for a rattlesnake myself. Look here, how about lunch? I'll say I need it, and you look as if you did, too."

Willy-nilly, incapable of protest, Mr. Maxwell was swept along. Actually, he didn't really mind. He needed some Dutch courage to face the terrifying Miss Flora at 2.30.

"As, of course, you know, Miss Kersey helped my client at intervals over a considerable period," said Crook, skating lusciously over thin ice. For he had only the Tea-Cosy's word to go on, and there were only two explanations of the Tea-Cosy's non-appearance, to a reasonable mind, and he liked neither of them.

"Quite, quite," agreed Mr. Maxwell, inspecting *specialité de maison à la Woolton* that was clapped before him. "And it was her intention to do so for so long as he required assistance."

"Meanin' to the end of the road," interpreted Crook, simply. "Well, that'll be a weight off the old boy's mind. What figure did she suggest?"

"It was always on the modest side. Mr. Kersey has no extravagant tastes. In her will she proposed an annuity of two hundred a year which, with what he himself possesses, would be sufficient for his needs."

"That settles his hash," agreed Crook. "How about Watson? She seemed to be afraid she might be left out in the cold."

Mr. Maxwell looked a little offended. "My client has also made provision for her," he said. "Similar provision, in short. She also left the house, Swansdown, but . . ."

Crook whistled softly. "The devil she did. That won't please Miss Flora. What does she get, by the way?"

"The residue of the property," said Maxwell, who had no more chance against Crook than a parachutist against the Home Guard.

"Nice," commented Crook. "She'll be relieved, too, won't she? I mean, there's all the jewellery."

Maxwell brightened a little. He seemed frightened of having to break the provisions of the will to the tough-looking woman he had seen at the inquest. "I understand that is quite valuable," he said. "Actually, I have never seen it, and in any case, I am not an expert. But Miss Kersey always gave me to understand that it comprised the major part of her capital."

Crook's red brows rose. "That so?" he murmured.

Mr. Maxwell became more confidential. "The fact is," he said, "my client was a very unusual kind of woman. She always gave me to understand that her employment of a lawyer was little more than a concession to the conventions. Those that come after me, she would say, will need someone to keep a hand on affairs. I'll have no bickering about what I leave. I like my yea to be yea and my nay, nay. But for herself she never took advice or indeed asked for it."

"And her income?" prompted Crook.

"Sprung from no known source. That is to say, she had a little money, certainly, invested in certain stocks, but some of these have depreciated owing to war conditions, and are practically unsaleable, while others are paying reduced dividends, and naturally the income-tax makes heavy demands . . ."

"You mean, she lived on her capital," condensed Crook, briskly.

"She didn't keep a large balance at the bank as a general rule," Maxwell explained. "But when it got low she would pay in a sum of money, usually a considerable sum."

"From the sale of shares?"

"No, no. She would explain that she had received payment for an outstanding debt—as I've said, she was rather reticent about her affairs, but it seems that at one time she had lent a good deal of money to friends, etc., and those accounts were being gradually paid off. Or else she would say she had sold something."

"The jewellery, for instance?"

"Possibly. But she didn't go into detail. At the time of her death, her balance was extremely low. In fact, she was overdrawn, but she promised the manager she would be paying in a considerable sum shortly. She said there was money due to her in London and she was going to collect it."

"Did she tell how much?"

"I understand not less than a thousand pounds."

"Is that the amount she generally paid in?"

Maxwell looked a little confused. "It wasn't by any means unusual."

"Did she spend a lot?"

"She liked a certain amount of comfort, though she wore the most peculiar clothes. And I believe she was very good to former employees. I understand she kept in touch with them, and often helped them when they were in poor circumstances."

"She didn't let you handle that side of her affairs?"

The old man shook his head. "She was very secretive. I doubt whether she confided much in any one."

"Any sign of that thousand pounds turning up since her death?"

"None," said Maxwell. "And what perplexes me is that among such of her papers as I have been able to examine I can find nothing to indicate that such a sum is due."

"And you say there's precious little in the bank?"

Maxwell nodded without speaking.

"In that case, how about my client's annuity?"

"Miss Kersey left depositions that it was to be regarded as the first charge on her estate. There is, of course, the jewellery. I always understood it was very valuable, and the purchase of an annuity for a man of Mr. Kersey's age would not be considerable."

"It'll look the size of a house compared with assets if my guess is true," Crook assured him. "Not had the jewellery valued yet, I suppose?"

"I intend to do so immediately."

"I take it, it's insured?"

"I did make that suggestion to Miss Kersey on more than one occasion, but she told me she was perfectly capable of conducting her own affairs and attending to her own best interests. I must confess that I have so far found nothing to indicate that any insurance was ever effected, nor has the bank any documents of that kind. And yet, and yet if the stones are worth what Miss Kersey believed, it seems madness not to insure them."

Crook tilted back his chair and looked at his companion speculatively.

"There's times, Maxwell, when it's less risky not to insure."

Mr. Maxwell looked as if he thought the other had gone mad.

"I'm afraid I don't follow you."

"If it gets about that you possess certain well-known pieces you may as well chuck them out of the window and be done with it. Your only hope is to stay dumb and not do a thing about protectin' them. And then, of course," he added slowly, "there's always the police to remember."

"The police?" Mr. Maxwell looked horribly startled.

"Yeah. They're a nosey lot, and you'd be surprised how much interest they take in things like jewels."

"But—you are hardly suggesting that my client had stones to which she had no right?"

"Come, come," Crook reproved him. "You're a lawyer yourself. You know there's a lot of funny business going on where jewels are concerned. And I don't mean Miss Kersey was head of a safe-busting gang. Come to that, I don't see how she could be. But suppose she has got some famous stones—and I fancy at one time the Ronald Cross figured in her collection—don't you see the curious might wonder how she got hold of them?"

"If there had been anything not—not absolutely above-board there would have been—publicity," observed Mr. Maxwell in a dignified manner.

"And there wasn't. I know that for a fact. Don't that suggest anything to your innocence?"

But whatever it may have suggested it was obvious that Mr. Maxwell was still a million miles from the truth.

Crook let that pass. "I take it, Miss Flora is an also ran. I don't mind telling you, Maxwell, I wouldn't give that for her chances," and he snapped his fingers derisively.

Mr. Maxwell observed feebly that the situation was a little unusual.

"Damned unusual," agreed Crook with his normal vigour. "But damned interesting for all that. But, of course, between ourselves and without prejudice, you smelt the rat a long time ago, didn't you? I mean to say, these elderly ladies who suddenly pay large sums in cash into their accounts—it's all too true to be good."

Mr. Maxwell here advanced a new suggestion. "I had thought that perhaps Miss Kersey had an illusion that the stones were more valuable than actually they are. It's by no means uncommon. . . ."

"If that's the case, I shall be disappointed," said Crook, who honestly hadn't thought of this solution. "Still," he added on a more cheerful note, "I don't think Miss Kersey was a lady with many illusions. Who's doing the valuation for you? Percy Fulham's the chap you want. Fakes that deceive nine experts out of ten don't get by him."

II

Bill Parsons had known Percy Fulham for years. In the old days they had been of mutual service on a considerable scale, and even now Bill was sometimes able to put a good thing in the way of his one-time ally. So it was natural that Fulham should hand on the information about Miss Kersey's treasure-hoard.

He came to see Crook and Bill after hours in their office in Bloomsbury Street.

"Had for a sucker," he announced, lowering his long body into Crook's only comfortable chair. "That is, if the chap who did the old lady in was hoping to get the proceeds of the sale. I never had a greater shock in my life. There's not one genuine piece there—nothing worth while, I mean. One or two brooches and lockets—just drawing-room stuff—but nothing solid, nothing showy at all."

"What's its worth?"

Percy Fulham shrugged his shoulders. "Precisely what the collection meant to the lady," he said.

"I didn't know Miss Kersey well," Crook assured him. "In fact, you could say I only knew her at second-hand, but there's one thing I'm damn certain about, and that is she wasn't the sort of dame to cherish imitation stuff for sentimental reasons. I should say she hadn't got an ounce of sentiment in her composition. If she had shoddy stuff, there's a yarn behind it."

"That's what I've come to get," said Fulham, knocking the ash off his cigar. "All that fake stuff is a copy of something good. For instance, there was the Brockenhorst Ruby." He looked slyly at Crook, but Crook's face was impassive. "Not playing ball?" Fulham suggested. "All the same, you tell me this. Miss Kersey wasn't any one special, I mean, no one you knew anything about. She wasn't in the ring, none of the trade knew her—that is; one of 'em must, the chap who made the copies—but the rest of us didn't. So how did it happen that she should have even a copy of the Brockenhorst Ruby in her possession?"

"There was a hell of a stink over that some years ago, wasn't there?" asked Crook, thoughtfully. "Weren't you . . . ?"

"I didn't make this copy. I made the original one, made it for Lady Brockenhorst. She said her husband was afraid of her taking the real article on a sea trip. Very sensible, too. The gangs that work these luxury cruisers— but I needn't tell you. You've got 'em off often enough in your time." Crook grinned, but still didn't speak. "Well, I made it and thought no more about it—till it began to get about that the jewels had been stolen. Lord B. raged like a lunatic. . . ."

"And suddenly shut up like a fan. I imagine that was when he realised that if there had been a theft it was goin' to involve his nearest and dearest."

"Meanin' Lady B. sold the ruby herself."

"Parted with it, let's say. Oh, I don't doubt Miss Kersey had it at one time. Even a man like Brockenhorst doesn't give his wife *carte blanche* to draw cheques for a couple of thousand, and Miss Kersey had big ideas— even bigger than that."

Percy Fulham nodded. "Likely some of the other stuff

changed hands in the same way," he suggested. "As a matter of fact, the Brockenhorst Ruby was in the market about a year back."

"The trouble with takin' your replies in kind," ruminated Crook, "is that when it comes to turning 'em into cash you're bound to be done brown. Now, Miss Kersey couldn't go to an ordinary jeweller and ask for a valuation. The ruby would be recognised at once, and any fellow in the trade of any standing would go to the police. Miss K. must have known that. It follows, then, as the night the day, that she sold through a fence—and you know, Percy, I'm damn sorry the old lady's snuffed it. She'd have been my money all right."

"If you ask me what the whole lot's worth, I should say, in the highest market, two to three hundred pounds. And that's being generous."

"How about the pearls?" asked Crook.

Fulham looked surprised. "There weren't any pearls."

"That's funny. The police haven't found them either. But then they haven't found her luggage—or her hat—or her nephew. In fact, the police seem to have their hands quite full at the moment—or empty, whichever way you like to look at it."

In this Crook was right. The police had got their hands full. They had sent out a public call for the driver who had taken the self-styled Mr. Kersey from the Warburg Court Hotel on the night of Miss Kersey's death, and for some days they had no results. Then a driver turned up at a local police station to give evidence.

"Why didn't you come forward before?" he was asked by an irritable officer.

"Because I didn't know it was me you was looking

for," he retorted with equal spirit. "Paddington's not my district, see? I come from Hampstead. I'd brought a party down to Paddington—special job, that was—catching a night train—well, queerer things than that happen in a war—and this chap hailed me from the pavement. 'Can you take me to 18 Bayswater Crescent?' he asks. 'I've got to catch a train to-night and my luggage is there.' 'Where did you want to go, sir?' I asked him. 'I've got to get back. It's too late as it is. I've got to get to Euston to-night,' he tells me. 'I've had a wire, it's life or death and there isn't a cab on the rank. I'll make it worth your while,' he says. Well, you 'ave to take a chance sometimes, so I said I'd do it, and he said, 'It's No. 18. Just cruise on till I tell you to stop.' It was a black night, see, not a star anywhere. I was driving with my brains as much as anything else. I never knew it was a hotel. Of course, it was all blacked-out, and when we arrived he says, 'Don't you move. I've got everything in the hall and I'll be back in a jiffy.' He was a bit longer than I expected, and I was beginning to wonder if he was another of these bilkers, when back he comes, saying something about having to telephone. I was going to get down for the luggage, but he said, 'No, it's not much. Drive like hell or I shall miss that train.'"

"And you drove him to Euston?"

"That's right. Said he had to go west. Something about rejoining his battalion and cutting it fine."

"Did you see him at all clearly?"

The driver shook his head. "I've told you, there wasn't a bit of light, and the police are down on a chap for showing a glimmer of his torch. When we got to Euston he gave me ten bob and fairly ran into the station."

"Didn't notice if he had a porter, I suppose?"

"I don't remember one coming to the cab. Porters are hard to get these days."

"Wearing uniform, was he?"

"Now you come to mention it, I don't believe he was. A tallish chap, big black hat. Didn't notice anything else."

The police, much hampered by the delay, that they felt was unreasonable and a scurvy loading of the dice against righteousness and order, made all the routine inquiries and examined the baggage deposited at the station, but without result. They got hold of the clerk in charge on the night in question and put him through it, but again without satisfaction. The clerk was practically certain no one had left luggage at that hour of the night. The chap must have been foxing, he said sulkily.

Benham next turned his attention to the Lost Property Office. He knew that it is the easiest thing on earth to get rid of a piece of luggage at a railway station, particularly in the black-out, when no one can watch a fellow's movements. All that is necessary is to deposit the case in some dim corner and stroll out of the station. One of two things will then happen. Either the case will remain untouched, to be rescued in due course by a porter, who will place it in the Lost Property Office, or it will be found by someone less scrupulous, though possibly more enterprising, who will appropriate it. Since there was no trace of the missing bag at any of the station offices, it seemed either that the criminal was tossing dust in the eyes of the police, and had removed himself and the bag by another entrance, or the thing had been stolen. In the latter case there seemed no reason why the case should not proceed indefinitely, since the thief would presumably realise that he was now in possession of goods for which the police were searching, and would, therefore, prefer to keep his own secret.

They interviewed Miss Flora again, and also saw Watson, with the object of learning what the case contained. Watson said that her lady had not intended to be away more than two or three nights and had only taken a change of under-linen, a nightdress and her toilet necessities. She (Watson) had done the packing overnight. All the garments were marked with Madam's name, but were not otherwise of a cut or quality in any way remarkable. A description of the missing articles was circulated in all quarters that might be expected to bear fruit, but without result. The police also communicated with all jewellers regarding the missing pearls, but although one or two strings were subsequently reported and examined both Watson and Miss Flora declared that these bore no resemblance to the wanted gems.

Altogether, they displayed a great deal of energy and initiative, and it was not fair to say, as the Troglodyte did, that they were simply spending public money without giving adequate service in return.

CHAPTER EIGHT

I shall come back at last
To this dark house to die.
—EDWARD L. DAVISON.

I

ON THIS matter of police intervention Miss Fitzpatrick was becoming fanatical. The occasional visits they still paid to the building became magnified in her mind to a perpetual coming and going of officers in uniform, and even in her dreams strings of men in blue wreathed in and out of the front gate and up the steps.

"What we pay the police for is to prevent murders, not fail to solve them when they've been committed," she told Garry, the pertinacious canary, who regarded her with a solemn, unwinking black eye, and, like a wise male, kept his thoughts to himself. "Besides, I don't feel safe with all these men about."

When she was a little girl, Miss Fitzpatrick's mother had "warned her about men."

"Don't you have anything to do with them," was the burden of her cry, and, "It's safer to keep yourself to yourself," and indeed Miss Fitzpatrick's sole excursion into romance had been a celibate curate who eventually died of consumption on a far from adequate income. If, on his death-bed, you had murmured the Troglodyte's name, it would have meant nothing to him. To celibate curates, women cease to have individuality; they are lumped together as "the faithful," and that's all there is to it.

By the time the Kersey Mystery was a week old, the old woman had got it into her obstinate head that she herself was in real danger. One afternoon, looking round her domain, her eye had been caught by an embroidered motto over the chest of drawers. "All is not gold that glitters," the motto proclaimed, and from that stage to the realisation that all men in uniform are not policemen was a short step. Thereafter, every time the creaking gate announced another arrival, she would not merely lock her door, but would drag an old settle across it. Her precautions were not without point. Once a man was in the hall, it would be simple to come down the basement stairs and attack her in her lair. Why such a prospect should hold out encouragement for any one she did not stop to consider, but, after all, criminal annals are full of tales of old women in lonely inns and solitary rooms, murdered for the money they have presumably concealed in deed-boxes under their frowsy beds, and although she was seventy-four she was by no means tired of life.

"Got to see this war through," was a favourite remark of hers. "Can't let that Schickelgruber put one over me."

She even abandoned her favourite device of sitting in the window and watching the house's traffic. Now that the police (and others) knew it was her custom, it had become dangerous. So she drew the thick, dark curtains and sat by the scanty fire, that, with the aid of a nightlight, was all the illumination she permitted herself. She employed a good deal of her time now in writing long letter to the press on the inefficiency of the police force and the increasing tendency to violence loosed by the war; and she wrote crookedly on a large card

NOT AT HOME

and put it on her back door.

So, like the little underground creature she tended more and more to resemble, she lived alone in the dark.

Presently her troubled mind, ranging hither and thither, persuaded her that the young girl, Sigrid Petersen, was the cause of all her present discomfort, and she resolved to tell her so. On her first visit, Sigrid had left her address with the old woman, and Miss Fitzpatrick now routed out this scrap of paper, and found a black-edged envelope that was part of the stock her mother had laid in on the occasion of Mr. Fitzpatrick's demise forty years ago.

The letter, unstamped to ensure its safe arrival, reached Sigrid the following day. It said:

> "You are warned to be careful how you inter-
> fere in the lives of others. Take care. You are
> in danger. Let the dead rest in peace."

That, Miss Fitzpatrick had thought with satisfaction, as she folded the sheet and put it into its yellowed envelope, will teach her to come meddling and filling my house with men in uniform. Even if it is against the law to put a body in an empty flat, what business is it of hers? She looked just like a witch, nodding her big head with its battalion of steel curlers, a little triangular shawl (also dating from her mother's time and, in recurrent seasons, the joy of generations of moths) knotted round her throat. The next day she sent a postcard.

"One sows and another reaps."

And, as a final effort:

"Believe a friend who tells you that, if you should ever again stumble on something not intended for your eyes, it is wiser to pretend to have seen nothing. Who knows where this may end?"

Sigrid was startled by the first letter that, not unnaturally, she supposed to have been written by someone who knew a good deal more about Miss Kersey's death than did the police. The second, coming the next day, increased not merely her curiosity but also her apprehension. When she received the third, she decided it was time to get advice. The obvious person to approach was a knowledgeable friend, but the only one she had cared for had disappeared in the Norwegian debacle. She wondered for a day or two what course she could best pursue, and then remembered the lawyer who was representing the missing Mr. Kersey, who also had rooms in No. 1 Brandon Street. She thought, ingenuously, that since he was putting himself to so much trouble for an old man he had only met once, he might be prepared to give advice to a girl who had never hitherto needed a lawyer, and wouldn't know where to find one now.

Her mind made up, she left her work punctually that evening and hurried down the tube steps. It was five-twenty-five when she reached No. 1 Brandon Street. Naturally, she couldn't be expected to know that Crook seldom came home from work until after dinner, and equally naturally she imagined he would have a servant of some kind to take a message for her. In her bag were the three anonymous communications; the front door of the house was unfastened. This was not usual, but since the coming and going of the police, Miss Fitzpatrick had refused to go upstairs and unhasp the latch after dark, with the possibility of having to open it again if authority should take it into its head to pay another visit.

The hall was very dark. A niggardly landlord had placed minute blue bulbs in the sockets and these, when turned on, were guaranteed to burn for one minute only and to give no light worth mentioning even then. Sigrid switched on her torch and began to make her way carefully up the stairs. A painted board in the hall showed her that Mr. Crook lived on the top floor, and the slot next to his name said IN as it invariably did.

"Never be out officially," was one of Crook's dicta. "You may just have stepped round the corner or be engaged—but you're never out. It ain't business."

As the beam from the little torch flickered on the first landing, she dropped her eyes and hurried forward. It was absurd, of course, but she had a feeling that the door might suddenly open and the Thing she had discovered behind it totter forth to meet her. She knew, naturally, that this was out of the question. Clara Kersey's mortal remains had been decently interred some days earlier, but the impression stayed in her mind. She ran up the next flight and was brought to an abrupt halt by unmistakable movements on the landing ahead. Casting the beam of her light over the banisters, she tried to assure herself that she was now approaching the top floor, but this was manifestly not the case. Above her she saw stairs winding into darkness. Below her, the darkness was complete, the shadowy blue glow having expired with a little click as she reached the first landing. It seemed to her that the gleam of the torch was now fainter than it had been, and even as she thought this, it paled and paled and went out altogether. Frantically she pushed the button of the switch, but nothing happened. She had no spare battery with her, and she stood for an instant, frozen by panic, in a sea of blackness that washed all about her.

"It's no good going down," she told herself, sensibly. "I'd much better go up and perhaps Mr. Crook will have a torch and will guide me to the street."

She took a farther step upwards, miscalculated the height of the tread and clutched wildly at the banisters. As she regained her balance the torch fell from her hand and rattled on the stairs. Bump, bump, bump, it went, sounding like a spectral creature leaping into space. It was now quite impossible to see anything at all.

She stood for a moment gripping the banisters. Above her head an invisible door opened. Then a faint beam wavered on the wall above her head. "Is any one there?" whispered a voice, as uncertain as the beam itself.

Sigrid recovered herself with an effort. "I—I didn't know there was any one in the flat," she whispered. "I was coming to see Mr. Crook and my torch went out . . ."

"Mr. Crook is not at home," said the voice on the same vague note. "I was hoping to see him myself."

"Oh!" Relief brought her several steps nearer to her companion. "But I expect he won't be long."

"He keeps very irregular hours, I believe," said the voice, doubtfully. "But—please come up and wait for a little."

She came round the bend of the stairs and saw the tall hesitating figure in black, as Crook had described him. Thin, tall, wearing a wide black hat that somehow gave him a ghostly look, and a black overcoat buttoned rather tightly round him.

"I have just come in myself," he said. "My name is Kersey. This is my flat."

"The Tea-Cosy!" exclaimed Sigrid. And blushed to the roots of her hair. "I mean," she added in some confusion, "it's what he calls you, Mr. Crook, I mean."

"So you know Mr. Crook?"

"I—I saw him at the inquest."

"The inquest? But I don't understand. Whose . . . ?"

"Your—your aunt," said Sigrid in surprise. "Didn't you know?"

"It will seem absurd," said the old man, "but the fact is I know nothing, or, at least, very little. I was hoping Mr. Crook might prove of assistance."

He backed as he spoke, inviting the girl to follow him into the flat. This had a great air of dust and desolation, which was only to be expected. The Tea-Cosy looked as macabre as everything else on the premises. He put up one hand and stroked his chin and then said, "Mr. Crook was kind enough to offer to assist me to find my aunt. We had an appointment—an appointment I was unable to keep."

"He has been wondering about you," Sigrid told him.

"I must have seemed most discourteous." The old voice sounded troubled now. "I hope he had not put himself to any great inconvenience." Then he seemed to remember. "You spoke of an inquest."

"Yes. It was I who—who found the body."

"I'm afraid I don't recognise you," the old man apologised.

"My name is Sigrid Petersen. I came to look at the flat and—and found your aunt there."

"But—which flat?"

"The one below. Oh, don't you understand? Someone had killed her and left the body there."

"Killed her in the flat below? But why should she be there at all? You know her hat was found here. It is all very confusing." .

"I don't feel very clear myself," Sigrid admitted. "I mean, I don't know how she got there. Nobody does."

"She was in a nursing home," said her companion. "So, at least, I was assured. But that, no doubt, was part of the plot."

"Who told you about the nursing home?" Sigrid demanded.

"Perhaps I had better explain. But you will sit down? I had hoped that Mr. Crook could throw some light on the situation. It is very difficult for me. I do not even know what time it is."

"It's a little after half-past five," Sigrid told him.

"I mean—the year, the day. For me time has been blotted out, I don't even know for how long."

"What happened to you?" Sigrid asked. "Don't you ever see the papers?"

He shook his head.

"Don't you realise the police have been looking for you?"

"The police?"

"Yes. Because of her hat, I suppose. And no one could find you. Where have you been?"

He shook his head. "I do not know. How absurd I must seem, but the fact is—I was on my way to the nursing home." He stopped dead. "But there was no nursing home. That was part of the trick. There was no nursing home."

Sigrid began to feel very much as Crook had done on the occasion of his sole encounter with the Tea-Cosy. The old man seemed about as consequential as a kitten chasing its own tail. "Then where have you been for the last week?" she inquired, in the dubious hope of pinning him down to some definite statement.

"That again I cannot tell you," was the mournful response. Suddenly his head shot up, like the head of a tortoise plunging from its shell. "Did you say a week?"

"Yes. It's more than a week actually. And during that time every one has been looking for you."

"Really!" said he, with a new note of interest in his voice. "That is most interesting. A whole week and no one knows anything about it. Certainly not I. A whole week blotted out of life. But then," his voice was now stronger and more enthusiastic than before, "what in essence is a week? A period of time. No more. And since the nature of time remains a mystery. . . ."

"What did you do when you left the flat?" interrupted Sigrid.

"It was all very strange. As I say, I had agreed to accompany Mr. Crook to King's Widdows the following morning. This was the evening, you understand. He was to call for me at half-past nine. After he had gone I bolted my door—yes, I am convinced I bolted the door —and I went to bed. Suddenly I was awakened by a telephone ringing. It had been ringing for some time, but I did not know that then."

"How do you know now?" inquired Sigrid, curiously.

"The man told me he had begun to think I was away or at least would never wake."

"You mean, the man at the other end of the line?"

"Yes." The Tea-Cosy beamed.

"But who was it?" Sigrid's voice was urgent with exasperation.

The old voice wavered again. "I—really I don't know. He asked if I were Mr. Kersey and when I said I was he told me that my aunt, Miss Clara Kersey, had had an accident in the black-out, and was in a nursing home. She had just recovered consciousness and was asking for me. Would I please come at once? Her condition was serious."

"How did he say you should get there at that hour?" asked Sigrid, practically.

"He said he would send a car that should stop at the corner. I was to come down quietly and not to disturb the house. He said she had lost her hat somewhere, and I said she had left it here and I would bring it along with me. So I dressed and unbolted my door and came down. That would be about half-past three or four o'clock, I think. There was a car just round the corner and a man was waiting. He came on to the pavement and opened the door and told me to get in. It was quite dark, you understand, so I could not see him well, but he seemed quite young. He told me that my aunt had been knocked over by a bus, and they had tried to find out if she had any relatives in London. But her bag must have been snatched in the black-out, for they had no notion who she was, until she regained consciousness and asked for me."

"Had they told the police?" asked Sigrid.

The Tea-Cosy seemed definitely taken aback at this suggestion.

"It did not occur to me to ask. We drove for some time, but where I could not tell, as the night was so black. I asked my companion if my aunt was very bad, and he said, I wouldn't have got you out of bed at this hour, if it hadn't been important. So I said nothing, and presently the car stopped and we got out. My driver had told me that he was a doctor in charge of the nursing home to which my aunt had been taken. It was still quite dark, and he held my arm as we went up the steps, and then he found a key and opened the door and we stepped into the hall. We went up some stairs, he guiding me because, though he had a torch, it was very faint, and presently we stopped in front of a door, and he opened it and we went into a room." He paused and was silent for so long that Sigrid thought he had finished.

"You have no idea whereabouts you were?"

"We—were in London, I think," replied the Tea-Cosy, in hesitating tones. "I am sure we had not travelled far enough to have reached the suburbs. My sight at all times is poor and, as I have said, it was a very dark night. I remember my companion remarking that there was no moon."

"What was the flat like, if it was a flat? I thought you said he was going to take you to a nursing home."

But the Tea-Cosy made a poor witness. "I don't say it was a flat," he said. "I only said we went up some stairs." He hesitated again. Finally, he brought out in triumphant tones, "There was a parrot. A big green parrot." He paused again. "It was a very ornamental flat," he said.

"And could it talk? The parrot, I mean?"

The old man looked staggered. "Oh no, no. There could be no question of that. You see, it wasn't alive. I turned to my companion to ask if I could be taken to my aunt at once, only to find that I was alone. I supposed that he had gone to pave the way for my arrival, and I moved across . . ." His voice trailed into silence. "I remember thinking it was so quiet, so very quiet. I thought I heard the man who called himself the doctor coming back, and I turned my head to speak to him. In all probability, that movement saved my life."

"Saved your life?" Sigrid stared with wide blue eyes.

"Yes. For at the same time something struck me with great violence and accuracy. I remember I had one moment of consciousness when I was surprised—oh, greatly surprised—and then I wished I had left a note for Mr. Crook, explaining the situation. He would think it so strange that I should disappear without even the courtesy of a message."

"So that's why you didn't come before," exclaimed Sigrid. "But where have you been all the time?"

Sadly the old man shook his head. She saw his face more clearly now under the shadow of the hat-brim. It had a strange pinched look.

"That, alas, I cannot tell you. I have no recollection."

"But you can't drop a week out of your life like that."

"It is probably inaccurate to talk about dropping a week," her companion assured her. "It may be that for me, owing to the effects on the skull of the blow that I received, time, as they say, stood still. It simply ceased to be. My next moment of life began when I realised who and where I was."

"Where were you?" asked Sigrid, with interest.

The feeble voice brightened again. "That is perhaps the strangest part of it," he said. "My next instant of consciousness was in this flat. I was here, presumably I walked up the stairs, but I have no recollection of it. But perhaps," he added, hopefully, "Mr. Crook will know. Mr. Crook was most helpful before. I pin my faith on Mr. Crook."

Sigrid pinched herself to make sure she was not asleep. A refugee from Norway, she had, during the past two years, seen many strange sights and met many peculiar people, but the Tea-Cosy was outside her experience. She didn't know if he were mad or simply a human being of a fresh type. It was possible that there were others like him, but that she had never encountered them. Crook would have told her that the bat-houses are full of them, and their particular idiosyncrasy isn't important.

When she heard him say, "I pin my faith on Mr. Crook," she thought of someone broadcasting Dickens during Children's Hour. Clutching hold of reality she said, "Perhaps Mr. Crook's back now. Or perhaps there's someone who can tell us when he will be back."

"We should have heard him if he had come up," said the old man. "But there is his office. Perhaps they. . . .

166

Oh yes, I see. You are looking for a telephone. You will find it in the hall."

"You don't know his number?" suggested Sigrid.

"I—I fear not. But his office is in Bloomsbury Street. I remember. . . ." He bumbled into the hall after her to indicate the telephone directories on a low shelf beneath the instrument.

"I can find it," Sigrid assured him. She was beginning to feel she needed to establish contact with a normal human being.

The light was bad, and she had to bend double over the book. So it was that she never saw what struck her. Only, suddenly, she felt a terrific pain in the head and dizzied under the blow, crumpling slowly at the knees. As she went down, clutching vainly at the darkness, she found herself paraphrasing the famous cry of another murderer.

Who would have thought the old man had such strength in him?

II

It is an axiom of those who spend their lives grappling with criminals that men show a tendency to repeat their crimes, just as novelists show a tendency to write the same story in a different jacket over and over again. Finding himself with the body of the unconscious girl at his feet, it was the murderer's intent to remove it to the comparative security of the first-floor flat that, having been examined at length by the police, would presumably remain unexplored for some months to come. No one was likely to rent it with its present reputation, and a body might easily remain there for weeks, if not for months, without being discovered. Even if it were found, there was no reason (he thought) why he should be associated with the crime. Now that the girl was out of the way, no one knew of his stealthy visit here. He could take advantage of the house's emptiness to drag her down to the flat below. Remembering the last time he had concealed a body, he felt the sweat break out on forehead and lips. No one who hadn't tried knew what it was like, getting an inert thing down a double flight of stairs, terrified at every moment of possible interruption. He knew, however, that nothing would shift the Troglodyte from her lair, and Crook was unlikely to return so early in the evening. It was too late for the postman or any local tradesman's delivery. All that was needed, therefore, was a cool head and patience.

To hurry matters now might prove fatal. His answers to the girl had been far from satisfactory, and he knew that she had only accepted them because she thought him a lunatic. A man like Crook would have probed. No, no, he wanted no encounter with Crook. Let them say what they liked about Theodore Kersey so long as Theodore Kersey was glimpsed by none of them.

He stooped over the girl to make sure of her condition and, as he did so, he heard an unmistakable sound—the cheerful slam of the big front door. The tall figure straightened itself. There could be no doubt. Those were Crook's footsteps on the stairs. The little lawyer came bouncing up in his usual jaunty fashion, paused a minute at Flat No. 1, then rounded the corner and came more slowly up the next flight. Outside No. 2 he stopped, as had become his habit, and pressed the electric bell.

The man on the farther side of the door remained rigid. He thanked his stars that Crook hadn't been a moment later, and thus have charged on to a crowded stage. He had had the forethought to turn off the electricity when he heard those threatening feet, and he quieted his leaping nerves by reminding himself that even Crook couldn't see through a wooden barrier.

Crook, rather surprisingly, rang again. The man looked down at his victim. She was motionless, without colour or any sign of life. Only on one temple a great area was darkening, where the weapon had struck home. Seeing him now, Crook wouldn't have been reminded of some ageing noble bird. There was no nobility in that face. It was hard, calculating, cruel. And indeed, the man was racked with fear. What, he thought, if Crook remembered the key that should be under the mat, should stoop to feel for it? He strained his ear to discover what was going on out of sight.

His gaze came back to the girl at his feet. He thought, "If she moves, if she cries out . . ." But at least no cry of hers should penetrate the black silence. There was no light in the hall but the watery beam of his downflung torch. Not even Crook could discern a reflection through the glass transom above his head.

At last Crook seemed satisfied that the flat was untenanted, and tramped on upstairs. The man on the floor below took a deep breath when he heard a door shut loudly. Nevertheless, it was now out of the question to risk taking the body downstairs. Crook was home unwontedly early. That might mean he was going out again, or it might mean he was expecting a visitor. Now his only course was to leave the body on the premises,

169

and slip away while he still had the time. But first there were preparations to be made.

He was in the living-room when the telephone rang. He turned his head over his shoulder in a kind of fascinated horror. The temptation to answer it was almost overwhelming. But wisdom told him it might well be Crook on the other end of the line, so he let common sense persuade him, and left it ringing. Hurriedly he dragged the girl into the living-room, scuffling the rugs on the way. Heaving her up, he flung her on to a chesterfield and tied a thick scarf over her mouth. There was no time to be lost. Perhaps some diabolical agency had warned Crook there was something amiss in the flat below. He seized a cushion and pressed it over the unconscious face, binding it with another scarf. The girl might take a little time to die, but she was no source of danger to him now. He found himself thinking, three for luck. . . . Three? Three to die? He shivered and came back to the hall.

He looked round to discover if he had left any incriminating clue but there was nothing. Pulling the wide-brimmed hat yet farther over his face, he noiselessly opened the door. Outside everything was pitchy black. He stood there a moment, straining every nerve, but the house was still as death. Still as death, he whispered, and another great shudder ran through him. Cautiously he closed the flat door, dropping the key into his pocket, and tiptoed down the stairs. The front door had been slammed, but he dared not risk calling attention to himself by a further bang, so he drew it softly to behind him, and so came out into the impenetrable night.

CHAPTER NINE

Everything's got a moral if only you can find it.
—ALICE IN WONDERLAND.

I

HE WAS only just in time. Not many minutes after the dusk had swallowed him up, Crook emerged from his flat, carrying a small tool in his hand. He stopped at the door of Flat No. 3, and felt under the mat, but the key was still missing.

"This door seems to have a fatal fascination for me," he ruminated, "and every time I open it I wonder if I'm being had for a sucker."

The tool grated softly in the lock; there was a yielding sensation; Crook turned his implement carefully. From the hall floor someone pressed a bell and then steps came up the stairs.

"Come right in," called Crook. "Don't stand on ceremony. If it's me you're wanting, that is."

A voice said hesitantly, "Mr. Crook?" and Crook said, "Yes, what is it? Forgotten something?"

The feet came round the bend of the stairs, and their owner was revealed as Hilary Grant.

When he saw what Crook was doing, he stopped, looking at him quizzically.

"Don't let me interrupt," said he in polite tones.

"Sure I won't," said Crook. "Come right in. I may want you."

"Do you mean to say your friend, the Tea-Cosy's, re-appeared?"

"That's what I want to find out." Crook had opened the door and switched on the blue light. "Well, some-one's been here," he said. "That telephone book's been shifted. It was on the shelf. No, don't touch it, man. It may have finger-prints on it. We want to help the police all we can." He looked round him. "Place is thick with dust," he said, and opened the sitting-room door.

"I suppose," began Hilary Grant, and then stopped. "My God, what's that?"

Crook didn't stop to answer him. Moving with extraor-dinary rapidity for a man of his bulk, he was across the room and bending over a figure that lay stretched on the sofa, with a cushion bound over its face.

"Who is it?" muttered Hilary Grant.

"We'll hope it's not a corpse," said Crook, unbinding the cushion. "Here, get some water, untie her feet. . . ."

He was removing the gag, lifting the girl into a more comfortable position, as he issued these orders. The young man came back with a cupful of water, and stood staring at the white, lifeless face.

His heart contracted. This was frightful, frightful. . . .

"What next?" he asked.

"Next?" repeated Crook, absently.

"I mean, is she going to be all right?"

"I'm not a doctor," said Crook. "Have a bit of pa-tience."

"Patience!" shouted the young man. Then calmed down again. "What put you wise anyhow? How did you guess there was any funny business going on?"

Crook straightened himself. "Whoever's responsible

couldn't guess I was coming back early to-night," he re-marked. "I don't blame him for that. But the rest's sheer carelessness. That's unpardonable."

"Carelessness!" said Hilary Grant, in surprised tones. "How's that?"

"The torch. That's how I knew someone had been up either to this flat or to mine. I stepped on a torch at the bend of the stairway. Now, it didn't seem to add up that any one should be coming to call on Flat 3, when the police have advertised all over the country for its oc-cupant, so the odds were that whoever it was meant to call on me. And whoever was in Flat 3 to-night was damn-all anxious she shouldn't get there."

"What on earth could she know that's so incriminat-ing?"

"P'raps later on she'll pull round sufficiently to tell me."

"Poor little girl!" Hilary Grant's flexible voice was very soft. "Whoever did that was pretty devilish."

"Pretty well up against it," amended Crook. "I'm not one for copybook mottoes, but there is somethin' in the bit about self-preservation bein' the first law that rings the bell every time. Besides, you have to remember we're presumably dealin' with a murderer, and that's always dangerous. You can't be hanged more than once, so if you're for it, you may as well have two violent deaths to your credit as one."

"But—she won't die, will she? Good Lord, Crook. . . ."

"I'm not God Almighty," said Crook thoughtfully. "But no, I don't believe she will."

"Oughtn't we to be doing something? I say, it's the girl who found—— Good Lord."

"I wonder what's keeping the police so long," murmured Crook, hauling out his turnip of a watch.

"The police! I . . ."

"You rang 'em, didn't you?"

"No. That is—I mean, I will." He dashed into the hall. Crook smiled a little grimly.

"Tell them to send along a doctor and an ambulance," he shouted. "The girl's a hospital case."

"Wonder what the devil she was doing here anyway?" hazarded Grant, who had picked up the telephone directory and was thumbing hurriedly through it.

"I told you, she must have been coming to see me."

"She must have known something. I mean to say, she didn't get that clump on the head by accident."

"Perhaps she annoyed her host. It could be, you know, Grant, it could be. As for the number you want . . ."

But Grant, throwing down the directory, said, "What the devil? Of course I know it. Whitehall 1212."

Crook heard him snatch up the receiver and bellow the number at the operator. "It's a dial phone," he called.

There was a suppressed curse and then the dial began to spin. Crook stayed where he was, but he could hear one side of the conversation and it wasn't difficult to imagine the other.

"Scotland Yard? That's right. Look here, there's been an attempt at murder. What? Oh, Earl's Court. Well, I am ringing the police. . . . But I tell you this is murder. All right, all right. What's their number? Any one would think I was an old maid reporting the loss of her Pom."

He got through at last and returned to the living-room to find Crook still maintaining his vigil by the side of the unconscious girl.

"You didn't touch anything, I hope?" said Crook, without turning his head.

"No. That's to say, only the telephone. I say, this is a nasty bit of work. Your house'll get a bad name. First Auntie—by the way," he stopped as if struck by a new idea, "this isn't *the* flat, is it?"

"Where she was found? No. That's underneath. Where she was killed? Most likely."

"You mean, this is Cousin Theodore's bolt-hole?"

"It was."

Grant looked round him apprehensively. "You don't suppose he's jammed into one of those cupboards, do you?"

"Not unless he's treated with invisible paint. The police have gone round with a microscope."

"It looks uncommonly as though you've got a maniac on the premises," the young man continued. "I mean, there doesn't seem any motive. Unless, of course, she had the pearls."

"You do imagine things," Crook congratulated him. "Anyway, she hasn't got 'em now. And what's more to the point, she doesn't seem to have a mother either."

"A mother?"

"When I was a young man, mothers warned their girls it was dangerous to go visiting unmarried men in their own quarters. But I suppose mothers have gone out, like everything else feminine. These days you can hardly tell 'em from their daughters."

Grant nodded, his eyes on that white, expressionless face. "You're right," he said. "A girl as pretty as that needs someone to look after her."

"And you'd like to be the chap? Don't tell me. I

wonder why it is that most men fall for the nincompoops. I suppose because the other kind can look after themselves."

"You've no right to call her that," expostulated Hilary, hotly. "She may have a marvellous brain."

"With a face like that? Don't make me laugh. Well, what sense would there be in that? Nature's not so prodigal as you seem to imagine. She doesn't throw in brains and beauty. She knows that would be over-doing it. Of course," he added complacently, smiling at his companion, "it's different for men."

Hilary Grant didn't seem interested. "Those damned police!" he exclaimed. "Do you suppose they thought I said a hearse instead of an ambulance?"

But at that instant the bell pealed and there sounded the noise of feet on the stairs. Then two men came in, with two others behind them.

"What's all this?" demanded the first.

Hilary Grant looked at him with fascination. Just thus did his favourite detective writers and film actors speak in similar circumstances. You couldn't imagine the living man running so true to type. The second man, after a rapid glance, crossed to the sofa. The third and fourth waited for instructions.

Crook explained the position, admitting coolly that he had broken into another man's flat on what appeared, on the surface, quite inadequate evidence. But when the officer suggested this, Crook breezily swept his arguments aside.

"Hand of Providence," he declared. "What did Providence leave that torch on the stairs for if not to guide me? Like the star, you know . . ." he added a little obscurely.

"You could have given us the information," said the sergeant coldly.

"It's expensive, being a little gentleman," Crook told him in earnest tones. "Now, suppose I'd taken your advice? First of all, I'd have had to overcome my natural scruples about disturbin' an overworked body like the police on such slight evidence. I mean," he added, more earnestly still, "I'm like that chap they have in Germany. I have mystical instincts, and I felt my place was in this flat, just as he feels his place is in London, but the difference between us is that I'm right and he ain't. Now, I ask you—by the time I'd got through to you and you'd talked it over with your superiors and looked up the Queensbery Rules, it 'ud have been a hearse, not an ambulance we'd have wanted."

"The police are a fine lot of chaps," he confided later to Hilary Grant. "No one knows that better than I do, and I'm always tellin' them so, but they're like that pal of the poet—a primrose by a river's brim a yellow primrose was to him, and it was nothing more. Whereas it's no good hopin' to get by in our set unless it's an orchid at least. If I'd phoned that I'd found a torch on the stairs, d'you think they'd have come ramping round, hell-for-leather? Stop me on the street and ask me, old boy. Of course they wouldn't. No, no, the police follow the straight and narrow way, and who am I to discourage 'em, but there are times when a short-cut across open country saves leather and lives, even if it does involve a bit of trespassin'."

"If this girl comes through you'll have saved her," said Hilary Grant, jerkily.

"And shall I get the Albert Medal? I give you three guesses. I shan't even get the personal thanks of Detective-Sergeant Benham. As for X—our criminal—I leave you to imagine what his feelings will be when he reads the morning bulletin."

The police-surgeon, who had all this time been busy with the prostrate body on the couch, now straightened up to say, "Concussion's what she's suffering from. As far as I can tell at present, it's not serious. Though, naturally, I can't give a foolproof diagnosis right here. But I fancy she'll be all right, bar a bit of a head and her beauty a bit spoilt, by this time to-morrow."

One of the officers inquired if any one knew who she was or where she lived, and Crook replied that she had looked over the flat on the first floor but, in view of the tenant she found there, she'd decided not to move in.

The officer next inquired the identity of the two civilians, and Crook, with beguiling meekness, introduced himself as the tenant of the top flat and his companion as a client.

"Comin' to see me," he added. "I'm like that chap, Carlyle. A sixteen-hour day is nothing to me. As a matter of fact, the young lady may have been coming to consult me, too. I wouldn't know. P'raps she'll be able to tell us in due course."

The girl's handbag was lying on a chair, and the identity card gave the police her full name and present address; they also found the three anonymous communications and took them into custody. Then they summoned the ambulance men and had the unconscious creature taken down the difficult stairs in a folding chair.

"What are they going to do with her?" demanded Hilary Grant, in anxious tones.

"Fallen flat on your face, haven't you?" said Crook, in his inelegant way. "Well, ask yourself. Where can they take her? What do we support the County Hospital for?"

"The Hospital?"

"St. Magnus. Not that it'll be any good your camping on the step for the night. She won't be in any state to see visitors at present, and when she is, Little Arthur's at the head of the queue, see?" He tapped his chest significantly.

After the police had finished with them, Crook invited his companion to share a quart of beer on the top floor, and Hilary Grant accepted.

"Was I right in assumin' you were comin' to see me?" Crook inquired, as they nodded amicably over the stoneware mugs that would, as the younger man observed, have stunned a policeman.

"As a matter of fact, I was. I don't suppose you can do a thing about it, and in any case, it's not your pigeon, so why should you, except that you seem to like poking about in other chaps' backyards—but the fact is it's Miss Flora. Heaven knows, she's no pet of mine, but—well, she upsets your theory about women having either beauty or brains. She seems to have been behind the door all through the session."

"Don't you make any mistake," Crook warned him drily. "There's plenty of brains there."

"Well, she's put 'em into cold storage for the time being," persisted Hilary Grant. "She's going round telling the world or as much of it as will listen to her, that Cousin Theodore murdered his aunt and collected on the pearls."

"Has she happened to mention it to the police?"

"Er—well, that I couldn't say. Should she?"

"If she's got evidence, of course."

"I don't fancy she has."

"In that case, my client's got grounds for a slander action. I shall advise him to that effect."

"I have tried to point out to her the danger of making these wild accusations," Grant told him. "But, as you could see for yourself, she didn't love me much in the old lady's lifetime, and now she behaves as though I'd been Cousin Theodore's accomplice. Varied with the suggestion that, since I didn't inherit a fortune on the old lady's death, I don't care a brass button what happens to her murderer."

"Why should you?" inquired Crook, pleasantly. "What d'you want me to do about it?"

Hilary Grant laughed in rueful fashion.

"Put like that, I do sound rather a fool," he acknowledged. "No, I suppose actually you can't do anything. But I did wonder if she'd listen to you. You see," his brow furrowed, "she seems to have no friends, no relatives, no one to advise her. She had made her aunt her whole life, and now she's stranded and—I suppose it sounds damn silly to a chap like you, but I do in a way feel responsible for her."

"Drop that notion at once," Crook told him firmly. "The woman's over forty, and if she can't accept responsibility for herself at that age, well, what's the bat-house for?"

"You do sound like the Spirit of Christmas," Hilary complimented him.

"I'm not goin' to carry Miss Flora on my shoulders and give her the chance to tear out what hair I've got," Crook assured him. "And if you take my tip, you won't let her get in your hair either."

"You really think . . . ?"

Crook banged his mug on the table with a noise that sounded like the echo of an air raid.

"Tell me this," said he. "D'you want to marry the girl?"

"You mean . . ." His face changed ludicrously. "Good Lord, Crook, you don't mean Miss Flora? What the devil . . . ?"

"I may be libellin' the sex," continued Crook in his blandest voice, "but my impression of them is that when they get to that age, no man's safe."

"I couldn't marry any one on what a grateful Government pays me," observed Hilary in a rather grim voice.

"And if your thoughts were that way inclined, I take it Miss Flora would hardly be your choice?"

"Well, hardly," agreed Hilary. "Thanks for the beer. You think I'd better keep off the grass?"

"If you take my tip, you'll keep on the other side of the gate altogether. After all, the world's wide."

Hilary Grant shot him a sidelong glance. "Quite," he said. And then, "You do think that girl's going to be all right, don't you?"

"If she doesn't go paying any more of these mysterious visits to strangers. It's about time someone took her in hand. These unattached young women cause half the trouble in the world, and the devil of it is," he added gloomily, "they're not even remunerative."

Grant laughed. "You ought to have gone on the stage yourself, Crook. You'd find it more restful than your present job. At least, you wouldn't be asked to act twenty-four hours a day as you do at present. All right, all right," he added, getting up cheerfully. "Don't trouble to point out the door to me. I noticed it as I came in."

He held out his hand; he seemed agog with excitement. His eyes shone. The hand that Crook clasped was warm and a little sticky. After he had taken his leave, Crook remained where he was for some time, thinking of a girl in a blue coat, with a blue scarf tied round her hair. Hilary Grant, travelling back by tube, thought about her too. Of their diverse reflections, one was common to both —a fixed intention to see the young woman next day, though the heavens fall.

II

Crook knew something of the ways of hospitals. He knew, for instance, that visitors are not popular at nine-thirty in the morning. He also, knowing the ways of the police, guessed that he wouldn't be allowed to see Sigrid until Authority had had first pickings. He even wondered if the zealous and humorless sergeant who had so greatly disapproved of him the night before had compelled one of his underlings to occupy a hard, wooden chair in the passage outside the ward all through the night.

The idea entertained him.

"All through the night," he warbled happily, casting his razor aside.

He thought what a lot of fun there is in life, and what a lot most people miss. He telephoned the hospital to make inquiries and was told that Miss Petersen was conscious but not yet allowed to receive visitors. That would depend on the doctor.

"And the police," added Crook, slamming the receiver back into place. "I'll be seeing you."

On the way downstairs the happy thought struck him that he might have an advantageous word with the Troglodyte, so he teetered down the basement steps and rapped on the door. The curtains were drawn forbiddingly across the windows and no one answered his rapping. Undeterred, he banged afresh, and now a voice shrilled, "Not at home. I don't rent this flat for the police to treat it like their guard-room."

"It's me, Arthur Crook, your neighbour," called Crook, stooping to put his lips to the letter-flap that had been cut in the back door. "I've come to warn you."

"What do you mean?" hissed the invisible Miss Fitzpatrick.

"There was another violent crime in this house last night," mouthed Crook.

The door flew open instantly. She must have been standing just the other side.

"So it's you," she said. "I thought it must be. What do you want to warn me about? I've got no money and I never see any one. I couldn't give evidence if I was paid."

Crook stepped inside and slammed the door smartly behind him.

"Don't you know better than to write poison-pen letters?" he demanded.

She turned on him like a flash. "I don't know what you're talking about."

"Oh yes, you do. The letters you wrote to Sigrid Petersen. If you don't end with a rope round your neck, it won't be any thanks to you."

"A rope? You're mad, that's what you are. I've always known there was something queer about you." Her little eyes darted at him, her voice was shaking with emotion. "I wonder what the police know about you."

Crook chuckled. "Not near so much as they think," he told her. "All the same, you're in a jam. You wrote to that girl telling her to keep away or she'd be hurt. Well, she didn't take your advice, and she has been hurt."

Miss Fitzpatrick folded her hands like paws, as though she could fold herself up inside them; she looked up at him sideways. "You're trying to frighten me," she said.

Crook shrugged. "The police are on the case. Didn't you hear them last night?"

"I heard a disgraceful amount of noise."

"And an ambulance? That was to take—her—away."

Miss Fitzpatrick struck out at him feebly. "I don't want you here," she said. "You've never meant anything but bad luck to me. I've never had anything to do with the police before, but you attract them like a honey-pot. It's not nice. I don't like it."

"When they've read those letters," continued Crook, mercilessly, "they'll want to know how you could tell that harm was coming to that girl. Remember, they haven't got the assailant yet . . ."

"I was down here all by myself, with my doors locked," Miss Fitzpatrick defended herself swiftly.

Crook jerked his head in the direction of the basement stairs.

"Easy to get into the main building, even if they were," he suggested.

"I didn't anyhow," the Troglodyte told him. "I'd be afraid. I don't like death. That's why I stay so snug here. Whatever happened upstairs last night, I don't know anything about it."

"You can tell that to the police," returned Crook, equably. "I'm your friend, you know. That's why I'm here. I want you to have a chance to think up a good answer before they arrive."

"Answer to what?"

"Your reason for writing those letters."

Miss Fitzpatrick looked at him defensively; she looked more than ever like a little animal, a ferret or something.

"I didn't want her to come back," she snapped at last. "The first time she came I had a queer feeling; the second time she found a body. And you say she came again. . . ."

"And there was nearly another murder," agreed Crook. "If it hadn't been for me, there would have been," he added in modest tones. "Tell me something, Miss Fitzpatrick. How did you know something grim would happen if she came again?"

"I have intuitions," said Miss Fitzpatrick, mysteriously. "I've had them all my life. When I was a girl I always knew when my father was going to arrive out of the blue and ask my mother for money. And I was always right. I don't like unpleasantness. And I don't like murder. It was for all our sakes I wrote those letters. There was nothing wrong in them," she added fiercely. "I just wanted to save her, and that's what I shall tell the police if they come interfering with me."

"I should," said Crook, cordially. "You might get away with it at that. No one admires the police more than I do, and what they can swallow would stagger an ostrich. Well, I must be getting along now. Just remember what I told you, though. And one last word. You stick to your story through thick and thin. After all, the police can't PROVE you had any other reason for writing the letters. But be like the chap in the Bible—don't let 'em persuade you to add or subtract anything from your original statement."

CHAPTER TEN

I do begin to have bloody thoughts.
—THE TEMPEST.

I

HAVING confirmed a suspicion whose truth he had never doubted, Crook walked round the corner in Earl's Court District Station and travelled up to his office. It was going to be a momentous day. He felt it. And, like Miss Fitzpatrick, his intuition did not let him down.

As he marched into his office he found the telephone ringing its head off. When he answered it a voice he knew well said in agitated tones, "Crook, I thought you were one of these early risers. Where have you been all the morning? I've got something for you."

"Bring it along," invited Crook. "Another bit of stolen goods?"

For the man at the other end of the wire was one Thomas Armitage, and the most respectable thing about him was his name, that he'd taken by deed-poll thirty years before. Crook (and, of course, Bill Parsons) had known Armitage for some years as one of the cleverest fences in the country. The police had been after him for a considerable time, but on paper he was the most honest man that breathed.

"That's the devil of it," said Armitage in worried tones. "You know, I wouldn't have had this happen for ten thousand pounds."

"What have you got yourself landed with?" inquired Crook, genuinely enthralled. "And why ask my advice anyway? It'll cost you six-and-eightpence, plus purchase-tax. . . ." Then he stopped. "Don't tell me," he said, and his voice was low with what he later told Bill was reverent amazement, "don't tell me it's the pearls."

"That's what I'm afraid it is," said Armitage. "Of course it had to happen this way. All the police in the country looking for the things, and I had to get landed with them."

"All perfectly simple," Crook told him briskly, "go to the police, make your report. . . ."

"You wait till you've heard my report," said Armitage, glumly. "The police'll die of laughing when I tell them."

"Give me first refusal," said Crook.

"Mind you," exclaimed Armitage, the business-man in him instantly asserting itself, "it's doing you a favour, letting you in on the ground-floor like this."

"I'll chalk it up on the credit side," promised Crook, obligingly. He hung up the receiver and grinned at Bill. "Providence has got a sense of humour," he told Bill. "Fancy Nobby Armitage being landed with the pearls." Putting a finger against his nose he said in what music-hall comedians believe to be a Semitic accent, "Chentlemen, chentlemen, I tell you I know nothing. Dese pearls are not pearls at all. They were laid last night by my little daughter's pet chicken."

"I wonder what his yarn will be," said Bill, thoughtfully. "It'll be better than a beefsteak to see Nobby on toast. When you think how slim he's been all these years. That can't be him already? He must have borrowed Father Christmas's reindeers."

Nobby Armitage was a tight, compact little man, very carefully dressed, with a pearl pin in his tie and rather pointed patent-leather shoes. He looked like a no longer very young chorus boy, and was exceedingly slim in build as well as by temperament. As soon as he was seated, he plunged his hand into his coat pocket and brought out something that made Bill lounge forward with a soft murmur.

"Nice work, Nobby," he said.

"You'll be the most famous man in England before nightfall," Crook congratulated him.

"Don't be funny," Armitage begged. "Or, if you must laugh, wait till you've got something to laugh at. But first of all, what do you say to these?"

Crook glanced at the necklace and passed it to Bill, the expert.

"Five grand," said Bill laconically, who liked people to know that he could talk American, if he chose. "Question is, are they *the* pearls?"

"They could be," said Crook. "I never saw the others so I can't be certain, but—where did you get them from?"

Armitage said in a hollow voice, "My son, Tom, sent them to me."

"Tom!" Even Crook's crust of sophistication cracked for a moment. "I thought he was in the Air Force."

"He is," said Armitage.

"I always heard they were an enterprising lot." Crook's voice was warm with admiration. "But how did he get 'em? Don't tell me he looted 'em in Berlin."

"If you didn't talk so much, I'd get a chance," protested Armitage. "Then you can tell me what you think the police are going to say when they hear." He settled himself with the precision of despair and told his incredible story.

It appeared that Tom Armitage was not his father's son for nothing. When it came to choosing a girl friend, he found one who hailed from Glasgow, and knew how many coppers a man should get for a shilling.

"Jean has her head screwed on all right," Armitage assured his audience. "She knows better than to let the boy go wasting his money on pictures and all that. Tom was always one for talking—talk, talk, talk, all the time he'd be. Well, this girl's a rare one for listening, so you can guess for yourself how well-suited they are."

It appeared that young Armitage's idea of taking a girl out was to walk, talking all the time, to the limit of the wide stretch of moorland, adjoining Tempest Green, and, weather permitting, rest in a little circle of bushes where, he said, no one ever disturbed them. "The other lazy lads, they take their girls to the Park," said Armitage, wrinkling his nose. "They pay tuppence for a chair, when all the grass is free. Who's to pay for the war if young men and women are going to act spendthrift in this way?"

"So young Tom's saving his money to pay for the war? Does him credit, Nobby, but even a girl like Jean would probably rather he saved it to buy her a ring."

"I have the very ring for them," said Armitage. "It was passed to me in payment of a debt years ago. . . ."

"And you've never dared show it in public since? I believe you, Nobby, I believe you. Well, I still don't know how Tom found the pearls."

"Yesterday he was taking Jean out as usual, but when

they got to their clump of bushes—where, mark you, no one else had ever been before—they found someone had usurped it."

"And had he got the pearls?" inquired Crook, patiently.

"Wait a bit," said Armitage. "Now, I should explain they didn't actually see the fellow's face. They simply saw that he was wearing a wide-brimmed black hat and a black overcoat."

Crook, who had hitherto displayed little interest in the recital, here stiffened and threw up his head.

"Tom says he got the impression that it was quite an old chap. I asked him how he could be sure of that, since he didn't see the old codger's face, but he said it was something about the slouch of the shoulders."

"You look out," said Crook, darkly, "or you'll be disgraced by having a son in the police force."

Armitage decided to ignore that. "So he said to Jean, 'You'd think he'd be ashamed at his age, sneaking our special corner.' Still, they went a bit farther and they found another place, not so good as their own, mark you, but they made it do. It didn't turn out a very good afternoon in the end; rain blew up after tea-time, and they came back earlier than they'd intended. As they came across the Green, Tom said, 'I wonder what happened to that old boy.' They had to go close by the bush, and as they passed he looked in that direction and, to his surprise, the old fellow didn't seem to have moved. Tom's not what you'd call superstitious, but he got an idea that something was wrong. He told Jean to wait where she was, and he went up to investigate. As he got near he says he called out, but nothing happened. He'd got proper cold feet by this time. But when he got round the corner of the bush he found what he'd never expected."

Armitage paused, apparently for dramatic effect, but actually because he was out of breath.

"Don't tell me!" begged Crook. "I'll guess. He found a ghost wearing the Tea-Cosy's hat and Miss Kersey's pearls."

"I wish you would not be so damned flippant, my dear Crook," cried Armitage. "This is a serious matter—to my son, to me and to my son's future wife."

"It's even important to the Tea-Cosy," Crook reminded him.

"What my boy found among those bushes on Tempest Green wasn't a person at all. It was . . ." He stopped, staring at Crook's brick-coloured face.

"In one minute," said Crook, "I'm going to take your silly head off your shoulders and bung it against the wall. Will you tell me in words of one syllable what your precious son did find?"

"Well," Armitage choked on an unexpected nervous giggle. "He found a black hat balanced on an old umbrella, and a black overcoat spread over the bushes. He said it gave him more of a shock than if he'd found a decomposed corpse."

"Wait till he's seen a few decomposed corpses, and then let him talk," was Crook's unsympathetic comment. "What did he say the umbrella was like?"

Armitage looked astonished. "Just a big, old umbrella, with a yellow, crook handle."

"Carry on," said Crook.

Bill struck a match and lighted a cigarette. You'd have thought Armitage was telling "The Three Bears" to his own grandchild for all the interest he took in the conversation. But you'd have been wrong. Crook knew that look; the police knew it, too.

"Well, what did he do? You've got so careful, Nobby, that getting words out of you has to be done with a corkscrew."

"He called Jean first and said what a—what a rum go it was."

"And Jean said?"

"Jean's a sensible girl. I knew that the first time I met her. She said, 'Well, Tom, seeing it's raining and I've my last year's hat on and seeing this gentleman doesn't want this umbrella any more, how about me borrowing it?' Tom says he still felt there was something queer about it, almost dishonest, he said, though that was ridic'lous, of course. But Jean's got a will of her own and there wasn't any one in sight, so he took off the hat and yanked up the umbrella and opened it and—and——"

"Quite the newest kind of fairy-tale," approved Crook. "In the old days, the pearls jumped out of the young lady's mouth."

"I told you how it would be," said Armitage. "You don't have to tell me it don't sound real. Why, I don't hardly believe it myself, telling you. Still, that's the way it was. He opened the umbrella and the pearls came sliding out like a snake. It was Jean who picked them up. 'Well, that's a queer thing to find inside an umbrella,' she said. 'But they're pretty beads, Tom. I wonder who left them here.' Tom took them from her and said, 'If you ask me they're not beads at all. They're pearls and worth a packet.' It was a long time before Jean stopped thinking he was pulling her leg. Pearls worth a packet aren't left hidden away in umbrellas, she said. But Tom was thinking.

" 'My father was contacted by the police the other day,' he told her. 'They were asking about a missing string of pearls. Something to do with a murder.'

" 'Do you mean, you think that may be the one?' Jean asked him and he said:

" 'I don't know. But I daresay Dad would. He knows something about pearls, see?'

"He was coming in with me if Hitler hadn't messed things up the way he did. Well, my boy told me candidly on the wire last night—and what that call must have cost him makes me feel as if it was December—when he thought of the police and all the fuss, he was for putting the pearls back and letting some other chap find them—and I wish to goodness he had," wound up Nobby Armitage, bitterly. "But Jean was always the business girl.

" 'Perhaps there's a reward offered for them,' she said, 'and if you don't tell any one, then I will.'

"Tom was flying last night—maybe he shouldn't have told me but he did—so instead of going to the police, he just packed those pearls into a box and shoved 'em into the post without even a stamp on them, for all the world like a pound of sausages."

"Wise lad!" said Crook. "That boy of yours is going to be a credit to you one of these days, Nobby. If you want to make sure a letter or parcel gets to its addressee, put the stamp inside instead of out. The fatherly post-office won't take their eyes off it, for fear of losing their fivepence."

"I suppose that's how it came through so quick," said

Armitage, grudgingly. "If he writes to me and posts it on the 5.30 in the usual way, it never gets to London first thing next morning."

Crook took the pearls once more into his hands. He looked at them as the police must have looked at the exhibits in the Poisoned Chocolates Case. They had just the same value for him, no more, no less.

After a minute he looked up.

"Well," he demanded, "what d'you expect me to do? I can't tell you if these are the pearls or not, and what's more, I can't suggest any one who can. Our only hopes are Watson and Flora Kersey, both of them amateurs. To the amateur imitation pearls and the real thing look pretty much the same. No, the umbrella's what we want. Where's that?"

"I suppose they left it where it was, unless Jean took it back with her. I didn't ask."

"Pity," said Crook.

"What's all the fuss about the umbrella?" inquired Armitage. "I should have thought the pearls . . ."

"They go together," Crook explained, "Bread and butter, liver and bacon, flotsam and jetsam, umbrella and pearls. One without the other is like . . ."

"I know, I know. I suppose it all means something."

"You bet it does," said Crook.

"I suppose you'll be able to prove the old gentleman had such an umbrella," Armitage went on. "Though, from what Tom says, it was ordinary enough."

"Not the old gentleman," said Crook, patiently. "Haven't you tumbled yet? The umbrella belonged to Miss Kersey, and she carried it around because she knew, if no one else did, what was in it. And I should say no one else did," he added, more to himself than his companion. "I ought to have thought of it, though. I had a client once who carried all her important bonds inside her umbrella. Said it was the one place where they'd be safe. Thieves might snatch your bag but they wouldn't sneak an old gamp like that even for firewood." Suddenly he began to laugh.

"Glad you think it's so amusing," observed Nobby, icily.

"Think of this fellow turning the place over for the pearls, and then chucking them away like that. Funny, what? Hope I'm there to see his face when they get him and he hears the truth. By the way, you say it was an isolated spot?"

"No one knew about it except Tom and this girl."

"We-ell." Crook demurred. "That's hardly the fact. One other chap knew of it, the chap who left the coat and hat there—to say nothing of the umbrella."

"Bill says he must have been about seven foot tall, if the coat was anything to go by. Well, Crook, now you've heard the tale. What happens next?"

"You go to the police, of course. It's such a damn silly story any one 'ud believe it."

"And you tell me you know the police?" Armitage's face was full of scandalised sorrow. "Why, they wouldn't believe a story like that from me if I was to swear on the Talmud."

"Never mind," said Crook, encouragingly. "You're goin' to make history, Nobby. And the police are goin' to have a gala-day—first, Miss Fitzpatrick and then you. By the way," he added casually, "if you can get in touch with your boy, I would. Get him to make his own report to the police and tell them you've got the pearls."

Armitage looked suspicious.

"That sounds a roundabout way of getting going," he remarked.

"Well, you don't want the police saying your boy was trying to palm you the pearls on the sly? You seem to have forgotten a lot of what you know about the Force, Nobby, and that was plenty. Not that I blame 'em altogether," he added in magnanimous tones. "They've got to be a bit smarter than the public, and every one's so smart now it isn't enough just to see what's there, you have to see a few things that aren't. You take my tip, Armitage. It's what I'd do myself."

His companion was regarding him with suspicion. "There's something behind this," he said. "You don't have to tell me. You're playing for time, Crook, and it's no use telling me anything different."

Crook sighed. "You read me like a book," he said.

Armitage stood up, reluctantly collected the pearls and announced, "I shall go straight to the police and tell them my boy's story."

"Have it your own way," said Crook.

"And I know, the moment I shut this door, you're going to think up a way to double-cross me. I can see it in your eye. But you take care, Crook. One of these days the police 'ull be too much for you."

"And p'raps, when I've gone, the people I'm protectin' the public from will be too much for the police. It's like the House That Jack Built. Still," he nodded farewell and waited for the door to close, "I don't suppose there are many umbrellas full of pearl necklaces lying round the countryside. This about clinches things, Bill. All I want now is a bit of proof, and that little girl in St. Magnus is goin' to provide me with that."

II

Eleven o'clock, therefore, found Crook at the hospital. He had already put in as much work as many men in an eight hour day, but for him the morning had scarcely begun.

His presence was hardly greeted with delight. In fact, a more sensitive man might have felt embarrassed. An auxiliary nurse passed him on to the ward-sister, a bustling lady with a bosom, who told him that it was quite impossible for Miss Petersen to see strangers.

Crook said he wasn't a stranger.

The Sister asked if he were a relation.

"Closer than that," said Crook.

The Sister looked at him with suspicion.

"I'm her saviour," said Crook, simply.

The Sister passed him on to the matron.

A single glance assured Crook that here was a sourpuss if ever there was one. She came, tall and frigid, looking as though she'd just been taken out of the frigidaire.

"What you suggest is quite impossible," she said.

"Anything else is impossible," said Crook, "but not that. This is a case of attempted murder, you know."

"I am quite aware of that, Mr. Crook. The police told me . . ."

"Hell!" exclaimed Crook, rudely. "The police couldn't have told you anything if it hadn't been for me. If it hadn't been for me, you wouldn't have had Miss Petersen here at all. She'd have been in the mortuary. It was her luck I came in when I did. If Miss Kersey had had that luck—but she hadn't. She came too early in the day. People I save from violence—apart from professional clients, that is—mustn't call before six."

The matron stared at him.

"Miss Petersen was found half-choked in the flat of a client of mine," Crook continued. "In the interests of justice, I've got to get a description of the assailant."

"And if he should prove to be your client?"

"Then greased lightning won't have a chance with me. He'll need everything I've got. Mind you, I don't admit yet it's anything to do with him, but I'm like all the English heroes, I don't believe anything's impossible—but if he is involved, then he needs me more than ever."

"You must know if your client is concerned in this dreadful affair," expostulated the matron.

To her horror, Crook leaned closer and shut one lively, brown eye.

"Between you and me and the gatepost, I know exactly who killed Miss Kersey," he said. "The job's goin' to be to prove it. Truth by itself's about as useful as a man with a tommy-gun up against a tank. And that's something that's not always appreciated the way it should be. Now then, I shan't keep the young lady long, and you can put a sister to play gooseberry, if you like. . . ."

The matron made a sound remarkably like a belch, as though this farouche visitor was too much even for her trained stomach, and said that if Mr. Crook would wait she would ascertain what could be arranged.

A few minutes later Crook was sitting beside Sigrid's bed. In the morning light, the girl's fair beauty was very apparent. The bruising was ugly and spoke of considerable violence. Crook thought she was fortunate to have suffered nothing more than slight concussion. Some instinct must have made her turn her head at the critical moment, and the blow had lost much of its force.

The little more and how much it is, he told himself. He liked cliches. He said only great men dared to use them.

When Crook explained who he was, she smiled at once.

"But I knew you," she said. "I saw you at the inquest. That is why I was coming to see you. . . ."

"I wish all my visitors had your wits," Crook told her.

"Wits?"

"Yes. It's a sound rule, any time you're visiting a strange gentleman, to leave a clue as to your whereabouts on the staircase. You've no notion what a help it is. That torch of yours, for instance. As soon as I found it, I knew we'd got a caller. Miss Fitzpatrick don't see any one after dark, the second flat's empty, the third should be, and you weren't in mine. Well, puttin' two and two together, I got a nice little sum. And now, let's get down to real business. D'you remember what this chap looked like? Anything special about him?"

He found Sigrid a helpful witness, the more so because she had recently been taken over this ground by the police who had, thought Crook unscrupulously, probably suggested several of the answers themselves. She explained her anxiety about the anonymous letters, an anxiety Crook speedily cleared up by assuring her that they were written by a semi-lunatic who couldn't help herself. He told her she needn't give them another thought. But when it came to a description of her assailant, she was on less sure ground. She said he was rather tall, and wore a black, wide-awake hat firmly pressed over his forehead. His manner was friendly and vague.

"You can't remember anythin' else strikin' about him? He didn't wear a peculiar kind of tie? or fur-lined boots? or a monocle?"

Sigrid shook her head. "None of those things. But he was the one you call the Tea-Cosy."

"What makes you say that?"

"He said so himself."

"I might say I was the Duke of Wellington, but they wouldn't pass that at Bow Street. The real thing is, did you see his face clearly enough to identify him if you met him again?"

Sigrid shook her head. "I do not think so."

"Y'see, he'll probably have some sort of alibi—these amateur criminals always do. It's what the police count on."

"I thought an alibi was so useful," murmured the girl.

"Useful to the police. Gives them something to work on, see? If you tell a man you can't account for your actions at a given moment, it's up to him to show that you must have been where he says you were, and that's not so easy to prove as you might suppose. But if you tell him you were in some particular place, well, all he's got to do is prove that you weren't, and that's a much simpler job. Your friend knew that."

"My friend?"

"Of last night. You asked him where he'd been for the past week, and he said he didn't know. See where that one lands you? Right in the pan. If he doesn't know, how the hell is any one else going to? He hasn't given us anything to build on. As a matter of fact, though, you might have guessed he was hazing you."

"Should I?" asked the girl, meekly. "What did I miss?"

"Didn't strike you as queer that he should remember all the details of the telephone-call and the assault that followed it—every single point, mark you—but nothing afterwards? Now, if he'd really been slugged on the head the way he says he was, so that he couldn't remember anything that happened afterwards, any medico would tell you that he wouldn't remember what happened immediately before, either. That's the worst of these artists. They will dot all the i's and cross all the t's. And that's what brings 'em in the end to the little covered shed."

"Do you mean, he betrayed himself last night?"

"Absolutely," Crook told her in cheerful tones. "Now, once more. You're sure there's nothing about his appearance you've forgotten? The police are very careful men. You and me might add two and two together and make it sixty-five, but the police know it makes four. It always has, therefore it always will. Talk to the police about progress. . . ." He shook his head sadly. "They learnt their multiplication table at their mother's knee and mother's knee is good enough for them for the duration."

But although she thought for some time Sigrid had to admit that she could add nothing to her previous evidence.

"I am sorry not to be more helpful," she apologised.

Crook stood up. "But you have been. You've told me the one thing I wanted to know. Now then, you take care of yourself. Don't see the press, whatever happens, and don't move out of this place till you hear from me. Never mind what any one else says, remember I saved your life once, and I'll go on doing it so long as you go on doin' what I say."

A new expression came into the girl's blue eyes.

"You mean, you think I may still be in danger?"

Crook stared at her in amazement. "Well, what do you think yourself?" he inquired reasonably. "This chap's taken so many risks that one more or less ain't goin' to worry him. Your safest place would probably be a convent, and even then he might slug the Mother Superior and turn up in her robes."

As he emerged into the corridor, he found himself once again face to face with Madam Sourpuss.

"Take care of that little girl," he said confidentially. "She's in a bad way."

The Matron looked as if she couldn't believe her ears.

"On the contrary, the doctor gives a most favourable account of her. It was simple concussion, following a blow or fall. In any case, we shall want the bed as soon as possible. One wing was bombed out during the raids, and we have very little accommodation for accident cases."

"I'll send for her soon," Crook promised. "She shan't be a burden to you much longer."

And he swept out.

III

Swansdown was Crook's next destination. Watson herself met him in the hall. "Oh, Mr. Crook!" She looked a little disconcerted. "I wasn't expecting you."

"And I shan't be staying long," Crook promised her. "I just want a bit of information."

Watson took him into the sitting-room in which Flora had conducted her rather stormy first conversation with him.

"I'm afraid it's too late," she said, turning and clasping her hands nervously. "Miss Flora's gone."

"Has she?" said Crook, putting up his red eyebrows. "She hasn't wasted any time."

"I don't think she felt she could forgive me for getting the house," Watson explained. "She was so sure her auntie would leave it to her."

"Did she want it particularly?" wondered Crook.

"I don't think it was a matter of wanting. Of course, she could always have sold it. One thing I do know, she never meant to live here, once her auntie was gone, that is. She said she hated the country."

"Very self-sacrificing of her to stay so long," Crook suggested.

"I don't think she'd have liked to leave Miss Kersey after all these years. Of course, she'll do some work now, I suppose. I mean, she's quite young as civilians go in this war."

"So she is," Crook agreed. "You're staying here, by the way."

"Oh, I shall stay," said Watson. "I mean, now I've got the house to myself—I've always wanted my own house, though I never expected to get it this way—I shall do nicely. I shall take in a few guests."

"You ought to get started while the going's good," Crook pointed out.

But Watson's horse-face stiffened.

"I wouldn't like to do anything till this mystery about Miss Kersey has been cleared up," she said. "Of course, I do hope the police will be as quick as they can. It's so very unsettling. And I'll have to get a few more beds, but in a nice safe part of the country like this—and it isn't really so lonely, for all Miss Flora calls it the 'Back of Beyond'—it shouldn't be hard to get guests. And I've looked after the catering for a long time now. Madam was very particular. She didn't like anything wasted."

"That sounds all right," Crook assured her. "What about young What'shisname? Is he going to start you off in business?"

"Mr. Grant? Oh well, there was some unpleasantness there."

"You're telling me," said Crook, cordially, settling down to enjoy himself. "Before or after Miss Flora went?"

"Oh, before, of course. She practically ordered him out of the house."

"Pretty cool, wasn't it, seeing it was your house?"

"She couldn't, somehow, seem to grasp that. Anyway, she was asking him what plans he was making, and he said, 'Was there anything against him staying here if I'd keep him.' And she laughed in a nasty sort of way and said, 'No, none.' And then she went on that any one could see he was in a Government post and knew how to do well for himself. I don't call that right, do you, sir? I mean, you shouldn't say just because a gentleman's in the Government he doesn't do any work."

"It's not a *sine qua non*," Crook acknowledged cheerfully. "Well, what happened after that?"

"Mr. Grant said, 'It won't inconvenience you if I stay, since you're going to London, will it?' And she turned on him and said, with me standing by, mark you, 'You've planned it all very nicely, haven't you? First you make your living off my aunt, and now you intend to go on doing the same off her housekeeper.'"

"I hope Mr. Grant gave her a good sock on the jaw," said Crook, "though I distrust these young men with B.B.C. voices. Always the little gentleman, and look where it gets you."

"Mr. Grant was very pleasant to have about the house," observed Watson, coldly. "Really, it's not to be wondered at that Miss Kersey liked having him here. Always good-tempered and so bright. . . ."

"Sounds like a popular advertisement," agreed Crook. "Has he—er—slung his hook for good?"

"I told him, any time he wanted a bed he'd be welcome, and he said he'd be glad to leave a change of clothes here in case of emergencies. He thinks he may be going abroad any time, though, of course, he doesn't like it talked about."

"Quite so." Crook was extremely grave. "It would never do to let the Axis powers guess his movements. However, the person I really want to see is you. Now, as I understand it, Miss Flora may have been her auntie's niece and Mr. Grant may have been her boy-friend, but it was you who really did the work. I mean, you looked after her and her things and probably packed for her and all that."

"Oh yes, sir," said Watson, a little shocked at the notion that any one else should interfere with this particular province.

"And you packed for her on her last journey?"

"That's right, sir."

"Do you remember, approximately, what she took?"

"Just her toilet things, sir, and a change of underlinen, the same as I said the first time I was asked. I put it up for her in good time; she liked things done on the early side, and I just left it open for her to add her brush and comb at the last minute."

"She actually put those in herself?"

"Yes, Mr. Crook. I came up to see what there was I could do, but she'd shut the case down and fastened it. It was one of these zipper cases, so I suppose shut down isn't accurate, really."

"How long should you say you were downstairs after your packing was done?"

"Oh!" Watson looked a little flustered. "I couldn't be sure. Quite a little time."

"That's all right," Crook soothed her. "Now, you know exactly what she took. And you know exactly what she had—how many chemises and so forth?"

"I did all her laundry," said Watson. "She never put it out. Laundries ruin your nice things so. And the only outside help we had was a woman from the village for the rough, and she's been away these last three weeks with the influenza, so no one but me's handled Madam's things."

"How all things work together for them that seek

truth," paraphrased Crook with a beaming smile. "Now, do something for me. Pop up and count Miss Kersey's things and make sure they're all present and correct."

Watson looked offended. "I don't have to count them to know that," she said.

"You're sure the police didn't do a bit of snitching on their own account?"

Watson's expression said that the mere suggestion was indecent.

"Or Miss Flora?"

"I don't rightly know who they belong to," Watson confessed. "Of course, I wouldn't think of wearing them. I thought perhaps later on I might give them away."

"Evacuees are a solution sometimes," Crook agreed. But once again he had said the wrong thing.

"I didn't mean any of those people," said Watson, coldly. "I'm sure Madam's things would be much too plain and decent for the lot we have round here. It's all lace trimmings and scalloped edges where they're concerned. And no shame neither. Hang them up in the front garden for all the world to see. No, I thought some of these decayed gentlewomen's societies, perhaps."

"A very good idea," Crook approved. "But, look here, before you do anything like that, do me one favour. Just count 'em and see if the total's right. No, I'm not suggestin' any one's gone off with 'em, but—it's all part of an idea I have."

Watson, now looking both perplexed and offended, went upstairs, and Crook wandered round the room, whistling cheerfully.

When Watson returned, he said, "Well? How was it?"

"Madam had eight of everything," said Watson. "She said then you always had six in wear and two for when the others began to get shabby. Whenever she threw anything away she bought another. Regular as clockwork."

"And how many sets are there upstairs now?"

"Seven."

Crook considered. "The police send back the ones she had in wear when . . ."

Watson shivered. "Certainly not. I wouldn't want them anyway."

"And the zipper bag hasn't been found?"

"You know it hasn't."

"And yet there are seven sets in the drawers upstairs?"

"Yes." Watson's resentment began to fade, as perplexity engulfed her.

"And you don't see what that adds up to? Think again. Listen. One set Madam was wearing. One set she took with her. Two from eight leaves six—and yet there's seven sets upstairs."

"Oh!" Watson's face seemed to elongate under his eyes. He thought, though he kept this to himself, that with a different temperament, she'd have done well on the halls. Her face, small and inclined to show its age, seemed to be made of india-rubber. "I never thought of that. You're right. It is queer. I remember just what I packed."

"And now it's back in the drawer. What does that look like to you?"

The woman looked at him quite incredulously, but his bold, brown stare never wavered.

"You mean, she didn't take them to London? That's

why you asked me if I'd finished her packing for her."

"Go on putting one foot in front of the other, and that's the way you climb the mountain," Crook approved.

"Then," Watson moved her feet carefully, "what was in the bag she took? I carried it downstairs, and though you couldn't say it was heavy, it wasn't empty."

"I never thought it was."

"Then—do you know what was in it?"

"I could make a guess," Crook told her. "When I'm sure—I mean, when I'm in a position to prove what I know, then we shall be at the end of the case."

"Will it be long, do you think?" inquired Watson, twisting her nervous hands.

"Depends on developments. There's one thing you can do, though. I suppose you'd recognise Miss Kersey's umbrella?"

"I'd know it in a hundred," replied Watson, instantly.

"Did she have her name on it?"

"Not her umbrella, no. Which was queer, seeing all her underclothes were marked. But she was funny in some ways."

"You're telling me," said Crook, politely.

"She sometimes got the idea that she was being followed or watched. She didn't want to carry anything that would identify her. Of course, her—her underwear was different."

"Quite different," agreed Crook, encouragingly.

"If she had half a chance, she wouldn't even carry her identity card, and as for putting her name in her gas mask, she just wouldn't hear of it."

"She must have had a riotous imagination," was

Crook's characteristic comment. "Look here, put on your bib and tucker and come with me to Tempest Green."

"Tempest Green?" The woman stared.

"They've got an umbrella there I think may belong to Miss Kersey."

"Oh!" Watson's eyes widened again.

"Surprised?" asked Crook.

"Well, I am really. I didn't know Miss Kersey ever went to Tempest Green."

"I never said she did. I only said her umbrella went there."

"She never let that umbrella out of her sight."

"Like a client of mine, who kept her documents inside hers, and then was killed stooping to pick it off a tramway-line. You could say the umbrella was the last thing her eyes rested on. It's pretty certain she never saw the tram."

Watson, a wary look on her face, went upstairs to put on her hat. Crook wandered aimlessly round the room till she returned. On the way to the station he apologised for the licensing laws of the country that prevented his offering her adequate refreshment, but Watson said stiffly she belonged to the Sisterhood, anyhow, so Crook stifled his natural feelings, and they each had a nice cup of tea at the Merry Mayde Teashoppe near the station.

On the journey to Tempest Green, with its inevitable change at Barnham Thicket, Watson spoke little. Only once she said, "I never thought of it ending like this, and her so clever at managing things," and the second time, "That poor girl. It does seem true what it says in the Bible, doesn't it, that no man dieth to himself. It's all terrible. It's fortunate you can't guess what's going to happen to you, or Madam would never have slept peacefully in her bed at all."

On the way to the station, Crook stopped at the post-office to send a telegram. It was half-past three when they reached their objective and Crook introduced himself in his usual breezy fashion. But the country police were less easily over-borne than their London brethren. Besides, Crook didn't mean so much to them as he did in town.

"Are you a relation of the deceased?" he was asked.

"Represent her missin' nephew," pattered Crook.

"We don't know anything about that," said the sergeant.

"That's the trouble," remonstrated Crook. "If you could unearth him, we'd be a lot further on."

"If he doesn't get in touch with his lawyer," began the sergeant, a bit nettled.

"Maybe he can't," suggested Crook slyly. "In which case, it's your job to find him. And maybe he won't, in which case we've got to get together and dig him out—or up, as the case may be," he added, *sotto voce*.

"Anyway, what can we do for you?" the policeman wanted to know.

"I hear you've found an umbrella full of pearls. No, don't ask me how I know. It's my job to know these things. Well, I've brought along the one woman in England who can identify it. The late Miss Kersey's housekeeper."

The sergeant looked somewhat put out, as indeed he was, at this unscrupulous stealing of the official thunder. He asked a lot of questions. He wanted to know why

Crook linked up the nameless umbrella with the dead woman. Crook answered him by explaining about the Tea-Cosy. He said that if he could see the coat and hat that had been found with the umbrella, he might be able to help even more. He was persuasive, blatant and indifferent by turns. But, as usual, he got his own way.

Watson recognised the umbrella at once by a number of scratches and other marks that would have been practically invisible to a disinterested eye.

"So that's why she wouldn't be parted from it," she said, looking as nervous as if she expected it to open of its own accord and deposit a snake on her lap. "All this talk about weather and not liking a stick because it gave you away . . ."

"Poppycock," agreed Crook. "I had my suspicions when Mr. Prince told me she never even came down to a meal without it. I wouldn't be surprised if she took it with her to the bathroom. It's what I'd do, if I had an umbrella worth five thousand pounds—and no nasturtiums to Mr. P., either," he added, with that vulgarity that the few refined persons of his acquaintance so deplored.

"It was a crazy thing to do," said Watson, still open-eyed. "Why, suppose she lost it?"

"Not much chance of that," said Crook. "She never took her eyes off it. Besides, who would want to pinch an antique like that?"

It did indeed look a shabby, battered affair; a tinker wouldn't have given you sixpence for it.

Crook blew a hearty sigh. "Pity X. isn't here," he said. "Nice to see his face—if you're a dab at human emotions, I mean. Think of huntin' through the old lady's handbag, then the zipper case, and—not a trace of the

213

pearls. And all the time . . ." he turned to the police, "I suppose you don't know where those are—the bag and the case, I mean?"

The sergeant said, "Well, no," and wished Mr. Crook would go away.

"We don't know what was in the case," interpolated Watson, in a shaky tone.

Crook looked at her in surprise. "Don't you see even now?" he asked. "Don't you really know what was inside when she got to Paddington Station?"

IV

Before he left the premises, Crook inquired whether he could see the hat and coat (he had already proffered this request and it had been politely ignored). But now the sergeant was defeated. The coat and hat were produced and Crook instantly identified them.

"Know 'em anywhere," he said, in his sweeping fashion.

"You mean, you've seen them before?"

"On the night of the 7th April, in my own house. See that greenish patch on the sleeve? I noticed that particularly. I suppose he thought, by putting 'em in a remote spot like Tempest Green, they'd rot before any one found 'em."

"He?" said the sergeant, lifting his brows.

"X.," replied Crook, lifting his a bit higher. "The murderer, the man the police can't catch. And if it hadn't been for a modest desire for privacy on the part of Sergeant-Pilot Armitage, they might have so rotted. Ah well, it's true what they croon on the air: Love is the mightiest weapon . . ."

214

He saw a tearful Watson to her train, then stepped into a telephone booth and called the aerodrome. When he was connected, he represented himself as Police Headquarters, and asked for young Armitage. When he heard the young man's voice, he said:

"Sorry you've been troubled, but there's one point to be added to this story of yours. What's the last time you were on Tempest Green, at the spot where you found the pearls?"

"A fortnight ago," said Armitage. "A fortnight and a day, to be precise."

"And there was no sign of any funnification then?"

"Not a trouser button," said young Armitage.

"Just as I thought," said Crook, and hung up the receiver.

CHAPTER ELEVEN

The shroud is done, Death muttered, toe to chin.
He snapped the ends and tucked the needles in.
                              —JOHN MASEFIELD.

I

AFTER Crook's departure Sigrid lay back considering the
position. With the remarkable resilience of youth, she
had already recovered in large part from last night's
brutal assault. The chief source of trouble was now
shock. When the police came to question her, and she
had falteringly retrodden the road of remembrance, she
had supposed at first that she had been a victim-designate
of what her neighbour at the office called "one of the
D.O.M."

"You look out for the damned old men, honey,"
Brenda Phillips had said. "They're much the worst. It
isn't," she added thoughtfully, "as though you get any
fun out of it, either."

Sigrid hadn't taken her very seriously. She was retiring
by nature and, not being of English descent, her friends
in her refugee country were few. At the end of the day's
work, she had been glad to slip back to the one-room flat
that she rented and had made so pretty. Of course, there
were young men in uniform, but a certain native com-
mon-sense assured her that a few pretty speeches, an
escort to a dance or so, or a ticket at the pictures did
not constitute a proposal. One or two had told her she

216

was the sweetest thing, and suggested she should wait till they came back from the war, but there had never been any one she could take seriously, except the young man in Norway, and no one knew what had happened to him.

Now it appeared that someone had tried to murder her, not because he had designs on her virtue, but because she constituted a danger to him.

"But how could I be dangerous?" she had demanded of Crook. "Me, I know nothing, I have never seen the old gentleman before. . . ."

"When you say you know nothin', you're understatin' the case," Crook assured her. "You know he was there at the flat yesterday afternoon."

The girl stared. "But why should he mind my knowing that? I don't know what he was there for."

"That's just the point. No one knows yet. It could be that he'd fixed himself an alibi, and you weren't to be there to disprove it."

"But they would have found me," she protested in a shocked whisper.

Crook shrugged his bulky shoulders. "Maybe, sugar, but when? If ever you take to a life of crime, you remember that the safest place to hide a thing is the place where the police have looked already. The odds are they wouldn't have gone through the Tea-Cosy's flat again till something fresh happened to distract their attention. "

"Do you think it was—him—I saw?" breathed the girl.

"What the soldier said ain't evidence. How do I know? Though, as a matter of fact, I have a pretty good idea. The trouble about amateur criminals," he went on confidentially, "is that they want to be so damn safe. It trips 'em up ninety-eight times out of a hundred. Now, suppose this chap had let you go past. You wouldn't have thought anything of it most likely, but there was the chance you were comin' to see me and you'd say there was a fellow on the second floor when you arrived. So, to make quite sure, he decided to put out your light. And all the good he's done the world is more or less to put out his own."

Sigrid lay brooding over this for some time. It was difficult for her to believe that some man, some maniac perhaps, regarded her as so dangerous to his own security that he was prepared to commit murder to keep her out of the way. There had been an unwonted gravity about Crook's face when he told her to await his instructions that had impressed her. She was still thinking about him when a nurse came in, carrying a bunch of flowers.

"How lovely!" breathed Sigrid.

"For you, dear," said the nurse.

"For me?"

"And the gentleman that brought them's waiting. I don't know what Matron will say, you having all these visitors. But he said could he just have five minutes?"

"Do you think Matron would mind? Oh, but Mr. Crook said—you don't think he's from a newspaper?"

"He wrote something on the card," said the nurse, who had read it.

Sigrid looked. "I helped Crook to rescue you last night," the message ran. "Let me see for myself that you're really still alive."

Completely mystified, Sigrid said, "Well, if Matron wouldn't mind . . ." and lay back, wondering.

A minute later Hilary Grant walked into the ward.

There was a gasp of excitement at his presence. He was the man most girls dream of both before and after they're married, before, hoping they'll find him, and later, when they're realising that a copy is never so good as an original.

He came straight to Sigrid's bedside.

"It's awfully good of you to let me come in," he told her. "I say, are you really all right?"

"I shall be soon. How lucky for me you happened to be there last night."

"I'm afraid I didn't do much. It's Crook you have to thank. I say, you're the girl who found Miss Kersey, aren't you? All right, all right, I'm sorry I asked. But I wanted to make you feel we aren't quite strangers. A thing like that sort of binds people together, don't you think?"

"Yes," said Sigrid, softly. "I think so, too."

"Look here," said Hilary Grant, a little awkwardly, but with so much charm that her heart turned over, "are you sure you're all right? I mean, when you get out of this place, have you got people or any one?"

"Not in England," said Sigrid in the same gentle voice. "My people are in Norway. My old grandmother, my brother and his wife—and my friends."

"But you've got someone here?"

"There are the girls where I work. They are very kind. . . ."

He shook his head impatiently. "I don't mean that sort of thing at all. I mean, someone who'll look after you."

She shook her head gently. Her blue eyes looked bigger than usual, because she was so pale. She seemed incredibly innocent, incredibly young. It was hard to believe that the most hardened scoundrel could harbour murderous thoughts against her.

"No," she told him. "There is no one like that."

Hilary put out his hand and dropped it for an instant over hers. "You're wrong," he said. "There's one man who'd move Heaven and earth to keep you safe."

And he spoke the truth.

Before he went he asked another question. "Crook doesn't bother you, does he?" he said. "You mustn't mind his manner. It doesn't mean anything. He's a good chap, really, and it's he who saved your life, not I. I'd never have broken into another man's flat on the strength of a torch lying about on the stairs. You can trust that chap, if he is a bit of a rough diamond."

"He seems to think that whoever it was, and he says I am to be careful not to say what I may think, will try again. That is why I am to stay here until he sends for me. He said he did not think it would be long now."

"Look here," exclaimed Hilary Grant, in instant agitation, "have you got a police guard at the door or anything?"

"A police guard!" She laughed. "How absurd you are."

She had a way of rolling her r's a little that was very fetching.

"Not in the least. If this chap's made one attempt on you and there's any chance of your recognising him again, then Crook's right. He won't take any risks."

"Mr. Crook says he takes a risk when he sets himself up against him—against Mr. Crook, I mean."

"Crook thinks he's damned clever and, from what one hears of him it's probably true. All the same, it's generally admitted that to him the case is all and the individual precious little. You want to be careful. Do the people here know how critical things are?"

"I am safe here," Sigrid protested.

But Hilary went on looking worried. "I hope so. I admit I'd as soon face a tank as your matron, but you have to remember that this chap is probably wanted by the police anyhow. . . ."

"That is what Mr. Crook says."

"What did Crook tell you?" demanded Hilary, still looking troubled. "If he'd been acting for you, he'd have told you to say you wouldn't know this fellow from a Plymouth Rock, but as it is . . ."

"He told me to say nothing until he could prove what he believed."

"You think he knows who it was? Or that you do?"

Sigrid hesitated. "I have promised . . ."

"You're quite right. Now promise me something. You'll stay put till he or I come for you?"

"He has told me to remain until he sends. And actually I have nowhere to go. My week is up to-night, and my landlady wants the room for a niece who is coming to London. I was going to get myself another one this morning. A girl who works with me gave me the address."

"I realise you've promised Crook," said Hilary Grant, "but, just for my peace of mind, promise me too."

"I promise," said Sigrid, gravely.

He caught her hand. "Did any one ever tell you how sweet you are. How old are you, Sigrid? Sixteen? Seventeen? You look a mere infant. I feel like your father."

Sigrid began to laugh. "You would not say that if you

had ever seen him. He died when I was a little girl. He had a beard and very big eyebrows. He was—oh, not at all like you."

"Thank God something made me call on Crook that night," exclaimed Hilary. "Was it really only yesterday? It seems as if days must have passed. You might call it the Hand of Providence."

The ward sister came up to them. Visiting hours were over, she explained. She tried to look severe, but Hilary disarmed even her official gravity.

"I shall come to-morrow," he said. "And—you won't forget your promise, Sigrid?"

"No—Hilary. I shan't forget."

He stooped and caught her hands. Before she could realise his intention, he had set his lips to hers. Then before she could so much as gasp, he had turned and was striding down the ward, followed by the adoring glances of its other occupants. But though Sigrid had given him her word in the best possible faith, she broke it all the same.

II

It was about five o'clock when the telegram arrived. In Mercy Ward the tea-hour was over. Tea came round at three-thirty in big white and gold cups, with bread and margarine and biscuits, or cake, and the only other excitement before lights out was the cup of milk or cocoa at six. Sigrid was settling down, counting the hours till visiting-time next day, when Matron herself came in, carrying a telegram.

It was addressed to Sigrid but had been "opened in

error." It said: "Meet me Charing Cross 6.30 main book-
ing-hall. Urgent. Crook."

"This is very irregular," said Matron, "but in the circumstances it might be as well for you to keep the appointment. We have just been notified of an urgent case
coming by ambulance immediately. . . ."

"You mean, I am not to come back here?" Sigrid's face
was blank with dismay.

"I hardly think this Mr. Crook would have sent for
you unless he had already made plans for your accommodation," was Matron's composed reply. "I understand he
is your legal representative."

"Y-yes." Sigrid sounded doubtful.

Matron stifled any doubts she might have cherished.
There were agencies and to spare to help young women
from occupied countries. Besides, the girl had been in
England for more than a year, she could hardly be
counted as a stranger.

Sigrid, trusting and quite incapable of fighting for her
own hand, said, "Oh yes, I am sure he will take care of
me. But, please, there is one thing. . . ."

"Yes?" said Matron a little more kindly.

"That young man—Mr. Grant—who came to see me
this afternoon—he was coming to see me to-morrow, and
now he will not know where to find me."

"You can ring him up," said Matron, coldly.

Sigrid blushed a little. "I do not know his address. If
you would let me leave a note that could be handed to
him when he comes to-morrow. . . ."

It was all very irregular, said Matron again, but in the
circumstances, she would see what could be done. In
any case, there would be no necessity for Sigrid to leave

a note. A message should be sent to Mr. Grant to the effect that he should get into touch with Mr. Crook for news of Miss Petersen's present whereabouts.

Hilary Grant, an enterprising young man, had left his address and telephone number at the office, in case, he said, of emergencies.

III

When she reached the street Sigrid was surprised to find how shaky and strange she felt. Charing Cross seemed a tremendous distance away. The hospital was about five minutes distant from Earl's Court Station, or she could walk as far as Kensington High Street and catch a bus to Charing Cross. But actually she did neither. Four or five steps convinced her that she would never reach her destination by either method, so she signalled a convenient taxi, and crawled inside. A moment after the driver had received his instructions, a small black car that had been waiting unobtrusively outside a closed public-house turned into the main road and followed it.

Sigrid reached the rendezvous two or three minutes before the specified time. A good many people seemed to be travelling, in spite of Government prohibitions, and she wondered whether Crook would be able to identify her in the multitude. She decided that the main booking-office was not an ideal place to have chosen; so many people hurried past, cannoning into her, pushing her aside, that she felt the breath would be banged out of her body before Crook appeared.

The hands of the big station clock pointed to six-thirty precisely when a man whom she had never seen before came up to her. He was tall and well-dressed, wearing a black hat and a black overcoat. He had the face and appearance of a gambler, and all her instincts kindled against him. He belonged, she thought, looking at that once-handsome face, to those men who, she was warned, are always on the lookout for an attractive girl, particularly one who is alone and has apparently no friends.

"Waiting for someone?" inquired the stranger, tipping the black hat, politely.

Sigrid looked despairingly round her. "I—yes. He's sure to be here in a minute. The—the telegram said six-thirty."

"It's that now," the stranger pointed out.

"He—he may have been delayed. He's a very busy man, is Mr. Crook."

She hoped that the mention of the wily little lawyer's name might drive her companion away but to her horror he only said, "So you're Miss Petersen. I thought I couldn't be wrong."

"Wrong?"

"Yes. Crook told me to meet you in this place. He was detained. You come along with me and I'll take you to him."

Sigrid stepped backwards. "No, no," she said. "I—I can't."

"What do you mean, you can't. You were expecting to meet Mr. Crook, weren't you? That's why you're here."

"Yes. But you're not Mr. Crook."

"I've told you. I've come instead of him. He said to fetch you to his place. It's not so far."

"I'm afraid I've made a mistake," panted Sigrid. "I mean, in leaving the hospital. I shouldn't have come. I— I'm not fit. I've had a bad accident."

"I know," said the stranger, soothingly. "But I've got the car here. I'll just tool you down. It's only a few steps. I can't leave her absolutely in front of the station."

He put out his hand and caught her by the arm. Panic overwhelmed her.

She struggled to free herself, but though the grip was apparently gentle she felt herself a captive.

"Now don't be silly," said the man, persuasively. "You trust Mr. Crook, don't you? So come along."

She had a wild idea of crying out, of calling for the police, of imploring help from other travellers, but even as she opened her mouth her companion spoke again.

"Now, you don't want to go back to that place, do you?" he said, in a rather loud voice. "You do as you're told. No one's going to hurt you."

One or two people, who had been watching the couple rather curiously, smiled in a comprehending manner at one another and moved on. That sort of case, those smiles said. A pity with such a lovely girl, but you could never tell. Sigrid was beginning to feel faint with terror when suddenly a new figure came striding through the crowd. He aproached the pair of them and caught Sigrid by the other arm.

"What are you doing here?" he demanded, and his voice was angry. "I thought you promised me not to stir out of that hospital till Crook sent for you."

"I don't know who the devil you are, sir," observed the first man, "but I'm here on Mr. Crook's instructions to fetch the young lady."

Hilary shot him a look of mingled disbelief and contempt. "When did he give you those?"

"A short time ago, since you're so interested."

"I had a telegram—at the hospital," interrupted Sigrid. "I left a message for you."

"I rang up the hospital to ask if you were all right, and they told me you'd left for Charing Cross, that you'd had a telegram. Matron said she was going to ring me. I wonder." He was paying no attention whatever to Sigrid's companion. "Have you got that telegram, by the way?"

Sigrid took it out of her bag and handed it to him. Hilary laughed shortly and passed it to the stranger.

"Perhaps you recognise this," he said. Then he turned back to Sigrid. "That telegram was handed in at Trafalgar Square at 4.30. At 4.30 Crook wasn't in London. I telephoned his office and they told me he'd left town at 12.30 and wasn't expected back before eight, possibly later. So, you see, he couldn't have sent it."

Sigrid seemed to crumple against his arm. "Then you mean . . . ?"

"I told you that whoever was after you would have another try," exclaimed Hilary with a sort of weary impatience. "I daresay he rang up Crook's office too, and thought that while the cat was away, he'd steal his mouse."

Sigrid was shivering now and he slipped one arm round her.

"Then this man . . ." she whispered.

The man laughed shortly. "You've got nothing on me," he said. "Call a copper if that's what's in your mind. Well, why don't you do it?" He laughed again. "I'll tell you why. Because he'd tell you to go home and sleep it off. You show him that telegram. Who's to prove I sent it? I say I haven't been near Trafalgar Square this week. I'm not Crook. . . ."

"But you knew he'd sent it," interrupted Sigrid, quickly. "You said so when we met."

The man shook his head. "Not me. I just opened the gate and you came tearing up the path."

"You told me you'd come on his behalf. You said you had your car here."

"Who says so?"

"I do."

"Where's your witness? Look here, young lady, you call a policeman and say I was trying to kidnap you and see what you get. Yes, and your gentleman friend, too. There's a lot of blackmail going on in London, and this is one of the first steps on the ladder. But you don't get me like that."

And with a sudden movement he disappeared.

"Where has he gone?" whispered Sigrid.

"I don't know," said Hilary, peering through the crowd. "You may be sure he'll keep out of our way for a bit, all the same. Why, you're shivering, sweet."

"Hilary," she whispered, "it isn't true."

"What isn't true?"

"That he'll keep out of our way. Don't you see, things are even worse than they were. Now he'll regard both of us as his enemies."

"Is that all you're afraid of?" he rallied her, gently. "Do you really think I can't look after you—and myself?"

"I'm frightened," she said. "This is a thing that has never happened to me before. When the Germans came into my country I was angry, I was ashamed, but I was not afraid. When they spoke of the Germans coming into this country that has taken care of me and let me work and live here at peace, I was fierce, because it is a good country and kind to the unfortunate, but I was not afraid. Even when I found the body of that old woman I was shocked, I was sick, but I was not afraid. Not as I am afraid in my soul now."

His arm round her tightened. "Look at me, Sigrid, and tell me something. Are you afraid of me?"

She shook her head.

"Then will you do something a little strange, a little unconventional? Will you let me take you home with me to-night, knowing you're as safe with me as you could be under the roof of an archbishop? You speak of being afraid. I tell you, I'm afraid, too, afraid of what may happen to you once you are out of my sight."

"I will do whatever you say," promised Sigrid. "But—don't leave me, Hilary. I feel he is waiting, and the moment you disappear . . ."

"I shan't disappear," said Hilary. "You can count on me from now till the day you die."

As they came out of the station it seemed to Sigrid that everything was suddenly unfamiliar, for a low fog had begun to drop like a curtain, giving surrounding buildings a dim and unearthly appearance. Though it would not be lighting-up time for half an hour, passing cars were taking no chances, and little golden paths of light travelled like will-o-the-wisps along the roadway.

Hilary yelled for a taxi.

"Where are we going?" asked Sigrid as they stepped into the cab.

"Back to my place. I can't be sure of your being safe

anywhere else. Even in an hotel there are servants who can be bribed. Besides, you'll feel less embarrassed with me."

The taxi nosed its way through the dark.

"Do you think he'll come back in the morning?" murmured Sigrid. "Does he know where you live?"

"I don't know," returned Hilary, slowly. "But I can tell you one thing. I'm going to telephone Crook when we arrive, and I'm going on telephoning him till I get him. He's so proud of this case—let him share the responsibility. Besides, he may recognise that fellow."

Sigrid stiffened. "Of course," she whispered. "I had forgotten."

"Forgotten what?"

"He told me he knew who the murderer is."

"Then why doesn't he do something about it?" demanded Hilary with sudden heat.

"Perhaps he is, and that's why he's down in the country."

"And meanwhile a second attempt's being made on your life in London."

"He can't be everywhere," said Sigrid in reasonable tones, "and, of course, he could not guess about the telegram."

While they talked thus, and Hilary strengthened and reassured the frightened girl, a desperate man in a little, black car followed the taxi up this street and down that, losing it once as the lights changed, putting on speed until he was once more within hail, thinking of the work that he must do before dawn.

CHAPTER TWELVE

Good wishes to the corpse.
—QUALITY STREET.

I

THE TAXI felt its way round corners, up hills, through the gathering dark—a tremendous distance it seemed to Sigrid, and yet nothing at all. She was aware of a curious light feeling, a sense of ease; to-morrow, she felt, danger would begin again, but for to-night she was safe. The taxi stopped at last and Hilary sprang out and opened the door.

"Here we are," he said. "It's not exactly Buckingham Palace, though actually it's more like that than you might suppose. Hitler doesn't admire the suburbs, it seems."

Through the dimness she saw a patch that was utterly blank.

"Two houses came down there," said Hilary, answering her unspoken question. "It's Static Water now. Lovely name, don't you think?" He paid the driver and tucked his hand under the girl's arm. "Hope you're in good shape. There are a lot of stairs."

The staircase was narrow and twisting; it was also very dark. They passed a black door, behind which no light gleamed, and came to another floor higher up. Hilary took out a key.

231

"You mustn't mind the furnishing," he said. "The last tenant must have been curator in a marine store."

"A marine store?" She turned to him, laughing a little. "What is that?"

"A junk shop. Flotsam and jetsam. You can pick up all kinds of things there from revolvers to china ornaments. My predecessor specialised in ornaments."

He switched on the light as he spoke. "Take a look round," he invited, going to draw the black-out curtains.

Sigrid stared about her, scarcely believing her eyes. On tables and desks, on stools, even on the floor, the ornaments flourished like extraordinary growths on the walls of an ancient temple. China and plaster, wood and stone, they stared and ogled and threatened.

"I've often thought I'd like to be a psychologist," said Hilary. "The study of the mind. Why do people do what they do? What turns their mental machinery? What conceivable pleasure could this fellow have had in choosing these horrors? That one, I suppose, is a copy of an Egyptian God. The parrot next to it is just the sort of ornament you'd expect to pick up in the Caledonian Market. This," he took a small statue from a table, "is a lovely bit of work, real jade. Don't you get a strange impression, looking at it?"

"It's Chinese, isn't it?" said Sigrid, taking it from him. She held it a moment. "It is like life," she said, softly, putting the little image down.

"What, the goddess?"

"No, I mean this room. Such a jumble. That screaming china parrot with outspread wings, that quiet Egyptian king, the goddess, so secret, so strange. Everything mixed together, so that you never know what to expect next, so that you are always looking for the thread that binds them."

"I didn't know you were a philosopher," said Hilary.

"This man who owned all these—why did he have so many, so different? And my life." She lifted her blue eyes to her companion's face. "My quiet time in Norway, the man I was to marry, who may be—who knows?"

"Killed?" asked Hilary, gently.

She shook her head. "We do not know. Sometimes I think he may come back, but . . ." She was silent a moment. "Then—my coming to your country, the work I do, and now this—this melodrama. You see what I mean?"

"I see." He held her hands a moment. "And now—who knows the next step?"

She shook her head. "How can we tell?"

"Well," said Hilary, becoming matter-of-fact again, "I should say a drink was next. What about you? Beer does for me, but—anyhow, let's see what I've got."

He went to a cupboard by the wall. "Sherry? No, no good. There isn't any. There's some madeira, though, that's not too bad." He tilted the bottle thoughtfully. "You try this, while I try and get in touch with Crook." He went out into the passage after he had poured out her drink. "Shan't be long."

Sigrid heard the click as the telephone receiver was lifted from its rest, and then the sound of the dial being spun. A moment later Hilary Grant looked in.

"Number's engaged, as usual. May as well polish off my beer." He drained it at a great draught. "Don't be frightened of the madeira," he said, and smiled. "I'll have another shot now."

Sigrid stayed where she was, looking round the extraordinary room in which she found herself. She had a curious sensation, as though all this had happened before, as though she knew the room quite well. Yet common sense assured her that this was her first visit here. Sunk in contemplation, she pondered on the doctrine of the reincarnationists. Perhaps those people were right who declared that life was a series of evolutions, always on the same planet, until a stage approaching perfection was attained. Perhaps in some previous existence she had actually stood in this house, or owned one of the innumerable ornaments jostling all around her. She thought of the Tea-Cosy and his strange theory of time—and suddenly she knew why the room felt familiar, why she believed she had been here before.

Nausea gripped her; the room seemed stifling. The light dependent from the ceiling was like a flame licking towards her. It had been like this on the night that her little home was bombed.

She staggered towards the window, pushed back the curtains and leaned out. It was the last quarter of the old moon, and the silver sickle had pushed a horn through the cloud, covering the outdoor scene with a shimmer like hoar-frost. The pale light shone on the emergency water supply opposite. It looked strange in a London suburb.

"Quite Venetian," thought Sigrid, hazily, who had never been to Venice. But already someone had thrown something over the enclosing wall. It looked like a dead cat.

From the street below a voice yelled, "Put out that light! Put out that damned light!"

They were shouting at her; two or three men had collected on the pavement below. She drew back an inch or two from the window and Hilary came pelting in.

"Someone's in for trouble," he began. "My God, Sigrid, what are you doing?"

She moved towards him. "Oh Hilary," she whispered, "I felt faint. I—I forgot about the light. I wanted the air. It was like the night—the night. . . ." She looked at him imploringly.

"What night? What's happened to you?"

"When I was bombed out. I felt—so close to death."

He jerked the curtain back into place.

"Lucky for us that wasn't a bobby," he said. "You really must pull yourself together, darling." He pushed her gently into a chair and put her drink into her hand. "You haven't touched that. I'll have another to keep you company. Whisky this time, I think."

"Skol!" he said, holding up the glass. "That is Norwegian, isn't it?"

She smiled. "Skol!" she repeated, in a small voice.

"What happened to you?" he asked. He was frowning as if he didn't understand.

"I think it's what they call delayed shock. It came over me suddenly. That man in the flat and then the man at the station to-night. Perhaps my brain doesn't register very well. It *is* like when I was bombed. I wasn't afraid at the time, not a bit, not even particularly sorry, but afterwards I cried and cried. Silly of me, wasn't it? I kept thinking of the little bits that were mine, all gone, all burnt and broken—the only home I had. It was almost as though I had lost my own life."

"You certainly look all in," he told her. "You'd better finish that and then lie down for a bit. I still haven't got Crook. I must have another shot. Or perhaps the office is closed. But I'll try the Earl's Court address now. He may ring the hospital and find you've gone, and Heaven knows what he'll do. Wreck the place, I shouldn't wonder." He rose and poured out yet more beer. With the glass half-way to his lips, he paused. Both of them had heard a sound on the stairs.

"Hallo!" exclaimed Hilary. "Someone's paying us a late visit. Oh damn, it's the police. I suppose some interfering old woman told them about the light."

"You must let me come and explain that it was my fault," cried Sigrid eagerly. "It's not fair you should be blamed."

But he pushed her back into her chair. "No, no, you stay where you are. My shoulders are broader than yours. It may be a plant, you know. I still haven't forgotten that fellow who was hanging about at the station."

He went out of the room and she heard the front door open in response to the prolonged pealing of the electric bell. On the step stood a policeman, his bulls-eye lantern casting an orange circle on the floor of the narrow hall.

"Light showing," said the policeman, stolidly.

"I'm sorry about that," said Hilary in his most engaging voice. "It was only for a moment. Curtain was accidently dislodged. It's all right again now. Anyhow it's not eight yet."

"It's gone black-out time," said the man in the same

236

unsympathetic voice. "And we've had a lot of complaints about light hereabouts."

"Not mine," returned Hilary in some indignation.

"I didn't say that, sir, but there's no doubt about it we've got a lot of refugees in these parts, and they're not all of them friends to us. We can't afford to be careless."

"Do you mean you're accusing me of spying?"

"Not at all, sir, but I'm afraid I must trouble you for your name and address."

Behind him the door opened noiselessly; a pale face peered out.

"Hallo!" said the policeman.

Hilary turned, a sharp movement on his heel. The girl had retied the blue scarf round her hair, her bag was in her hand.

"It's all right, Sigrid," said Hilary in soothing tones.

The policeman, who had been going to ignore her—after all, young gentlemen were young gentlemen—started at the sound of the name.

"Sigrid!" he said, suspiciously. "That's not English."

"Norwegian refugee," said Hilary in hurried tones.

"Got your identity card with you?" inquired the constable.

"It is here, in my bag."

As the girl bent above the catch, that was a little stiff, someone else came out of the blackness of the staircase. He was a tall man, with the manner and mien of a gambler, and he wore a soft, black hat and a black coat.

Hilary and Sigrid saw him simultaneously.

"What the devil are you doing here?" Hilary exclaimed. "Officer, this man is pestering us. . . ."

"I've come for Miss Petersen," said the stranger, in un-emotional tones.

"Miss Petersen's in my care," Hilary informed him.

"Not much she isn't," said the man. He turned to Sigrid. "I've come to take you to Mr. Crook."

"I don't understand," whispered Sigrid, faintly.

"You will soon. Any reason we should all hang about on the stairs?"

He pushed past the policeman, who was now standing between him and Hilary Grant, and he caught the girl by the arm as he had done half an hour earlier and pushed her gently back into the room. The glass of madeira was standing where she had left it on the table. It was now about two-thirds full. The stranger, walking with a bit of a limp, crossed the room and picked it up. "How much of this did you drink?" he demanded of the shaking girl.

"None of it," she whispered. "I—it tilted."

"Good thing you didn't upset the lot."

Hilary, suddenly breaking away from the policeman, leaped into the room and hurled himself on the stranger. The latter seemed ready for this move, for he backed hurriedly, handing the glass to Sigrid as he did so.

"Catch hold. Don't drop it."

She took it blindly.

"Now then," said the policeman, "what's all this about? Funny goings on, I must say."

"Officer," said the man in the black coat, "I charge this man with the wilful murder of Clara Kersey and the attempted murder of Sigrid Petersen. All right, all right," he stepped up to where Sigrid trembled and paled, "I'll take it now. I'd like to know why he was so anxious I shouldn't have it analysed."

"You'd better all come along with me to the station," announced the officer, who was feeling a bit out of his depth.

"Pleasure," murmured the stranger, putting his hand into his coat-pocket. "No, Grant, I wouldn't if I were you. A bullet in the midriff would be damned unpleasant, and I'd swear it went off by accident." Before they left the flat he went into the hall and dialled a number.

"That you, Crook?" he said, when he had got his connection. "Bill Parsons here. I've got your girl—and the goods. You'd better meet us at the station. We're going right along."

II

"When did you start realisin' you were runnin' in the Suicide Stakes?" Crook inquired paternally of Sigrid Petersen a little while later.

"It was in the flat while he was pretending to telephone to you. I can't explain why, but suddenly I felt I knew this place, not exactly that I had been here before, but I knew it. I mean, I knew about it. It did not surprise me. And then I saw the parrot—I had, of course, seen it already, but it was as if I saw it truly for the first time—and I remembered."

"What did you remember?" asked Crook.

"I remembered the last time I had heard someone speak of a green parrot—a parrot that could not speak. That was in the flat on the second floor in your house. The old man was telling me how he had been called out of bed in the middle of the night, and had been driven to a flat or house a long way off, a very ornamental flat, he said, and they had a parrot. I thought of the canary in the flat in the basement, and I remembered I asked if it could talk and he looked at me in such a strange way, and said, 'No, it wasn't alive.' And so, suddenly, I knew I was in a worse danger than I had ever been."

Crook was regarding her with open-eyed admiration. "You mean, that's all you had to go on, a green china parrot? No, don't tell me about your woman's instinct. I've bought that one before."

"It was a little more than that," said the girl. "I asked myself why he had brought me to this solitary place, alone with himself. If this man were to follow us, surely it would be more wise to take me to some place that was larger, where there were people. And then—I could see that no one was living in that room. It was an empty house, I think. And I listened to him at the telephone, and I thought, 'He knows Mr. Crook is away.' He said so not half-an-hour earlier, as we stood in the station. So then I was sure he was not really ringing you up at all. Oh, I cannot tell you how afraid I was then. You see, I knew he was my old man and he had tried once to kill me, and there was no chance, I thought, of any one interfering this time."

"I told you," said Crook, wearily. "I'm always telling people. Crook always gets his man. Do you suppose I was going out of London just to leave the murderer a fair field? Bill was on your tail all the time. He knew I hadn't sent that telegram, and when he saw you leavin' the hospital, he did a bit of arithmetic and guessed that our Mr. X. was takin' advantage of me bein' away."

Sigrid was silent for a moment. "What was he going to do—this time?"

"He'd doped your drink. But you weren't to die of poison."

"Then—how?"

"Notice that nice ornamental water just opposite?"

"I—I saw it."

"Well, I think, as soon as you'd passed out, you'd have left the place very quietly, and—well, it's a lonely neighbourhood, and things do get chucked into these ponds —bricks and what-not—and what's one splash more or less? Then, you see, if you had been found—and why should you till it was too late for any one to know who the dickens you were?—it 'ud look like death by drowning, and death by drowning ain't murder according to the act. Not unless some officious fellow saw him tip you in."

"You mean, they'd have thought it suicide?"

"Or accident. Some of these walls ain't very high. That one isn't, and the County Council ought to know by this time you've only got to label a thing Dangerous to have half the parish rallyin' round."

"Suppose," whispered Sigrid, "suppose I had drunk that madeira before your man arrived?"

"Never heard of a thing called a stomach-pump?" suggested Crook, but his voice was terse. The possibility had occurred to him also.

"And—the real Tea-Cosy?"

"Can't you guess? You know, most criminals, especially amateurs, always repeat their technique. The very fact that they get away with it once, instead of warning them not to tempt Providence a second time, seems to have just the opposite effect. They think they're so damned efficient, they can go on throwing dust in the eyes of the world for the rest of their natural. And when they find themselves up against it they blame their luck or the other side's unsportin' behaviour. Two-thirds of the chaps who end in the little covered shed commit suicide. The fact is, you've got to be damn clever to be a successful murderer. And you've got to have nerve. When you've committed your murder you're not done. You've got to carry on just as usual. And that's what most of 'em can't do. They're damn all anxious to cover their tracks, they want to look natural, so they go round laughing their silly fat heads off and talking at the tops of their voices, tryin' to impress every one with the fact they've nothing to hide, and of course they overdo it, and people start nudgin' one another and sayin', 'What's the matter with old Joe? Something on his mind, if you ask me,' and that's the beginnin' of the end."

Sigrid began to shiver.

"Cold?" asked Crook, solicitously.

"I was remembering that water. There was something in it—a cat, I think—floating on the surface."

"Not cat," said Crook. "Hat. A big, black, unmistakeable hat, with bows and flowers and brooches stuck all over it. Y'know, this has been an amateur's case right from the start, full of untidy ends and bits of botched work. Ever noticed how conceited amateurs are? So damn pleased with the one thing they've done right, they don't remember all the loose ends they've left. And it's the loose ends that choke 'em in the long run." He abandoned himself luxuriously to one of his favourite topics. "Ever seen an amateur water-colourist? Can't get a cow's

242

legs to look right, so plants the cow in a cornfield. Can't model a neck properly, so shoves a bunch of flowers under the chin. Finds hands difficult to model, so covers 'em up with a muff. Take my word, Kipling knew his onions. Same with amateur actors. Lots of gestures, waving hands like sea-anemones, waggling heads like mandarins, all to try and hide the fact they've got no technique. This is the same. That's why we've got 'em both by the heels now."

"Both?"

"Sure. It's a two-man crime. Didn't you realise that? Or rather, one man, one woman." And speaking more to himself than the girl, he added, "They'll hang Grant. Not a doubt of it. And he deserves it for being a clumsy fool. But she—oh, I take off my hat to her, and that's not a thing I have to do very often."

CHAPTER THIRTEEN

I make it a rule only to believe what I understand.
—DISRAELI. ("THE INFERNAL MARRIAGE.")

"THE FIRST TIME I visited that household, I said they were a gift to a chap like Freud," remarked Crook to his select audience of three. His companions were Bill Parsons, mainly on tap to supply the company with beer, Aubrey Bruce, the famous little redheaded Scotch K.C., who said there was no one on earth he liked better than Crook so long as they were both on the same side, and a rake of a man with an amusing unscrupulous face, called Cummings, editor of the *Morning Record*, a paper so famous it didn't even have to advertise its daily net sales. In the early mornings tubes, trams and buses seemed wrapped in *Records*. Every one carried them. They were sensational, scathing, sceptical, libellous and irresistible. It was even said of Cummings that he had once persuaded a man to commit a murder by reporting it in the most engaging terms before it actually took place.

The prosecution was retaining Bruce in the case of Grant v. Rex, and Bruce was glad enough to pick Crook's brains to the last morsel. While the lawyer orated, he drew his customary school of fishes on the pink blotting-paper, a great, coarse, eagle-eyed fish for Crook himself, a slender silver fish for Sigrid, a swordfish for Hilary Grant, an octopus for Clara Kersey.

"Think of the position," Crook went on. "Miss Kersey,

madly ambitious, resolved to pay back the world for what it hadn't given her at the time she wanted it, ruthless, unscrupulous, crazy with what Freud would call the lust for power, and lording it over as many people as she could collect. On the other side, Miss Flora, equally embittered, sick with impatience, knowing herself a tool in her aunt's hands, longin', I'm certain, to break away, but knowin' she's helpless. At the beginning, I daresay she was grateful enough to auntie. On her record she wouldn't have found it easy to get a job, and she hadn't, apparently, anythin' of her own. But after a bit she must have seen she was like a fly in a web, with Miss Kersey for the spider. Say she tried to get away—who'd take her without a reference, and what sort of a reference would her auntie give her?"

"She must have been pretty valuable," demurred Cummings, who throughout the conversation made odd hieroglyphics he called shorthand on the back of an envelope.

Crook agreed, "Miss Kersey couldn't carry on a show like that entirely on her own. There'd be books to keep, correspondence, telephone calls—she'd have to have one confidante."

"Who could blackmail her?"

But Crook negatived that. "Whatever she felt, Miss Flora wouldn't dare quarrel with her aunt. It was her bread and butter. And she couldn't expose the old lady without exposing herself. No, she was like the apostle, fast in prison, and there was no way out. I daresay Miss Kersey tantalised her by tellin' her that one of these days she'd be an independent woman, but in the meantime there was auntie hale and hearty, holdin' the purse-strings and the reins and givin' 'em a good tug every

now and again just to let every one know she hadn't
gone to sleep. Oh, she'd saved the girl from a six months'
sentence and given her a life stretch instead. And where
she made her mistake was she didn't realise what she was
up against, that money can't do quite everything, and
that Miss Flora was gettin' desperate and was just
watchin' for her chance."

Bruce looked startled.

"D'you mean to commit murder?"

"Let's say to get even. I don't suppose it took the concrete form of murder at the beginnin'. That came later,
after Grant appeared on the scene. Grant must have
seemed like a last chance to her. She'd lost her youth and
her chances of a love-affair—you can be sure Miss Kersey
would have nipped that in the bud if there'd been anythin' of the kind on the horizon (Crook never cared how
much he mixed his metaphors)—and here was a good-
lookin' scoundrel obviously on the make."

"You think she'd see that?"

"She was no fool. And a young man like Grant doesn't
suddenly plant himself on an old woman and her drab
companion out of the kindness of his heart. No, I made a
few inquiries about Master Hilary. It's quite true he had
been in the Diplomatic, but he left it rather hurriedly.
Lucky not to have a public inquiry at that, but the
authorities weren't sure how the B.P. 'ud stand for some
of the facts, so they contented 'emselves with givin' him
the Order of the Boot. He says he went on the stage
after that, and I daresay he did, he was a good actor,
but Miss Flora ruined him. Like nearly all amateurs she
would overdo it. But she gets the last laugh or I miss my

guess. I wonder!" He brooded a moment, his chin in his hand.

"Wonder what?"

"Whether she hated him as much as she'd hated her aunt when she found out he'd just been makin' use of her. Because, of course, though she may have been in love with him in a queer twisted sort of way, he never had a spark of feelin' for her. She was just a pawn in the game, and—well, it's sometimes the pawn that checkmates the king."

"Miss Kersey's heir, eh? Still, murder's a tall order."

"Yes. Y'know, it 'ud be a good story for these psychological fellows, those two women livin' in the same house for years, and Watson like a buffer between them. And then young Grant appears and the balance tips up and you get the whole boiling upset."

Bruce hunched his shoulders and bent over his sketching. Crook gave you these surprises sometimes. He seemed so hard-boiled and suddenly he'd display an understanding of circumstances and temperament that seemed absolutely out of character. He was glad he hadn't got the job of convicting the woman. Cummings, however, was never less than a newspaperman. What mattered to him was the story.

"What makes you so damned sure Miss Flora was behind it?" he wanted to know.

"I fancy the letter proves that."

"What letter? I say, Crook, what a story!" He was openly exultant.

Crook, however, looked a bit grim. "Even you won't be able to print this one."

"I can't? What the devil do you mean?"

"I know the *Record's* reputation, but even it couldn't stand up to the stink there'd be if you dragged Miss Flora's name into the headlines. Y'see, you've got no proof, and sink me if I see how you're goin' to procure any."

"I suppose," said Bruce, looking up thoughtfully, "you're referring to the letter Miss Kersey sent to her nephew."

"Wrote to her nephew. Right, Bruce. As dramatists say, the crux of the situation. Now, consider."

Cummings watched him, fascinated. In half a minute, he thought, he would thrust one hand into non-existent coat-tails and fling out the other in a Pickwickian gesture that would probably overset a quart can of beer.

"There are three things to remember about that letter," Crook continued. "1. It had been opened twice. 2. The postmark was King's Widdows April 3. 3. It was found on the 7th April on top of the morning paper in the Tea-Cosy's flat."

"What does that add up to?" inquired Cummings, perceiving that the speaker anticipated some comment.

"Figure it out for yourself. Take the points in order.

"1. Who opened that letter the first time? Obviously it was done to find out what the letter contained, and it was done by someone who was very anxious to know just when Miss Kersey was planning to visit Earl's Court. Now that letter passed through four hands. The first was Miss Kersey herself. Of course, she could have reopened it herself, but I don't think she did. For one thing, Miss Flora said she had to wait while the old lady sealed up the letter, and for another, there's no sense in opening an envelope unless you're going to enclose something or add a postscript. Now I saw that letter and there were no enclosures and no postscript. So that lets her out. She handed it to Miss Flora to post in Minbury on the 12.30 collection. But for some reason Miss Flora didn't post it."

"Who did post it?"

"That's the point. I don't think any one posted it. That's why it was found on top of the morning paper in the Tea-Cosy's room."

"Whoever put it there must have been the murderer."

"Exactly."

"And that wasn't Miss Flora, because Miss Flora never moved out of King's Widdows on the day her aunt was killed."

"Right again. There was only one member of that household who was in London that day and that person was Hilary Grant. Of course, there was the old lady herself, but even our enterprisin' police force haven't suggested she committed suicide."

"It's like the House that Jack built," said Cummings. "Miss Kersey gives the letter to Miss Flora, Miss Flora passes it on to Grant, he—how do you know he didn't post it after he'd read it?"

"Because the postmark says King's Widdows, April 3rd. But there's only one daily collection from King's Widdows, and that goes out at 10.30 before the letter was written, so it was obvious that the postmark was a fake. And you only fake a postmark to give the impression it's been through the post, when actually it hasn't done anything of the kind."

"Of course, they wouldn't want Theodore Kersey to

get it in case he did turn up. All the same, how could they be sure he wouldn't?"

"Because he was a creature of habit and he never came home at three in the afternoon."

"But how would Grant know that?"

"He made a point of findin' out. Remember the under-taker?"

"D'you mean that was Grant?"

"He'd been on the stage, remember. And he did show a lot of interest in the households at No. 1. I suppose if he'd heard that the Tea-Cosy generally showed up after lunch he'd have sent him a wire, askin' him to meet the 2.55 at Waterloo, and the old boy might be there still. That deals with points one and two. Point three—about the letter lyin' on top of the mornin' paper. Well, doesn't that prove it only arrived that day? Otherwise, it 'ud have been under the paper. And the Tea-Cosy's Daily Hindrance hadn't turned up that morning, so she couldn't have put it there, and if the Tea-Cosy had taken it in he'd have opened it. And even if he was double-crossin' me, he'd have shoved it up on the mantelpiece, because he'd just told me that all his unopened letters were put there as a matter of course.

"No, you take my word for it, that letter was deposited on the afternoon of the 7th, before Miss Kersey reached the flat."

"You're being damned definite," objected Cummings.

"The thing's obvious. If the letter had been put in position after the murder was committed—and the police agree that that probably took place in the kitchen, on account of the glass-cloth twisted round the throat and the tap left runnin' to reduce the chance of cries bein' overheard—then the murderer must have seen the hat on the back of the chair when he went in to put the letter in place. And if he'd seen the hat he'd have put it where he put the body, and the Tea-Cosy might be walkin' the earth as free as air at this minute."

"Half a minute," protested Cummings. "Are you suggestin' that it was the hat that killed the old boy? They got the body, by the way didn't they?"

"Out of a bit of London's Little Venice, as I expected. They got one or two other things too they've been lookin' for for some time. I'll come to them in due course. But if the hat hadn't been left in Tea-Cosy's flat he wouldn't have started bein' curious, and no one might have begun askin' questions for weeks. When Grant and Miss Flora were plannin' the murder they didn't mean any one to guess for ages, and between them they could have kept up the game with fake letters and telephone messages from the old lady for a time. Meanwhile, they'd have the pearls, even if they got nothing else, though I fancy they were both pretty sure that was only a beginning. Sooner or later, of course, the body was certain to be found and sometime or other identified."

"If it wasn't past identification by that time," suggested Cummings, grimly.

"They wouldn't want to wait too long. And anyway, there was Watson. She'd get anxious after a bit. You wouldn't get her to believe all was well if weeks went by without a sight of the old lady. And anyhow, what's the good of putting out a fellow's light if you can't cash in on what he leaves behind him? No, no, they could count on Watson to pull in the police, if it came to that. And once she was found, there couldn't be any doubt about it bein' murder. Old ladies, however dotty, don't hide themselves under rugs in empty flats, havin' first twisted tea-cloths round their necks."

"And what did they expect to happen then?" Cummings was like a dog on scent.

"Oh, that was where the Tea-Cosy was to come in. They meant all along for him to bear the brunt. That's why they left the letter in the flat. Well, clearly someone 'ud have to take responsibility, and they didn't mean it to be them. Without the letter, how would any one know Miss Kersey had ever thought of visitin' in Brandon Street?"

"And supposing he'd sat down and written to the old dame, apologising for missing her?" Cummings persisted.

"It 'ud be easy for Miss Flora to get hold of the letter and burn it, wouldn't it? And who's to know it was ever written? Oh, don't make any mistake about it. The hat was an accident, but that letter in Tea-Cosy's flat was one of the planks of the murderers' platform."

"They must have been reasonably sure Miss Kersey was going to leave her money to the niece," suggested Bruce, speaking out of a long silence.

"I fancy, whether she did or not, Miss Kersey meant 'em to believe it. She was always talkin' about the younger woman steppin' into her shoes. And it's just the sort of thing she would do, like holdin' the carrot in front of the donkey to egg it up the hill."

"And whisking it away when it's got there."

"She did leave Miss Flora the residue of her property," Crook reminded them. "Where they went wrong was supposin' she had much to leave. They were wise, really, to make sure of the pearls. But naturally they didn't know that. They thought it was a chance worth takin'. Only, you see, Grant made a bloomer about the hat, leavin' it where it couldn't help bein' seen and Providence made a worse one when it allowed that girl to find the body within twenty-four hours. As a matter of fact, Grant must have given a lot of thought to the affair, and laid his plans rather neatly. He didn't fall down on the general outline, only on the details, trying to add a bit of decoration that didn't quite match the rest of the picture. If he hadn't tried to be so damn convincing he might even have got away with it."

"Surely not, once the Human Bloodhound was on his track?" jeered Cummings.

"Why did he have to pretend he didn't know what the Tea-Cosy was like? He said he thought he was a little, fat man like a clock. But not half an hour later Watson produced a photograph of him out of the drawing-room. Grant must have seen that picture dozens of times, and known whose it was. Besides, if he didn't know what he was like, how did he know the sort of disguise to wear? Miss Fitzpatrick would give him something to go on, but—oh, he knew they were approximately the same build."

"There's one thing I'd like to know," said Bruce, "and that is how both he and Miss Kersey managed to come and go without being seen by the old witch in the basement."

"I've explained about Miss Kersey. The Troglodyte was busy rearrangin' her past with the girl just before three. If you've ever heard an ex-actress rememberin' aloud how she played the front half of a tom-cat in the Bovey Tracy panto. the year Edward VII came to the throne, you'll know they won't so much as notice it's got to to-morrow morning. As for Grant, I think she did see him both come and go, but she didn't recognise him as Grant. What she said to me was, 'There was no stranger came to this house yesterday except the girl.' She wouldn't realise Grant was a stranger, because he'd be got up to look like the Tea-Cosy. He'd come about half-past two, say—and lucky not to collide with the girl on the first floor; it must have been a close thing—let himself in with the key and then, I fancy, he hid and waited for Miss Kersey to arrive."

"Mightn't he have let her in?"

"I doubt it. He'd know there was a world of difference between deceivin' the Troglodyte down a flight of steps and through a basement window and pullin' the wool over the eyes of Miss Kersey, who would be as near him as I am to you, and was no fool most of the time. There'd be the difference in voice, too. He knew what the Tea-Cosy looked like but he'd have no guide as to how he spoke. No, I fancy he waited in the kitchen, and she let herself in and went in to the livin'-room. He'd taken the precaution of removin' the bulb and leavin' the curtains partly drawn, so that if they did meet face to face there wasn't much likelihood of his bein' recognised as the boy from her home town. Not seein' the Tea-Cosy, and knowing, of course, that bein' on time wasn't his besettin' virtue, she made herself at home, tossed off her hat, and decided to wait. How long she decided to wait we don't know but I'm reassured that Grant didn't come in after her, because if he had I'm pretty certain she'd have

254

tackled him in the hall, and I agree with the police that she was killed in the kitchen. I think most likely she began exploring and was attracted by the sound of the running water and walked straight into the trap. Benham thinks that the murderer was waiting behind the kitchen door and jumped on her before she had a chance to understand what was happening. There are signs, by the way, that that glass-cloth was used as a gag. She seems to have struggled a bit. The cloth's torn, as if with teeth, and there was a mark on her jaw and a spot of blood on the cloth that bears out that explanation. And then, I think, he probably lost his nerve. The amateur touch again, though there I don't blame him. It's difficult to be an experienced murderer. The police don't give you a chance."

He broke off for a moment and signalled to Bill to refill the glasses.

"I've had murderers in this very room," he went on, "and they all tell the same yarn. People take much too long to die, much longer than you expect. It makes you feel rocky. A gun's all right, if you happen to put your bullet in the right spot, but it's too damn dangerous. The police know too much. Hands round a throat don't leave finger-prints. Of course, what Grant should have done was go through the flat, make sure there was nothing left to give him away, but he got panicky, lost his head and couldn't think of anything but getting away. Y'know, murder plays the devil with your nerves, particularly in a more or less empty house. Every creak's a footstep and every breath of wind's a voice. Men have told me that once the job was over all they wanted was to clear out. I know they come back sometimes afterwards, but that's the second stage of panic. In the first stage, all they want is to get away. And that's what Grant felt. I daresay he'd opened the first-floor flat in advance. A baby could force that lock. There was always the chance of someone comin' in, a chap delivering Government posters or something, as he lugged the old lady down, but that was a chance he had to take. He was lucky just missing the girl, as it was. And then he bolted, leaving the hat in the sitting-room, the one fatal thing to have done."

"I suppose," said Bruce thoughtfully, "she took the umbrella into the kitchen with her."

"According to Prince of the Warburg Court she took it with her everywhere, probably even to the bathroom. Yes, she must have taken it or it would have been found with the hat. Unless, of course, she left it in the hall, where it attracted his attention. Anyhow, the fact remains that he did collect the umbrella, and he didn't collect the hat. He parked the body and he cleared out. If the Troglodyte saw him comin' down the steps—well, she'd simply think it was the Tea-Cosy. I don't know what he did next—went to the pictures perhaps. He had to fill in time somehow before it was dark enough to call for her luggage from the hotel and spin his yarn about an accident in the black-out."

"So that's why he waited so long. To think up a good excuse. Though he could have said there'd been an accident in broad daylight. They happen often enough."

"I don't fancy he wanted to be recognised by the taxi-driver or any one at the railway station. Of course, the lights would be on in the hotel, but that wouldn't matter, since he was representin' himself as the nephew. Everythin' must have seemed O.K. to him till he rang up

Swansdown to report. That was the call Miss Flora got, of course, not the one she said she had from auntie. He'd know she'd answer it. And then it came out about the hat."

"Suppose he'd ignored the hat?" said Cummings. "Mightn't that have been better for him?"

"Well, no, I shouldn't think so," said Crook. "Even the Tea-Cosy's human. If you came back and found a hat like that on your armchair, what would you do about it?"

"If I recognised it. . . ."

"You couldn't help yourself, if you'd ever seen it before."

"Then I'd look round in case the lady had left a note."

"And you'd find the letter and realise she must have come while you were out. . . ."

"And I'd write to say how sorry I was I'd missed her."

"And sooner or later someone would open your letter and start asking questions. Where is Miss Kersey now, for instance? What's the address of the nursing home? Besides you never can tell. The Tea-Cosy might have gone straight to the police, if he wasn't put off. I don't say he wasn't takin' a chance, but then how could he know I was on the trail?"

"So he proceeded to rub the Tea-Cosy out?"

"Yes. The story Miss Petersen heard is approximately the truth. It's a good rule to tell as much truth as possible. It's more confusing for the other chap. Grant rang the Tea-Cosy and spun him the yarn about the nursing home. Y'know," he sounded reflective and vaguely remorseful, "I must have heard that chap leaving the place.

That's what woke me, and like a fool I didn't think of drawing the black-out."

"Even you couldn't have seen the number of the car in the dark," Cummings consoled him.

"He must have driven the old boy to the empty house —Hendon way that was—I suppose he was staying there —and later on he deposited the poor devil in the hiding-place so thoughtfully provided by the L.C.C. Anyhow, that's where he was found, plus Miss Kersey's little zipper case."

Cummings' head shot up. "What was inside it?"

"What you'd expect."

"Stop wisecracking, Crook. We ain't all amateur sleuths."

"Some nice pieces of china and half a brick."

Cummings frowned. "Funny? I don't get it."

"Well, what did you think would be there?"

"Whatever she took to London with her."

"But you knew they were back in Swansdown. Watson told us that. She said Miss Kersey's complete outfit was on the premises with the exception of what she was wearing at the time she was killed. Don't you see? Watson gave us the facts when she said the old lady simply took a change of gear with her. But—ever wondered why Grant took such a large case to town just for one night? It was big, you know. I fell over it in the hall. And afterwards, when he got that phoney wire, he picked up the bag and said he wouldn't want anything that size for just one night. Well, if that wire had really come from the War Office, how did he know he was only going to be in town one night?"

"You mean, it wasn't a genuine telegram?"

"How could it be? It arrived about two o'clock. The post office at King's Widdows shuts from one to two-thirty, and no business is transacted. It was shut at 2.20 when we went past. So how did Mr. Grant get a telegram nicely written on an official form at two p.m.? Answer. He didn't. But he wasn't going to let me go to town without him. He wanted to keep an eye on my movements, so while I chatted with Watson he rigged up the message and produced it for my benefit. That was one of his worst breaks. He was so anxious about the main plan that he forgot to tidy up the details. He gave himself away a bit further while we were going down to the station; he said how crowded the trains were in the morning. Or perhaps he said it when we were in the carriage. As a matter of fact, we arrived on the same train, and my journey was easy enough. I could have had a couple of carriages to myself. So if his train was crowded, it shows he didn't leave Paddington by the 11.6. That gave me another idea."

He pitched away the stub of the fat little cigar he affected and lighted another.

"Y'see, some time or other he planted the umbrella and the Tea-Cosy's outfit at Tempest Green. Now why Tempest Green? It's not a place many people know exists, but a man travelling from London to King's Widdows would know, because it's one of the places where you invariably have to change."

"You mean, he left Paddington by an earlier train, got rid of the hat and coat and the umbrella at a place far enough from London, so he thought, for them not to be traced, and then caught your connection?"

"Looks like it," Crook agreed. "How the Powers That

Be must have laughed to see him stick that gamp in the earth and pelt off hell-for-leather for the station. He'd ransacked the case, no doubt he'd ransacked the hand-bag—he probably burned the contents and chucked it out of the window. And he couldn't find a trace of the pearls. He must have decided she'd already got rid of them, though she'd been p.d.q. if she had, seeing they didn't reach London till 12.30. Still, there it was. But like most people who've committed a murder, he didn't much like the idea that all his energy had been thrown away and that, possibly, is why he went back to the flat, obsessed by the idea that she'd hidden the pearls in some place so obscure that the police hadn't noticed them or so obvious they'd overlooked them. And it certainly wasn't part of his plan that the girl Sigrid Petersen should find him there."

"She seems to have been pretty nippy at throwing monkey-wrenches into the works so far as he was concerned," commented Cummings, dryly. "Anyhow, it's she who persuaded him to sign his death-warrant."

"The trouble about murder is that you can never be sure when the unexpected won't turn up," Crook told him in earnest tones. "That's what ruined Rouse. He never anticipated bein' seen by two young men comin' back from a dance at two o'clock in the mornin'. It ruined Mahon, too. He couldn't know his wife was goin' snoopin' through his pockets. It's ruined most of the big murderers."

Bruce spoke sombrely, laying down his busy pencil. "If it isn't that, it's generally something else. Do you remember the confession of Samuel Dougal, the Moat Farm Murderer? 'However clever one may be and however well one's plans have been carried out, there always is the suspicion lurking at the back of your head that you may have made one little blunder which will lead to the truth coming out.' "

"He made more than one," said Crook, dryly. "Trying to be clever, that was his trouble. The essence of crime is simplicity, but these bright lads won't realise it. How often d'you find a public-school-man making good in crime? I tell you, when you do he's a headline in the press. That right, Cummings?"

Cummings nodded. "Mayfair Killer's Many Crimes. You could sell an edition on a headline like that."

"Just what I was saying. Y'see, they've been educated. They know about things like strategy. The only strategy worth the name is the strategy that goes in and bumps the other fellow in the solar plexus, but that's all too easy for them. And so they go round elaboratin' and, of course, sooner or later they trip themselves up. Grant didn't have to murder that girl, but he reflected that she was on her way to see me. She was pretty sure to say she'd seen the Tea-Cosy, and he knew I'd met the original. Of course, he could clear before I had an opportunity of seein' him, but I'd know he was around. It was too dangerous. The girl might notice some detail that would identify him with himself, in my mind. So he decided to take the bold course and do her in. And once more Providence was too much for him. His heart must have been in his mouth when he heard me groping for the key that he knew was in his pocket."

"Didn't he think any one was going to ask questions about the girl?"

"Why should they? Girls disappear every day of the

week and this one had no people in England. Her work-mates would only shrug their shoulders and say, 'Some man behind it,' and they'd be right, though it wouldn't be quite the way they meant."

"There's one thing," said Cummings, who liked all his points explained as he went along. "How could you be sure it wasn't the real Tea-Cosy the girl had met?"

"She told me that. Warned me that though he was wearin' a broad-brimmed black hat there wasn't any-thing else noticeable about him. But the real Tea-Cosy wore a coat nearly to his ankles. You couldn't miss it. Remember what young Armitage said? The fellow who owns that must have been seven foot tall."

"And that's what gave him away?"

"That—and his hands. Y'know—know anything about actor's make-up? If you're a young man and you want to appear as an old codger, it ain't your face you have to worry about so much as your hands. Faces aren't diffi-cult. You can fix them with false hair and wrinkles and scars and whatnot, but hands are a different matter. You've got to make them up carefully. Grant could chase down to the Earl's Court Station lavatories, as I suspect he did, and throw off the wig and whatnot, and clean off the grease-paint. But time was strictly limited. He'd got to know if any one was trying to break into Flat 3, and he thought, 'It's the face a fellow goes by.' So he did nothing to his hands, and then just before he went I got one of his hands in mine and it was sticky—not gum-sticky, nor sweat-sticky, but cream-sticky. I may not," said Crook, flaunting himself like any robin, "be much of an actor myself, but actors are like other men. They get into trouble, too, and you can pick up a lot of hints from hearin' them talk. I knew Grant had been putting something on his hands and I knew what it was."

"He was taking a bit of a chance, wasn't he, racing back to the house he'd just left?"

"In a sense, that's not true. The Tea-Cosy left and Hilary Grant came back. If I wasn't on the move, then he'd sneak off and the girl would die alone in the dark. But if I was there, then he had some footling excuse for wanting to see me. Couldn't stand the suspense, see?"

"You can't blame him," objected Cummings. "Lots of chaps are afraid of the dark, and this way he could be sure of a ringside seat."

"With me and the police and the girl under his eye all the time. He pretended to fall hard for her, though why he should when he saw her trussed up like a chicken, when he'd hardly noticed that at the inquest, don't ask me. I ain't a sentimentalist. But, of course, that gave him an excuse to see her in hospital and pump her—find out my next move."

"And she gave him everything?"

"On a gold plate with parsley round it. She wasn't to leave the hospital till I sent for her, she told him. So Grant rings my number, finds I'm out, finds Bill's out, and plays his trump card. He didn't know, of course, that Bill was watching that hospital like a cat by a mouse-hole, and that was another bloomer on his part, and he thought this was his chance. By the time I came back to town, she was to have joined the Tea-Cosy in his water retreat, and who was goin' to connect Mr. Hilary Grant with her death? Why, when the truth came out, he was going to be just frantic with grief." Crook took another long pull at his beer. "Well, he's frantic all right, though not with grief."

Bruce was doodling like mad. Cummings looked over his shoulder. "In Heaven's name, Bruce, what's that monstrosity meant for?"

Bruce didn't look up. "It's symbolic," he said. "It's intended to represent Grant's frame of mind when he thought a few jewels were worth three lives."

Cummings experienced one of the few spasms of embarrassment of his existence.

"What made you take to the law, Bruce?"

Bruce smiled rather constrainedly. "You think I'm a misfit?"

"Well, hell," expostulated Cummings, "we only live once. May as well enjoy life. This is just a story to me, and it's a job to Crook, but to you . . ."

"Well, it's my life, too," explained Bruce. "There's one thing you haven't explained, Crook. What made you so sure Flora Kersey was involved?"

"Ever heard of the hen lapwing?" inquired Crook.

Cummings said, Well, no, he'd never thought about it, but he supposed lapwings were no more celibate than any other birds.

"When a lapwing thinks any one's near her nest, instead of having the sense to lie doggo, she kicks up a hell of a clutter and attracts everythin' within hearin' distance. She thinks she'll divert 'em from the nest, but they soon get to know that where she is there the eggs are also. In the same way, when Miss Flora blackguarded Grant on every conceivable occasion, telling me and Watson, the world and his wife, that she couldn't stand him, didn't trust him, that he was a sponger and a cad,

I began to wonder what her little game was. She protested too much. Amateurs again." He drew a long sigh.

Cummings, who liked all his i's dotted and t's crossed, put a final question.

"D'you think he ever intended to marry her?"

"If it was worth his while—certainly. But I can tell you this—that he never will."

"No one ever will," amplified Cummings, more soberly than he had hitherto spoken.

Crook looked surprised. "What makes you say that?"

"Well, they'll take her, too, won't they?"

"What for?"

Cummings stared. "Accomplice in the murder of her aunt."

"I know we've got an enterprisin' police force, second to none," Crook acknowledged. "But even they can't arrest a woman without evidence. I know the story she's going to tell the police, and it's a damn good one. Believe me, she's thought of everything.

"First of all, the letter. Her version is that when she got to Minbury on the 3rd she ran into Hilary Grant, who was goin' into the post-office, so she gave him her aunt's letter to despatch with the rest. How was she to know he never posted it?"

Cummings sounded sceptical. "You believe that yarn?"

"What the hell does it matter what I believe? All that counts is that no one can prove it ain't true."

"And the rest?"

"There's the fake postmark. Well, she says she knows nothing about that. She wouldn't know how to make one. Probably she wouldn't. The telephone message she got on the night of the 7th she thought was genuine.

She didn't think about the telegram from the War Office being a phoney one. Mr. Grant handed it to her but she didn't pay much attention. His concerns were nothing to her. She never thought about the post-office being closed. As for her auntie's gear being brought back to the house and put in the drawers in her room, well, she says Grant must have done that. She never saw the suitcase open after he brought it back—you know, he must have carried his own disguise in it, too—but he'd have plenty of opportunities of goin' into Miss Kersey's room when the others were out. Well? How about it, umpire? You can say it stinks of collusion, but you can't prove it. She knew nothing about the girl, she's had the sense not to put down a line of writing that Grant or any one else can produce in court. Watson can swear that she warned the old lady against the fellow, saying he was an adventurer and most likely a scoundrel into the bargain. She herself had been devoted to the old soul for years—no, I don't see how any court would dare offer a case against her."

"And she gets the pearls," said Cummings. "It's a whale of a story, Crook. Not that you need talk about risks. You take 'em yourself good and plenty."

"Murder's a risky game," Crook pointed out. "And so's detecting it. I might be as convinced Grant was guilty as a zany that he's God Almighty, but that's not good enough for the courts. They want proof, and even Grant, wriggle like the original serpent though he may, isn't goin' to find it easy to get past that drink he gave the girl. As a matter of fact, he isn't hanging for committing two murders so much as for being a damned fool. Why did he have to open his mouth so wide? If he'd never mentioned the parrot that couldn't talk the girl wouldn't have put two and two together, wouldn't have had any suspicions at all."

"My friend, Scott Egerton," observed Bruce gravely, "says that Fate always keeps the last trump up her sleeve and plays it on the side of the righteous."

Crook bridled a little. "These M.P.s, they think they know everything. Takes a war to show 'em they're not quite the wise guys they believe they are. Hey, Bill, keeping that beer to bathe in?"

Bill slouched forward to take the hint.

"Of course," said Bruce, a little maliciously, "we know Crook only backs certainties. The very fact that he's on a case . . ."

Crook grinned, all his good temper restored. "Look at the thing straight," he urged. "Everything's turned out for the best. Miss Kersey's no loss to the community and neither is Grant. Miss Flora will get off, and she's had a life stretch as it is, so I don't grudge her whatever the rest of her life may be worth. Watson's got the guest-house of her dreams, and the girl's well rid of a rascal. She'll get over Grant presently. I know her kind. Look delicate, but heaps of sand. If this Norwegian lad don't turn up again—and war's remarkably like a flat stone, in that you can never tell what won't come creepin' out from underneath—there'll be some other chap. She's not the kind to die an old maid."

"And the Tea-Cosy?" suggested Bruce. "Is being hit on the head; the best thing that could have happened to him?"

But you couldn't take the wind out of Crook's sails so easily.

"Look at the thing scientifically," he proposed. "What was the main business of his life? Speculating on the Time Theory. Well, a wallop on the head may be just death to you or me, but to him it's a short-cut to the millennium. By this time he must have learned the one thing he wanted to know, and it's a pity, it is, on my sam, that he can't give us a straight tip about it."

THE END

>>> If you've enjoyed this book and would like to discover more great vintage crime and thriller titles, as well as the most exciting crime and thriller authors writing today, visit: >>>

The Murder Room
Where Criminal Minds Meet

themurderroom.com

www.ingramcontent.com/pod-product-compliance
Ingram Content Group UK Ltd.
Pitfield, Milton Keynes, MK11 3LW, UK
UKHW040434280225
455666UK00003B/63